Tempest Tossed

Three Strand Cord Book 3

by

Tracy Krauss

Fictitious Ink Publishing
Tumbler Ridge, BC

Published by Fictitious Ink Publishing

Tumbler Ridge, BC, Canada

V0C 2W0

DEDICATION

This book is dedicated to Jesus. I'm so grateful that He continues to love and accept me despite my shortcomings—because I have them. In abundance. Despite the fact that I've been a Christian for a long time now, I still mess up. This is a theme I wanted to highlight in this book, (besides the mayhem, and romance, of course!) When someone accepts Jesus into their life, it doesn't mean they have it all together. Unlike the previous book in the series which is all about redemption, this one is about 'working out our faith'. I hope it encourages people to continue to fight the good fight, despite the obstacles.

Tracy Krauss

For I am convinced that neither death nor life, neither angels nor demons, neither the present nor the future, nor any powers, neither height nor depth, nor anything else in all creation, will be able to separate us from the love of God that is in Christ Jesus our Lord. (NIV)

Romans 8:38-39

PROLOGUE

"*D*o you think Mommy and Daddy will really let me get a pet?" Tempest thumbed through the book about dogs she'd gotten from the library. "If they do, I want a Great Dane!"

"Great Danes are too big for in the city," Martha said.

"It says here they're prone to hip trouble. I wonder if that's true?"

"Maybe. Now, can you be quiet? I'm trying to watch a show."

Tempest glanced at her babysitter. Martha was only a few years older than she was herself and usually spent most of their time together watching TV.

It seemed silly that Mommy and Daddy thought she needed someone to look after her when they went on their weekly date night. When she'd complained about it once, Martha said she should be happy her parents weren't getting a divorce. Poor Martha. Maybe she should cut her some slack.

Tempest went back to her book. The telephone rang. Tempest snatched the receiver up before Martha could make it to the phone. "Hello?" It was Great Aunt Rose.

Two words resonated with the low pitched frequency of a horror film. Accident. Dead.

Tempest twisted, screaming and clawing out of the demon's grasp until she fell to her knees.

It was the night the world stood still. The night that changed everything.

Tempest

Tempest unlocked the door to her apartment and opened it just enough to slip through. Her two dogs bounded forward immediately, Jupiter's low 'woof' forming the bass line for Paddy's high pitched vocals. They hovered excitedly, tails wagging.

"Hello to you, too!" She gave each head a pat. "Now, go sit," she commanded with cheerful cadence, pointing to the futon in the middle of the one room suite. The dogs trotted obediently to their spots. Jupiter, the Great Dane, sat down on the floor beside the futon while Yorkshire Terrier Paddy hopped onto its surface.

With practiced accuracy, Tempest clicked the deadbolt in place with a 'thack' and then leaned against the door, allowing herself a moment, eyes closed. With a cleansing breath she slowly opened them, letting her gaze wander to the view out the large window, the trees rustling in the breeze beyond its frame. The filmy drapes hung limp and unmoving, just as they should, with nothing on the other side to cause alarm.

It was foolish, really. This apprehension she felt every time she entered her own dwelling. It had been months since the terrible day she'd found her cat Zoe swinging listlessly from a noose on the other side of a different window.

Pets - and people - died.

It was time to get over it. Put it behind her.

But it wasn't that easy.

Dirk had asked for her forgiveness, and she had given it. He was a Christian now, and as a believer herself she had to show him that she'd let it go.

Except she hadn't. Not really.

If it had been a stranger who'd done the dastardly deed - angsty teenagers playing a sick prank, or even a psychotic neighbor who hated cats - maybe, just maybe - she could've handled it. But no. It had been someone she trusted. Someone who claimed to love her. And that made it all the worse, not just because he had betrayed her, but because she felt like a hypocrite.

With an extended breath, Tempest pushed off the door and walked to the small kitchen counter where she deposited her handbag and laptop. Next she checked her phone one more time to see if she'd missed a message from Ryan. Nothing.

She slammed the phone on the counter - perhaps too forcefully - and winced. What had she expected? As an FBI agent, her boyfriend, Ryan O'Toole, often worked erratic hours, sometimes not communicating for days, or longer, because he was on some secret assignment.

It was how they'd met. She'd been posing as her friend Cherise - an innocent favor that almost turned tragic - and Ryan had been working a drug case undercover. The fact that they made it through the ordeal alive and together seemed like a miracle. Ordained by God.

Or maybe just wishful thinking on her part. She and Ryan lived in separate worlds, and the longer they were together the more she realized it.

With a sigh, she headed to the futon to minister properly to her pets. At least they were the one constant in her tumultuous life.

"There you go, boys. Miss me?" Using one hand per dog, she rubbed behind their ears. "We'll go for our walk as soon as I change." Jupiter leaned into her hand while Paddy yelped, jealous for his share of attention. Tempest laughed. "I promise."

She felt badly sometimes that they spent so much time cooped up indoors, but it couldn't be helped. It was the best she could do for them right now. She missed their walks on the beach her previous location had allowed, but it was beyond what she could ever afford on her own.

This was reality, not some fairytale where everything turned out happily ever after.

PADDY TROTTED by Tempest's side, his toenails clicking out a happy rhythm on the cement. Jupiter led the way, only slightly in front as he sauntered to match his mate's pace. He had learned to be patient during their walks. Tempest knew he longed for some free rein so that he could stretch those long legs, but it would have to wait until they reached the park.

Her current accommodations did not afford the same convenience as her old digs. When she'd first moved to LA, she'd lived in a detached house only a few blocks from the beach, housesitting for a wealthy friend of a friend. It had been perfect. Sea air, beautiful views, and plenty of space to exercise her pets. And it had spoiled both her and the dogs ever after.

The arrangement had set her expectations unrealistically high. She couldn't afford that kind of place on her own, so now they were relegated to a bachelor pad above her employer's garage and walking the residential streets each evening. At least there was a park nearby where she could let the dogs run free...

as long as there weren't too many people around. Jupiter's size made him an intimidating creature, so she had to be careful.

She maneuvered the leashes so that all three of them were in single file for a small stretch and ducked under a low hanging branch. A neglected yard had begun to spill onto public property, its hedge encroaching on the sidewalk and its mature trees in need of pruning. Most of the neighborhood was well kept, however. It was an older, well established suburban area, probably built in the sixties. Rectangular bungalows were the norm, interspersed with a few mid-century modern designs.

The breeze lifted her hair, and she was glad for the light jacket she wore. Even though it seemed like summer in Los Angeles all year round - at least as far as she was concerned - temperatures could still feel cool in January, especially in the evening.

They were nearing the park, just two blocks from home, and both dogs increased their pace, aware that they might be afforded a bit of freedom if there weren't too many other patrons out and about.

"Here we are, boys." Tempest stopped at a centrally located bench. She patted Jupiter's massive head and then Paddy's smaller one. "I'll let you off if you promise not to get into trouble."

She surveyed the area before unclipping their leashes. Both dogs waited patiently, tails wagging furiously as she retrieved a tennis ball from her backpack and tossed it as far as she could. Jupiter charged after the projectile, Paddy following, well out of reach by the time the bigger animal snatched the ball and rock-eted back to where Tempest sat. He dropped it at her feet, tense and ready for a repeat.

"Good boy," she cooed, rubbing his head. She threw the ball again, and he bolted after it.

Paddy yapped incessantly, frantically spinning in circles as he attempted to fetch the ball first. The futility of his efforts made

Tempest laugh out loud. "Poor Paddy! There's no way you'll ever get there first, but you won't stop trying! Will you, boy?"

"Looks like they're enjoying themselves."

Tempest looked up in surprise. She'd been so intent on watching her dogs' antics that she hadn't even heard Ryan approach.

"Oh! You're back in LA?"

Ryan sat down beside her. "I told you I'd only be gone a few days." He leaned in for a kiss.

She reciprocated with a quick peck on the lips. "So you said, but I never really know for sure." She threw the ball again, effectively distancing herself. She noticed the slight frown, despite the fact that Ryan was very good at schooling his emotions into a perfect mask. He probably expected a more passionate greeting, but she just didn't have it in her right now.

"True enough," he said lightly and relaxed against the hard bench, watching the dogs at play.

He was as handsome as ever, with his dark hair, blue eyes, and strong athletic build. Almost too good to be true.

She shook her head. Her suspicious nature when it came to men was a hard habit to break. This was Ryan, not one of the others.

"Fetch," she called and tossed the ball again. She purposely threw it directly near Paddy so he could have a taste of success. He was back with the ball in two seconds flat, tail wagging. "Clever boy," she said in that voice reserved for pets and small children.

"Here, let me do that for awhile." Ryan held out his hand.

"Sure." She placed the tennis ball into his palm.

"Hm, soggy," he said with a grimace. He stood and threw the ball well beyond Tempest's farthest mark before wiping his palm on his jeans. "You should get one of those ball launchers."

"You offered," she said. "And a little dog slobber never hurt anyone."

He sat back down, smiled, and reached for her hand. "Reminds me of when we first met. You all tangled up in their leashes."

"That only happened once." Her accompanying laugh was only slightly defensive.

The memory of that time was as clear as if it were yesterday. She and Ryan had taken many walks along the beach, with the dogs as their excuse. It was unbelievable to think that at the time she didn't even know who Ryan really was. Perhaps that had been part of the attraction - the intrigue and sense of danger that went with their rendezvous.

"It was adorable," he said, rubbing her fingers with his thumb. "You trying to convince me you were Cherise, and me going along with it because I was undercover."

"What a way to start a relationship. Both pretending to be someone else."

There was silence between them for a few seconds.

Ryan squeezed her hand. "You okay? I get the feeling you're mad at me."

Tempest sat up stiffly. "Of course not. Why would I be mad?"

"I don't know. That's why I asked." He released her hand. Jupiter was back with the ball, and Ryan threw it again before continuing. "I get that you feel frustrated sometimes with the demands of my job. But I don't always have a choice."

"I know," Tempest said.

"Then what is it?"

"It's nothing."

"It's obviously something or you wouldn't be mad."

"I'm not mad."

"Then what's wrong? You seem quiet. Aren't you glad to see me?"

"Of course I'm glad to see you." She hesitated. "It might be nice to know in advance, though. That you're even safe."

"So, it *is* about the job," he stated.

"Not the job per se, but the lack of knowing." That was actually only a half truth. The realities of his job terrified her. The prospects of him getting killed while on assignment kept her up at night, even when he was safely in the city working behind a desk. She'd witnessed firsthand the types of situations he could find himself in. Like the time in Italy when Cherise was kidnapped, or more recently when he helped crack a drug smuggling operation in Mexico. It was just too dangerous.

"You know I can't divulge certain things." Ryan threw the ball again. "Think of it this way. As a journalist, you know better than most the importance of protecting your sources. In my case, I need to put those kinds of protective measures in place, too, and sometimes that means not texting or calling. It could put lives at risk."

"I know that." She looked down at her hands, picking at one of her nails. His tone was so logical. Almost patronizing.

"You just never know who could be watching," he added.

"Of course I understand," she said and stood up. "I think it's time I head home, now, though. And for the record, I'm not mad."

Ryan stood also. "You sure?"

She nodded.

He bent to kiss her again, and this time she let herself respond, kissing him back. Ryan was a good man. He wouldn't lie to her.

"Wanna go out for a bite to eat first?" he asked.

"Not tonight. I've got an article to finish before morning or Frank will have my head."

"Sometimes I regret getting you that job. Frank's expectations are unrealistic."

"You didn't get me the job!" Tempest protested with a slight smile. "I got the job purely on my own merits."

"After I gave you the tip that he was looking for an assistant," Ryan reminded.

"True."

"You sure? You have to eat," Ryan said encouragingly.

"How about tomorrow?"

Ryan furrowed his brow. "Not sure tomorrow is going to work for me. We'll see."

And so it went... Tempest pasted on a smile. "Okay." She turned to her dogs. "Sit!" she commanded.

"Want a lift back to your place?" Ryan asked.

"Thanks, but no. This is their only exercise, and its close." She bent to clip both dogs back onto their leashes.

"I'll see you tomorrow, then," Ryan said.

Maybe she would and maybe she wouldn't. That's just the way things were.

TEMPEST TUCKED a strand of chestnut hair behind her ear, pushed her glasses up on her nose, and squinted at the computer screen. Although she now wore contacts most of the time, by evening her eyes felt scratchy and her old glasses came out of their case. Unfortunately, her vision wasn't as clear with the glasses, but it was a small sacrifice.

The article she had promised her boss, Frank Dunlop, was as polished as she could make it. She'd hold off sending it until morning though, just in case some new inspiration came in the night.

Jupiter was curled at her feet, and Paddy snuggled nearby on the futon. She reached to scratch Paddy behind the ears and then clicked the laptop shut and unfolded her legs. Jupiter lifted his head in question.

"Sorry to disturb you, boy. I need a snack and maybe a nice cup of tea." Her dinner of ramen had hardly been satisfying. She probably should have taken Ryan up on dinner. It might have eased some of the tension she'd felt when they parted.

To be honest, their relationship had been awkward for some

time, now. He was always on assignment, and she didn't like the secrets that created a barrier between them - even if she knew it was necessary. She wanted a man who could share his life with her, not just select parts.

Of course, she also understood the reasons for his secrecy. Like he'd pointed out, it was part of his job, and therefore part of the package if she wanted to keep dating him. But it didn't mean she had to like it.

Their whole relationship was built on a shaky foundation. It all started with a ruse that she never should have agreed to in the first place. Pretending to be someone she wasn't had landed her in a heap of trouble. Her friend Cherise had begged her to pretend to be her for what sounded like one innocent meeting with an old family friend. Cherise was off chasing her latest flame and couldn't go, so, like a loyal friend, Tempest had agreed. It's what got her entangled with Cherise's brother Dirk, nearly got Cherise killed, and did result in one fatality - her cat Zoe.

Ryan, unbeknown to her or Dirk, was undercover and posing as the family friend. And so the game of lies had begun. She'd been tongue-tied by his good looks. He was not the middle-aged man she had expected. To top it off, he kept showing up in unexpected places - Boston, Los Angeles, Rome... Despite her better judgment, she'd been hooked. Ryan O'Toole had gotten under her skin and hadn't emerged. And when she found out he was also a believer, well, it seemed like God had ordained it all along.

On their first real date, she'd told Ryan about Zoe and how she could hardly stand to stay in the house where she'd been hung.

"I know a few people. Let me check around," he'd said.

And he had. Within a week he'd found a lead for a job, which led to a new place to live, and even recommended a church. His.

And now she had Ryan, too. Sort of.

She just couldn't help the doubts that continually rose up in her mind. What if his secrecy about his work went beyond protecting the case? Yes, he was a Christian, but he was a man, too. What if he he had to do things sometimes, to maintain his cover? It had happened to her friend, Cherise. Her lover Roberto had turned out to be a nark and sleeping with Cherise had been part of the deal.

Tempest let out a frustrated growl. Jupiter looked up and whined. "It's okay, boy. I'm just being stupid. Go back to sleep."

Ryan wasn't Roberto and she wasn't Cherise. She just had to keep reminding herself of that fact.

CHAPTER 2

*T*empest's eye caught sight of something hanging outside the glass patio doors. It arched gently in the breeze like the pendulum on a grandfather clock. She squinted, moving closer. A few more steps and her hands flew to her mouth as she stifled a scream.

Zoe's lifeless body swung lazily from the end of a rope.

Tempest backed up, bumped into a dining chair, and inadvertently sat with a plop.

TEMPEST WOKE IN A SWEAT. Jupiter whined while the rhythmic swell of Paddy's little frame continued uninterrupted. She patted Jupiter's head, and he laid it once more upon the edge of the futon.

There would be no more sleep tonight. Dream free slumber was a luxury that occurred too infrequently.

"HM. I think I can use that piece you sent this morning, but how's that article on Judge Cromwell coming?"

Tempest yawned before looking across the top of her computer at her employer. "Just fact checking."

"Not getting enough sleep?" Frank asked.

"I'm fine. I'll send the article to you as soon as I finish."

"Ever heard of deadlines?" Frank mumbled gruffly, more to himself than to Tempest. "It's the problem with you young people nowadays. Don't know the meaning of deadlines."

Tempest's lips twitched and she forced her mouth into a straight line. To an onlooker, Frank Dunlop seemed gruff - the typical crusty newsman from back in the day. After working for him for several months, she knew better. Most of it was bluster. Armor designed to protect.

Frank was an independent journalist who managed to sustain himself as a freelancer mostly due to his reputation and sheer determination. He'd been looking for an assistant when she'd applied. Someone willing to do some digging, not afraid of hard work and long hours, and most importantly, someone who could follow orders. It wasn't the arts and culture scene, but it was work. Writing work.

Frank was in his early sixties, with salt and pepper hair, a drooping moustache straight out of the eighties and rumpled clothing that spoke of too much time sitting behind his desk. He was best described as boxy; square hands, barrel chested, granite shoulders - probably an intimidating figure in his younger years with a gravelly voice that cut right to the heart of the matter. Tempest was grateful for the opportunity to learn from his experience.

The office was cramped with two desks, a couple of filing cabinets, a photocopier, a printer, and a coffee station - all in one room, accessible up a long stairway over a small florist shop. Not the most glamorous location, but it sufficed. Truthfully, she could have done most of her work from home - and sometimes did -

but Frank was old school. He liked the idea of keeping an outside office.

Their first meeting had been right here in this office - Frank on one side of his desk and she on the other, sitting in a wooden, hard-backed chair. He'd examined her with close scrutiny, as if to gain as much information from her body language as from her resume. "I was impressed with the piece you sent me. Not too frilly. Good hook; nice gritty feel, but sympathetic, too. You sure you wrote it?"

"I assure you, I wrote it," Tempest had replied. She'd held her hands together in her lap, determined not to cave under his penetrating stare. He was staring at her over the tops of his reading glasses, her sample article in hand. "I assume you also checked my references and some of the other freelance work I mentioned?"

Frank had nodded, glancing back at the piece of paper. "Impressive."

"Thank you."

"And you found me how, again?" He'd looked up.

"A mutual acquaintance."

"Not willing to divulge?"

"You know how it is. Giving up one's sources and all that."

"Good, good. I like that."

In this case there was really no reason to keep her source secret. It had been Ryan. But something Ryan had said kept her mouth shut.

"He fancies himself a vigilante of sorts, keeping an eye on the pulse of the city. Our office has a mutual agreement, you could say. He provides us with intel from the street and we direct his sniffer in the right direction when we can. He said recently he was looking for an assistant. Someone to do some of the grunt work, as he put it. I almost hate the thought of you getting involved with a guy like him. Not saying he's not above board, but sometimes I wonder where he gets his information..."

Frank had tapped on the desktop with a pen. "I can't pay you a regular nine to five wage. I pay for work done. You'd be freelancing, but with a guaranteed outlet for your stories should I like them. Kind of like a sublet. You bring the stories, I have the contacts."

"But you *are* looking for a steady stream of work?"

"First rights are mine, and if I don't want them, you can go ahead and try to sell elsewhere."

"I can do that. It's a deal."

"I don't recall offering one yet."

"Oh, of course."

Frank had squinted past her head into the distance. "Ross... that name sounds familiar. I knew someone back in the day with that name. Marvin... Milton... A darn good reporter, too."

"Merlin?"

Frank had snapped his fingers. "That's it."

"He was my father."

"Is that so? Whatever happened to him? Retired?"

"He and my mother were killed in a car accident when I was a child."

"Yes, yes." Frank's chair squeaked as he shifted. "I remember now. So sorry to hear it."

"Thanks."

Frank had cleared his throat and shoved a stack of papers toward her. "Have a look through these and see if you find anything worthwhile. They're just tidbits. A bit of this and a bit of that. Not sure if there's any real news in there, but that's what you're for. To sift. Kind of like panning for gold."

Tempest had taken ahold of the stack, trying to gather it together into an ordered semblance. "Okay... so you want me, then?"

"Of course."

Relief had flooded Tempest's being. "Thank you. You won't regret it." She'd hugged the folders next to her chest.

"Well, get going, then." Frank had made a shooing motion. "I expect to have something worth printing on my desk first thing tomorrow."

That had been months ago, and things hadn't changed much. Frank still expected quality work in record time, and she wouldn't have it any other way. These days, Frank didn't insist she work exclusively on his leads, although he wouldn't guarantee anything. If she wrote enough from his slush pile, she could also work on pieces she was more interested in.

Sifting through Frank's semi-finished ideas for articles had been exhausting. There was a huge variance in Frank's pile of tidbits, and she knew her first article would be a test of sorts. She'd finally decided to go with a human interest story about a woman who lived on the beach and collected bits of plastic. Over the course of a year the woman had collected close to a ton of stray garbage that would have otherwise ended up at sea.

Tempest had stayed up all night working on the piece and subsequently arrived late the next day - another serendipitous event which had turned out for the best.

Frank had nodded as he read the article. "I like it. Not too bleeding heart to scare anyone away, but not making excuses either."

"So, it meets with your approval?"

"Absolutely." Frank then looked up, pinning her with his penetrating gaze. "You were late this morning. Not too impressive on your first day."

"I'm so sorry. I live quite a ways from here and then one of my dogs got loose and I had to fetch him and get him back in the house before I could leave."

"Next you're going to tell me the bus was late."

"No, I'm borrowing a car. It's part of the deal where I live. I'm house sitting for a…" she'd hesitated on the next word, "a friend."

"I know. Noticed the car yesterday. I wondered why someone

driving a car like that needed a paltry job like the one I'm offering."

"Trust me, the sooner I can get out of that situation, the better."

"Any reason why?"

She'd found herself telling Frank everything - about Dirk and Cherise and Zoe. Even Ryan. It surprised her in hindsight. It must be why he was so good at his job. He had the uncanny ability to get people to talk to him. To tell him things.

"Now that's quite a story," Frank had said.

"I didn't mean to tell you so much."

"Don't worry. It helps me see where you're coming from, and I might have just the answer. I have an apartment over my garage. My son used to live there, but he's moved on, and now my wife and I are looking to let it out."

The rest was history. Frank had become the father figure she'd been craving. She owed him her job and her independence. He was the one man she wholeheartedly trusted.

TEMPEST LIFTED the lid to the mailbox attached right outside Frank and Edna's front door. Edna usually retrieved what belonged to her and Frank earlier in the day, but left Tempest's mail behind for her to get herself on the way home from work. It was easier than having to ask Edna for it. Frank's wife didn't go out much.

Frank was slowly ascending the cement steps behind her. "Anything interesting?" he asked.

"The usual," she replied. "Bills."

"I thought you young people did everything online."

"Mostly." Tempest smiled, still sifting through the letters. "Oh! Here's an unmarked one. Edna must have forgotten it." She held out a plain brown envelope.

As Frank took it from Tempest, three photographs slipped out onto the step. Tempest bent to pick them up.

She couldn't help looking. Sudden recognition hit her in the gut, and she gasped like she'd been sucker punched. "Frank?" she asked as she slowly straightened.

"What is it?" Frank took the photos and flipped through them. "Hm."

Tempest peered over his shoulder. They were taken in front of a storefront with an awning over the window. A figure leaned up against the brick of the building. He was wearing dark glasses. She waited for Frank to say something.

Frank nodded his head. "Sure looks like your boyfriend," he confirmed. He perused the blank envelope. "Wonder who sent them?"

"What if he's in trouble?" Tempest turned wide eyes toward Frank.

"It's probably nothing. I'll figure it out and let you know. I'm sure there's nothing to worry about."

"How can you say that? The guy he meets up with looks so... shady!"

"He works undercover and has all kinds of contacts," Frank said reasonably. "That person could be anyone."

"I suppose..." Tempest frowned. "But why? Why were these in your mailbox? And who put them there?"

"Those are the questions of the hour, aren't they?"

"Do you think it's a warning? Maybe an undercover operation he was working got found out, and someone is warning him - through you... or me." She stopped and blinked. "He could be in danger. We should tell him right away!"

"Slow down." Frank took Tempest's flailing hands and calmed them into stillness. "Or maybe whoever put them there thinks there's a story."

"What... what do you mean?"

"I'm not saying anything for sure," Frank responded. "Just leave it to me."

"No! You're not telling me what you really think. I can tell you're holding back, and I need to know."

Frank let out a gust of air. "Sometimes cops get jaded. They see a lot of people benefitting when they don't get the same compensation for doing the right thing..."

Tempest's jaw tightened. "Just what are you implying?"

"I like to think I'm unbiased. That I can see both sides of things."

"Ryan is *not* a dirty cop!"

"I never said that. But we have to be smart about this." Frank's gravelly voice held reason. "I don't know him as well as you, and he seems like a good sort. But..."

"But what?" Tempest prodded.

"I did some digging about a drug operation he helped crack recently, and some things didn't add up."

Tempest started to shake. "It can't be."

Frank patted her hand. "Listen, I'll do everything I can to get to the bottom of it."

"Let me see those pictures again." Tempest reached for the photos. The time stamp showed the day before yesterday. She turned to Frank. "Where do you suppose these were taken? Do you recognize it?"

"Not off the top of my head, but it shouldn't be hard to find out."

"He was supposedly out of town for a few days," Tempest said, more to herself than Frank. "Do you think he was lying?"

"Who knows? I won't know until I do some digging." Frank took the pictures and stuffed them into the envelope.

"You keep saying 'I'. Well, I have a few questions for him myself!"

"Not sure how smart that is. If he *is* lying, asking directly won't help. It could end up getting you into trouble, and I won't have that."

"But… what should I do?" Tempest whispered.

"You leave it to me. I'll handle it. When I find something, you'll be the first to know."

"Promise?"

"Yes, I promise. In the meantime, just act natural. It could be nothing."

Frank stepped past her and unlocked his own door before going inside. The deadbolt clacking into place jolted her back to reality, and she skipped down the front steps to make her way to the side entrance of the garage which led to her own apartment.

Act natural?

Scenes from every horrible past relationship came rolling back. Every suspicion; every doubt she'd had about Ryan, followed. What if she'd just been fooled again?

CHAPTER 3

*T*empest wasn't sure which was worse - horrible dreams or not being able to sleep at all. She slipped ever so slowly from the bed so as not to disturb the dogs and tip-toed to the sink for a glass of water. The tepid liquid - for she couldn't risk letting the tap run - slipped down her throat. With a sigh, she set the glass down and leaned against the counter, head bowed.

Every time she opened up to a member of the opposite sex, it turned out to be a disaster. Even though she didn't believe in curses, it felt like one had been cast on her at birth. After all these years, one would think she'd have learned something. Maybe she had. Men couldn't be trusted.

She had loved Ron, her college boyfriend. Or at least, she thought she had loved him, but maybe he'd just filled the role of the male lead in her fantasy about having a family. He was a security blanket. A proper Christian with the same beliefs who elicited very few sparks.

Someone in one of her literature classes had invited her to a youth event on campus and she'd gone. It was there that she'd met Jesus. Her best friends Cherise and Stella were skeptical at first, so she'd learned not to talk about her faith too much around them. She didn't want to drive them away.

When she'd met Ron at church, it looked like God was on her side after all. Ron was honest, upright, and a man of deep integrity. A bit legalistic, but that didn't matter since he loved God and wanted to serve Him - just like she did.

Everything was going according to plan. Until Ron found out she wasn't a virgin.

Oh, he said it didn't matter to him, but she could see it in his eyes. The disappointment. Aversion, even. She was tainted, and he made a clean exit to the mission field. So much for grace.

Now, Jake was another story...

⁓

TEMPEST CLUTCHED the books a little closer to her chest and kept walking. She'd made the mistake of taking a peek at the good looking guy who sat in front of her in her classic literature lecture. Not that that was anything different. He was handsome, and she often snatched glimpses of the back of his neck while he lounged only a few feet away. When he smiled - at one of his own friends, of course - the entire room lit up. Talk about cliche. The guy was a walking, talking metaphor for 'college hunk'.

Except that college hunks didn't pay any attention to spectacled librarian types, as Cherise would have observed, which was why her friend was always trying to give her a make-over. And now she had gone and drawn attention to herself. She had actually looked him in the eye on her way out of the lecture theater. She was mortified and decided then and there she should probably sit in a different section of the room from then on.

Except she didn't. Bucking up her courage, she decided to stand her ground - or sit as it were - and stay in the same seat. So did he. The next time they met he actually smiled at her before he sat down. Tempest's heart fluttered in her chest, and she was glad that he didn't turn around again or he'd see the flush that had taken over her face from roots to collar.

On day three he actually said hello, and the day after that he added a quip about the course. "Here for my daily dose of Keates. My mother says it's good for me."

She said something idiotic like, "Keates is good for the soul," and then hid her nose in her books.

Day five of contact arrived, and he introduced himself. "I'm Jake, by the way." Tempest stared at the hand protruding into her space across the top of the seat in front of her. The moment lasted a little more than even normal awkwardness would allow until she finally grabbed his hand and gave it a perfunctory shake. "Tempest."

"Tempest? That's a nice name."

Tempest blinked, not trusting herself to blurt a thank you.

After a full week of pleasantries, Tempest relaxed, thinking long into the night about what clever quip she could say the next time they met. He always laughed at her comments, saying something like, "Whoa! You're so smart!"

It was a Thursday. The autumn leaves were thick upon the campus grass, and the wind made it nippy enough to need a warmer jacket or at least a thick sweater. It was the day she came alive and then died.

Class was over. Tempest gathered up her books. Jake stood, hands in pockets. From what she could tell, he only used a tablet for notes, and it was tucked into the backpack slung over one shoulder. "I was thinking. Maybe we should go out for coffee? That last lecture had me sleeping. I think I need some caffeine to wake me up."

Tempest pushed her glasses more securely onto the bridge of her nose. "Okay."

The moment the two syllables came out of her mouth she wished them back. Desperately. Now he'd know for sure that she was a bumbling fool around good looking guys. Besides, she usually went to the library for another hour after class. She liked routine.

The popular bistro frequented by college students was just two blocks away. Tempest didn't remember what they talked about. At the time it seemed like they had so much in common, but in hindsight she supposed he just pretended to like the same things she did - classic literature, music, animals... The one thing that did come back to mind was his fascination with her roommate.

"It's cool that you get to room with one of your 'besties,'" Jake said. "Lots of times you don't get a choice."

"Cherise has connections," Tempest said, using air quotes.

"Cherise? That's her name?" Jake asked.

Tempest nodded. "Cherise Hillyer. We've been friends since we were twelve. Went to the same boarding school. She's my best friend, except for Stella, who is also -"

"Cherise Hillyer, you say?"

"Yes. That's what I said."

"Does she have an older brother? Dirk Hillyer?"

Tempest squinted in thought. "Um, I think so. You know him?"

Jake shrugged nonchalantly. "Maybe. You'll have to introduce us and then I'll know for sure."

"Okay."

Jake looked at his watch. "I'll walk you back to your dorm."

"You don't have to do that."

"It's getting dusky. I wouldn't be a gentleman if I let you walk alone after dark."

"It's no trouble, really -"

"I insist." Jake smiled in that charming way he had. He paid the bill, and as they walked along he even took her books so that she didn't have to carry them.

Tempest could hardly string two words together let alone carry on a conversation. The best looking guy on campus liked her! Her stomach was in knots, and she felt tongue tied and suddenly shy, despite the pleasantries of the past hour in the coffee shop.

"Well, this is it." They stopped in front of her building, and she pointed to the wide glass doors at the top of a flight of cement steps.

Jake started up the steps, her books still in his arms.

Tempest scurried after him. "I can take those."

"No trouble. I can take them right up to your room for you if you like." He stopped in front of the door. "In fact, maybe this would be a good time for you to introduce me to your roomie."

"My roomie?" Tempest squinted.

"Yeah, you know. The one who might be related to my buddy, Dirk."

"Oh. Right. We're not actually supposed to have visitors."

"Really? Isn't segregating the sexes kind of out of date?"

He'd called her out that time. He was correct. There was no particular rule about bringing members of the opposite sex to one's room. Cherise did it all the time - when Tempest was out, of course. She recognized the telltale signs left behind like the musky smell of male pheromones.

"Come on. Just for a few minutes?" He smiled encouragingly. "I won't bite."

Tempest took a deep breath. "Okay." The rule was old fashioned, and she'd made it up anyway.

With her heart hammering in her chest, Tempest used her keycard to activate the doors, and they entered the building. Two flights of stairs and she did the same with the security lock on her own door.

"Cherise?" Tempest called as she entered the room. When no one answered, she turned to Jake and pointed. "You can set those over there on my desk."

Jake deposited the books on the small built-in desk and then looked around. "Nice digs."

Tempest frowned as she surveyed the small quarters. "You think?" Evidence of female clothing of all sorts lay on Cherise's half of the room. Tempest's was spotless.

Jake sauntered to Cherise's rumpled bed and picked up a lace bra.

"Oh! Don't do that," Tempest said with alarm. "I don't think she'd want you to touch her stuff."

"Sorry." Jake dropped the bra where it lay. "So, I take it this is her side and that's your side?" He gestured to Tempest's pristinely made bed.

"Um, right." Tempest twisted her hands together. "Well, since she's not here, I suppose..." She didn't finish the sentence, embarrassed. With any luck he'd get the hint and take his leave.

Jake took the two steps to Tempest's bed and patted the crisp bedcover. "I see you like a tight ship."

"Yes. Cherise says I need to lighten up, but..."

Jake looked around. "And when is she coming back again?"

"I... I don't know. It's hard to tell with Cherise."

"She wouldn't mind if we, just... you know. Hung out for a bit?"

"I, um..." Tempest pushed her glasses up.

Jake smiled. "You don't mind, do you?" He gently removed the glasses. "I'd like to see what you look like without them."

"Oh! I can't see very well without them."

"Who needs to see?" He smiled again and set the glasses down on the nightstand before looking straight at her. "Much better." He reached up to cup her cheek in his hand. "Do you mind?"

Tempest's eyelashes fluttered, and her stomach was in knots. He was going to kiss her. She knew it. She couldn't nod yes or no, just wait for his mouth to slowly descend on hers.

She felt awkward and clumsy, not knowing what to do when his lips grazed hers and he tried to open her mouth. She took a step back and her legs bumped into the bed. "Oh!"

It came out in a mumbled mess, since her mouth was covered with Jake's. Her mind told her she should stop it, but the warmth in her core said otherwise.

Suddenly she was sitting on the bed, then lying, Jake on top of her. "Oh! Wait. What if Cherise comes home!"

"Don't you want to?" Jake pushed up on one elbow. "I got the impression you were into it."

"Oh, well..."

Jake started kissing her again and was moving his hands up and down her sides in a way that she had never experienced before.

"What about -"

"Sh. It's handled." He silenced her with another kiss.

Tempest gave into the sensation. Maybe it was time she joined the twenty-first century.

When Jake was done, he simply rolled off and got dressed. "You didn't tell me you were a virgin."

"I... didn't know it mattered." Tempest clutched the rumpled sheet around her chin.

"See you at class tomorrow, then." He was already heading for the door. Not so much as a thank-you. Not that that would make it better.

This wasn't how it was supposed to be. Not like in the movies, when the couple made love for hours and then lay in each other's arms basking in the light of their love. It lasted all but five minutes - and it hurt. No fuzzy feelings, no heart-felt declarations of affection.

She lay there, too stunned to even cry for a good ten minutes. Then she rose and took her violated soul to the shower, where she allowed herself to cry for an hour.

It wasn't like he'd raped her. The sex had been consensual. But she felt just as dirty.

CHAPTER 4

*T*empest's hand was on the doorknob when her phone buzzed. She checked the number and her heart froze. Ryan.

Act natural. Act natural.

Tempest tried to keep Frank's admonition in mind. "Hello?" How could she act natural when everything inside her wanted to scream, "Liar!"

"Hi. It's me. Do you think we could meet up this morning?"

Tempest shut the door to her suite, cradling the phone under her ear as she juggled her purse and laptop. "I'm actually just heading to the office. Frank's waiting outside in his van."

"I never did understand that. Why you go to the office when you could do most of your work from home."

"Frank likes it." She launched down the wooden steps. "Speaking of, he might blow a gasket if I don't get a move on." As if to add credence to her statement, Frank tooted the horn.

"It's important. Can't you make an excuse?"

Tempest bolted out the side door of the garage. "Um... maybe. But we'd have to meet somewhere close to work."

"I can do that. How about the cafe at the end of the block?"

"Okay. What time?" She climbed into the passenger side of Frank's beat up minivan and did up her seatbelt as Frank simultaneously backed out of the drive.

"Ten?" Ryan asked.

Tempest glanced over at Frank. "Okay. See you then."

"Mr. FBI?" Frank asked as soon as she'd hung up.

"How did you know?"

"Been in this business too long not to know," Frank said. "So, you're meeting him at ten, I take it."

Tempest just nodded.

"Why?"

"I don't know for sure. He just said it was important."

"Don't say or do anything stupid. Ryan's no slouch. He'll know something's up if you're not careful."

Tempest let out a frustrated sigh. "And what *is* up, exactly? Maybe he just wants to see me. He *is* supposed to be my boyfriend. I'm sure there's an explanation."

Why was she defending him? He'd lied to her about being out of town. How many more lies were there? She straightened in her seat.

"You're too close to the story. Too much digging and he'll know something's up."

"Are you saying I shouldn't meet him?"

"Would you normally meet him if he asked?"

"Yes…"

"Then meet him. Just don't dig. Leave that to me."

"I don't know what you want from me, Frank," Tempest said with a huff. "You want me to act natural, but how am I supposed to do that when I know something is wrong?" She let out another frustrated sigh. "I'm a reporter, too, you know. And I'm closer to him than you. Maybe I could find something out without making him suspicious."

"Maybe."

"What's the matter? You don't trust me?" She glared at Frank's profile.

"Not true. You're a darn good reporter," Frank said. "You can dig with the best of them. But sometimes the pile isn't sanitary. I want to spare you that."

"I can handle it. I just want the truth."

RYAN POINTED to the two cups of coffee on the table the moment Tempest entered the small cafe. She wound her way past several tables and sat down across from him, shrugging out of her jacket as she did so.

"Hope you don't mind that I got you a coffee."

Ryan was as handsome as ever, accentuating her disgust that she may have been played - again. "Coffee is fine," she clipped.

"You sure? If you want something else, I'll drink both."

Tempest blinked and then tried schooling her features into a pleasant mask. She'd obviously been frowning, and he'd picked up on it. "No, coffee is good. I was just... it's just work." She took a sip to calm her nerves and then forced a smile.

"You should think about starting a blog or something. Find another outlet for your writing. Frank puts way too much pressure on you."

"Blogging isn't what it used to be," Tempest said. "Besides, Frank and Edna are good to me. I live over their garage for next to nothing, and I have a secure outlet for my pieces." She shifted in her seat. "So, you said it was important. What's up?"

"Can't I just want to see my girl?" Ryan flashed a smile and reached for her hand.

"Um... yes. I suppose. But..." Her pulse rocketed into high gear, and not from his touch. What if his lies went further? What is he *was* a dirty cop? She retrieved her hand and tucked a strand of hair behind one ear. "I don't have long. We're working under some deadlines."

"Okay." He sighed. "You caught me lying."

She choked on her coffee. "What?"

"Yes, I did want to see you because it seems like so long since we spent any real time together, but I do have another reason." He smiled sheepishly and squinted.

Tempest's breath caught in her throat. "Go on."

Ryan put both hands under the table. "There's something I need to ask you before I go on the next assignment."

"Another secret assignment? So soon?" Her throat felt tight and she clenched her jaw.

Ryan nodded. "In the works. When I get the call, I might not be back for awhile. I probably won't be able to contact you much, either, but -"

"And I'm just supposed to sit here, not asking any questions. Just wait for your return like a good girlfriend?"

Ryan's eyebrows rose, her uncharacteristic interruption obviously catching him off guard. "I know it's been difficult this last while, but…"

"Difficult? Is that what you call it?" She looked him in the eye, not wavering. She was no longer the shrinking flower she'd been all those years ago in college. Life had taught her a few things. "What if I'm not willing to do that anymore?"

"What are you saying, exactly? That you want to break up?" Ryan asked point blank.

She avoided his question by asking another. "Well, how do I know I can trust you? How do I know you're not flirting with other women while you're supposedly undercover?"

Ryan's eyes widened. "Is that what this is about? I would never do that to you!"

"But how do I know that? You flirted with me."

"That was different."

"How?"

"It just was! I've always been honest with you. About my feelings, anyway." He lowered his voice and sat forward. "Maybe we should take this somewhere else."

Tempest straightened her spine. "We're fine right here."

Ryan sat back and let out an exasperated sigh. "This isn't the way I had imagined things going. I knew you'd be unhappy about the situation, but you've never acted this way before."

"Stood up for myself, you mean?" Tempest asked.

"When you put it that way, yes. And in hindsight, it's probably about time. I'm proud of you. But that doesn't change the fact that I have a job to do."

"What other things have you lied about?"

"Being undercover and lying are not the same thing. You know I can't divulge certain things."

"Very convenient, I'd say."

"What do you want me to say?"

There was silence for a moment until she leaned forward. "Were you even away this last time?"

He narrowed his eyes. "What makes you ask that?"

"Oh, just some very interesting photographs I saw - of you!"

Ryan was all business now. Eyes of steel penetrated hers. "What photographs? Who gave them to you?"

Her confidence was beginning to vanish. "I don't know. Someone put them in Frank's mailbox."

"What was in them?" Ryan asked.

"Um… you. Meeting up with some shady person in front of a brick building."

"What else?" Ryan persisted.

"The building had an awning." She hesitated. "Ryan? Are you in trouble? What's going on?"

"Listen to me and listen carefully. Do not pursue this. Tell Frank not to pursue this. Things could get dangerous for you if you do."

"Why? Because you're a dirty cop?" The words were out before she could stop them.

Ryan stilled, blinking several times. "Is that what you think of me? Truly?"

She shook her head. "I don't want to believe it, but Frank says -"

"Forget what Frank says! Forget what anybody says. I need you to stay clear of anything you may think you know - or may not know." He brought something out of his pocket and set it on the table. "You're probably right. Breaking up *is* for the best."

She let her gaze move slowly to the small velvet box that sat between them, and her breath hitched.

"I was going to propose to you before I left, so you'd know I plan to do better in future. As soon as this case is wrapped up." He opened the box to a beautiful diamond ring, sparkling under the cafe lights. "But it's a moot point now." He snapped the lid shut with a decisive clack and put the box back in his pocket.

Tempest blinked, tongue-tied. "Ryan, I…"

"Save it. I know things haven't been the best recently, but I thought you knew my intentions were honest. Apparently not." He stood up. "That's why I said it was important. Glad I didn't waste your time."

Tempest watched him stalk from the cafe. Confusion swirled in her brain. What had she just done?

TEMPEST TOOK a cab and went straight home. There was no way she could face Frank - or anyone else.

How had it come to this? Ryan was going to propose! And she had driven him away because of her own stupid, unfounded suspicions.

She was nursing a cup of tea in one hand while scratching

Paddy behind the ears with the other, when her phone rang. She glanced at the caller. Stella.

She didn't feel like talking to anyone right now, not even her best friends, but her well ingrained sense of obligation got the better of her and she answered.

"Tempest!"

"Hi, Stella," Tempest said.

"How are you doing? Is everything all right?' Stella asked in her typical no nonsense way.

"I'm fine. Everything's fine," she lied.

"You sure? For some reason I just felt like I needed to call, to make sure you're okay."

Tempest let a wane smile turn up the corners of her mouth. She couldn't hide anything from her friends. They were like sisters. "Actually, if you must know…" She hesitated and took a deep breath. "Ryan and I broke up today."

There was a moment of silence. "What? Oh Temp, I am so sorry! What happened?"

"I, um… he proposed."

"And you said no…?" Stella probed.

"Not exactly." Tempest's voice hitched. "Oh, Stella! I am such an idiot!"

"It's okay, hun," Stella soothed. "Getting married is a big step. If you aren't ready, then that's okay."

"No! That's not it."

"Okay… Start at the beginning and tell me everything."

From their declining relationship, Ryan's continued secret activities, to the final blow when she'd seen the photographs, she left nothing out.

"Wow. I don't know what to say. Maybe you dodged a bullet," Stella offered. "Do you really think Ryan is up to no good?"

"I don't know what to think." Tempest sniffed.

"Personally, I can't imagine it's true."

"Neither can I," Tempest admitted. "But with all the doubts in my head… Oh Stella, I think I really made a mess of things this time!"

"Do you love him?" Stella asked.

"I thought I did. My radar isn't always the best, though."

"What are you talking about?"

"You know… past relationships."

"Forget about Ron," Stella said emphatically. "He was a colossal jerk."

"Not just Ron…"

"Who else, then? Dirk? You were never really a thing, so you can't count him."

"I know. And he's with someone who's really nice now. At least he was the last time I heard." She didn't mention Jake. Although both Stella and Cherise knew that she'd slept with him, they didn't actually know the whole story. It was too embarrassing to share in its entirety, even to them.

"If you and Ryan are meant to be, then it will work out. Just give it time."

Tempest nodded, even though Stella couldn't see her. "I know you're right. I just have to trust God more."

"Exactly. Look how He worked things out for both Cherise and me. Who would have thought we'd be married to brothers, no less."

"I know. Crazy."

"Zane and I will pray about this," Stella continued. "And I'm sure next time you talk to Cherise, she and Blue will, too."

"Thanks."

"Isn't it amazing that we're all Christians now?" Stella asked. "I remember a time when we thought you had gone off the deep end with religion!"

"I know. God is good," Tempest said. Her voice sounded flat, even to her own ears.

"Hey, listen…" Stella said softly. "I know you're hurting right now, but you'll get through this. I promise."

"Thanks. I love you," Tempest said.

"Love you, too."

She hung up and sat for a moment in quiet contemplation. She did trust God, but at the same time she was overcome with doubt, too. How could a mature believer in Christ be so double minded?

With a sigh she stood up. "Come on, boys. You ready for some exercise?"

Both dogs wagged their tails.

At least she still had them.

CHAPTER 5

*T*empest sidestepped the man in the church foyer, and they made eye contact for a brief second. He smiled but continued on his way. She waited a moment and then slipped into the sanctuary to find her normal seat before the service started.

Was it strange that she continued to attend the same church as Ryan? Not that it mattered much, really, since he was often away and apparently would be gone this time for awhile. She had every right to worship here. She wasn't the one who'd done anything suspicious.

The man she'd so carefully avoided in the entrance took the seat beside her only moments later. "Is this seat taken?" he asked as he made himself comfortable.

What if it were? But she didn't dare verbalize that thought. "No, it's not." She tried for an aloof yet confident smile. Inside, she just wanted solitude.

"Geoff Vanguard."

Tempest blinked, realizing after a second that he was speaking to her. She turned her head and focused on the man beside her. He was mildly attractive with a stylishly studious air about him - cropped hair, beard, relaxed but trendy clothes, hipster glasses... His hand was extended.

"Tempest Ross." Their hands barely touched before hers was back in her lap.

"I've seen you around." He smiled.

"Oh." She wasn't sure what else to say.

"The friend you come with sometimes... He's busy today?"

"Um... yes. You could say that."

"Have you been together long?"

"What makes you think we're a couple?"

"Aren't you? I just assumed."

Tempest clutched her Bible more tightly. "We're not together anymore."

Geoff took that in with a nod. "You should come out to the singles group, then," he said. "We have a Bible study every Thursday evening."

She flinched, ever so slightly, her radar on high alert. He was being awfully forward. What were his motives?

She released the breath she had been subconsciously holding. She shouldn't let her jaded view of the opposite sex dictate her every action. It could be a perfectly friendly offer.

"Thanks. Maybe I'll do that."

TEMPEST HESITATED IN THE DOORWAY. At one point in her life she had been too trusting, but now the pendulum had swung the other way. It was time she shed the baggage of suspicion and found some Christian friends in LA. Without Ryan, her immediate circle was small, indeed.

With one more deep breath, she stepped across the threshold into the church lounge where the singles Bible study was held. Several couches made the space feel intimate, even though it could probably hold thirty quite comfortably. Some people mingled around a coffee dispenser while a few were already seated.

Geoff spotted her almost immediately and waved, a pleasant smile splitting his features. She tamped down her first thought about his motivation and waved back. It didn't take him long to join her. "I'm so glad you decided to come."

"Thanks." She looked around.

"I'll introduce you to everyone before we start."

Tempest straightened her spine. "No need."

"We're all friends here," he said with a laugh. "Randall will ask anyway, so be prepared."

"Randall?"

"The leader." Geoff pointed to a dark complexioned thirty something man who wore glasses.

Tempest nodded. "Oh."

People started migrating to the sitting area, and she and Geoff followed. She found a spot on a comfy couch, and Geoff sat beside her. Randall started with prayer and then, as predicted, he welcomed newcomers. It wasn't as bad as she'd feared. He got each person to say their name in turn. She and another girl named Joyce were new, so at least she wasn't alone.

Once introductions had been dispensed with, they got right into the study. It was based on a passage from Mark Chapter 2 where Jesus ate with some tax collectors and sinners, and then got reprimanded by the religious leaders of the day for doing so. Tempest relaxed and listened, enjoying the friendly discussion. Maybe she could fit in here.

"Jesus wasn't afraid to hang out with the disreputable of the day," Randall said. "He came into the world to connect with people."

"I'm not arguing with you," Joe, another member of the group, said. "I just meant that we still have to be careful. It can be a slippery slope. Reaching out to people and then starting to participate in the sin can happen."

"Of course. I would never suggest someone get involved somewhere if they feel it could become a stumbling block - to them, or others. Just as long as we don't get hung up on the kind of segregation that's led to problems in the past. How are people going to hear about Jesus if we don't engage with them?"

"A little less judgment and a little more love," Geoff said under his breath so only Tempest could hear.

Tempest nodded and smiled over at him.

"What about the gay community?" someone named Brittany asked.

Randall turned his attention to Brittany. "What's your question?"

"Should the church be embracing people with different sexual orientation?"

"This is a timely - and tricky - topic in light of our current culture," Randall answered. "I don't pretend to know all the answers, but I think that loving people is our first and most important directive. 'Love your neighbour as yourself,' is the second greatest commandment after loving God. Jesus ate with tax collectors and prostitutes. I believe he would have done the same with those in the gay community."

"Wait," Joe said. "The Bible clearly states that homosexuality is a sin."

"It says that homosexual behaviour is sin, just like any type of sexual sin - or lying or stealing or murdering. But remember, the person and the sin are not the same thing. Jesus' offer of salvation is for everyone. Once someone comes to Jesus, they need to stop acting on the sin. That's what the word repent means. To 'turn away from.'"

"So, you're saying that gay people have to remain celibate for the rest of their lives if they become Christians?" Brittany asked.

Randall held up a hand. "Look, I know it's not popular. People have been told that it's genetic. That they're born that way. The media is on overdrive these days trying to convince us that same sex attraction is normal. I'm not totally convinced about that. While I agree that some people are born with certain propensities, let's say - some men are more effeminate and some women are tomboys - I think there's more to it than that. Background, upbringing, childhood experiences… these all play a part."

"What about the science?" someone asked.

Randall rubbed his chin between his thumb and forefinger. "Well, popular Science also says that the earth evolved over time, but I believe the Biblical account. That it was created by God."

There were murmurs of ascent from the group.

"Look, I don't pretend to know all the answers, but I trust that God would not force something on someone which He then forbids. We live in a fallen world, and we have to look at all the factors. Even then, sometimes God allows certain thorns in our flesh to strengthen us spiritually."

"That's just cruel," someone said.

"God's ways are not our ways," another person countered.

"Guys!" Randal held up both hands. "I realize this is a hot button topic. And like I said, I don't pretend to have all the answers. All I know is, I have to base my theology on what God's word says. God's grace is big enough to extend to everyone, but grace isn't the same thing as a license to sin. According to my Bible, sex is reserved for those in a marriage relationship."

"Okay. So what about gay marriage?" Brittany folded her arms across her chest. A surge of more disquiet filled the room. The friendly discussion had turned into something more. Joyce, the other new person, got up and left. Tempest looked over at Geoff. He was just listening, apparently not phased by the general disruption.

"Diane, you have a question?" Randall pointed as he called over the hubbub.

The room quieted. "I'm just interested in what you think gay people should do. Seek counselling? What?"

Randall ran a hand over his closely cropped head. "I suppose the short answer is yes. It might mean making hard choices, and even then, sin still has consequences. But with God's help, people can overcome any hurdle."

"Assuming you believe it's a hurdle to be jumped," someone murmured.

"You never answered my question," Brittany piped up.

Randall sighed. "Look, I'm just the facilitator. This might be a discussion for another day. I know of several well spoken people who have turned from the gay lifestyle after getting saved. It might be a good idea for us to adjourn for now, and perhaps we can all look into the topic a bit more. I'll ask the senior pastor to attend next time, if it will help."

"Sounds like you're on the fence, Randall," Joe said.

"Personally, I don't believe marriage between same sex partners is part of God's plan, but some might say that as long as it's a monogamous relationship, others have no right to an opinion about what happens in their bedroom. The truth is, there are mixed reactions and degrees of comfort, even within the church. I also know that there are people within the body of Christ who are struggling with this issue. It's not necessarily black and white and it's not a simple fix. Like I said, I'll get reinforcements next week."

Joe stood. "Well, I probably won't be back to hear it. I think I've heard enough."

"I'm sorry you feel that way, Joe," Randall said.

The group watched as Joe stalked from the room.

"Good riddance," Brittany said. "Joe is always so opinionated."

"He's not the only one," Diane murmured.

Tempest watched as Randall closed his eyes for a second. "I should probably go after him. Chase, would you mind closing in prayer?"

Chase, a slightly overweight young man with red hair and a beard, stood up as Randall took his leave. "God, we thank you that we can come together to study your word. Lord, you know that many of us have more questions than answers right now, but we pray, God, that your peace would descend on each and every person that attended here tonight. Help us to love one another unconditionally as we continue to seek your face. Guide us into your truth, in Jesus name. Amen."

A rumble of 'Amens' was followed by quiet conversation as people stood and packed up their belongings.

Geoff leaned toward Tempest. "Wow. Well, that was quite the study for your first time. I hope you aren't scared away."

"No, but it wasn't what I expected, that's for sure. I guess I never really considered the implications of becoming a Christian for certain people." Tempest tucked her Bible into her book bag. Many of the group had used their phones or other devices as Bibles, but she still preferred a real book to an electronic one.

"So true. Think you'll come again?" he asked.

"Probably. I could hardly leave it at that, could I? What's your take on the whole thing?"

Geoff shrugged. "I'm noncommittal."

Tempest frowned. "Really? You don't have an opinion?"

"Just being selfish, I guess."

"What do you mean?"

"I don't want to have one that's different than yours. At least not until we get to know one another better." He smiled.

"Oh." Tempest looked down. Her suspicions were true after all. Geoff was interested in more than just friendship. She looked up. "I suppose I have more questions than answers right now, too, but I think I agree with what Randall said. God loves everyone, so it's up to us to do the same. I feel for people who are struggling, but I guess I'm just glad I don't have to deal with it personally." She let a wane smile cross her lips. "That sounded shallow and selfish. Sorry."

"No problem. I totally agree with everything you said, so we're on the same page. Just glad it's not me, like you said."

"Geoff... Just so you know, I'm not ready to get into another relationship right now."

He laughed. "Perfect. Me neither."

Tempest's eyebrows rose a notch. "Is that so? Well, good. Then we really are on the same page."

"Seems so." Geoff looked at his oversized watch. "It's still early. Wanna go for coffee?" He smiled again. "Strictly as friends. I promise."

"Sure."

Geoff seemed like a nice guy. She didn't feel any kind of spark, but she needed a friend more than anything right now to help fill the gaping hole in her heart. It would be nice to have someone to talk to besides Frank and Edna. Someone without all the baggage that she, herself, carried around.

"So what brought you to LA?" Geoff sat forward slightly, elbows on the table between them in the secluded booth. They'd been at the all night diner for at least an hour already.

Tempest cupped her mug of tea with both hands. "I'm *from* LA, actually."

"Oh?" He looked surprised. "But you mentioned that you went to school in Boston - both grade school and college. That's a long way from here."

"I went to a boarding school."

Geoff's eyebrows rose. "Is that so? I didn't peg you for the rich type to go off to a boarding school. What do your parents do, anyway?"

"Um, my father was a journalist and my mother was a cellist."

"Was?"

"My parents are... they passed away when I was a child." Tempest looked down at the steam rising from her mug and clutched the warm ceramic more tightly.

"Oh, I'm so sorry to hear that. I didn't know or I wouldn't have been so insensitive."

"It's alright. That's how I ended up in Boston, in the care of my Great Aunt Rose. She wasn't much for children, so I got sent to the boarding school, which turned out alright since it's where I met my best friends."

Geoff nodded. "And then after college you decided to move back to LA?"

"It was a stretch, but I'm glad I did it."

"A stretch? How?"

"Believe it or not, I'm not very adventurous. But it's been good. I'm so grateful to my boss Frank - and his wife Edna. He gave me a job and even lets me live above their garage."

"That's nice of them. So, your dad was a journalist, too. Keeping it in the family. I like it."

"Yes, that's right."

"How did your parents die, if you don't mind me asking?"

Tempest swallowed some tea before answering. "A car accident."

"That's rough."

"They were hit by a drunk driver," she added.

Geoff whistled. "Doubly rough."

"It took me a long time to forgive the man who did it. I finally just had to put it behind me and move on. It was tearing me up inside."

Geoff gave a sympathetic nod. "I know what you mean."

Tempest frowned. "Really? Did something similar happen to someone you know?"

"Not just someone I know, but my own dad. He hit another vehicle and was accused of manslaughter - driving under the influence causing death."

Tempest's eyes widened. "You mean he hit another vehicle and someone died?"

"Yes, but as I said, he wasn't actually drunk. Not really. His blood alcohol level was barely over the legal limit, and according to him he wasn't in the wrong. The other car pulled right out in front of him without warning. Like they wanted to get hit."

"Still, he shouldn't have been driving if he'd been drinking."

Geoff's voice took on a defensive edge. "There wouldn't have been a problem if the other vehicle hadn't swerved right into his lane. But no one would believe my dad's side of the story. It got thrown out in court as unsubstantiated. So, he spent some time in jail for it when I was little. Not the happiest memories, I can tell you."

"I'm sorry." Tempest did feel badly, in a way. But Geoff's father shouldn't have been driving under the influence. There was no excuse for that...

"Yeah, it was pretty rotten. A lot of stigma for my family - my dad being labelled a killer and a drunk, when the truth is he hardly ever drank in the first place."

"What about forensics?"

"As far as the police were concerned, it was cut and dried. My dad hit them and they were dead. End of story. Besides, this isn't the movies."

"How is your father now?"

Geoff shrugged. "I don't talk to him much."

"Why's that?"

"After he got out of jail he distanced himself. I see him occasionally, but I try to avoid it. It's just not worth the effort."

So much for a nice Christian guy with no baggage.

CHAPTER 6

*T*empest sat on the futon and curled her legs underneath her as she opened her laptop. Jupiter and Paddy knew what was coming and immediately took up their favorite spots nearby. Her fingers clicked on the keys, entering a search for 'Vanguard' and anything she could find about Geoff's father's manslaughter case. No matter what she tried, it came up blank.

She tried a more general search from the same time frame and several options appeared. With a sharp intake of breath, she recognized newspaper articles from her own parents' case among the list. Almost of their own volition, her fingers clicked on one of the articles.

It was a short piece, not garnering a front page or even much space. The headline read 'Couple Killed By Drunk Driver'. Tempest froze. It was written by Frank Dunlop.

Why hadn't Frank told her he'd covered her parents' deaths? She skimmed the article. It wasn't anything she didn't know already, but even after all this time, it brought back a sharp stab of pain.

She went to another piece written by a rival newspaper and

skimmed it as well. Same basic facts. Except... She paused and went back to a certain line that caught her attention. *"Although Mr. John McGowan's blood alcohol was close to the legal limit, it was not over. His claim that the other vehicle drove directly into his path was unsubstantiated."*

Why hadn't she noticed that line before? What if Geoff's father's name was John McGowan? Just because they didn't have the same last name meant nothing.

TEMPEST DESCENDED the apartment stairs that flanked one wall in Frank's garage. The garage itself was made of unfinished studs and contained some shelves, unused sporting equipment that hung from the rafters, and of course, Edna's 1973 Monte Carlo, which never seemed to leave the safety of the interior of the building. Frank had to park his own beat up minivan on the driveway outside.

She went outside via the side entrance and into the narrow breezeway that connected the garage to the house. Tempest knocked on the side door and waited. She heard the scurrying of feet and within seconds Edna Dunlop answered the door. "Oh, hello dear. What can I do for you?" Edna's hair, dyed a dark and unnatural shade of red, was next in line for shock factor to the ruby red lipstick she always wore.

"Is Frank available?"

"He's just about to watch his favorite crime show on TV."

"Oh. I hate to interrupt..."

"Get your butt in here," Frank bellowed from the other room. "I'll put the darn thing on pause."

Tempest suppressed a smile and stepped over the threshold. Frank and Edna's home had probably been very stylish at one point in time, but the tired wallpaper and outdated furnishings told a different story.

Edna led the way from the side entrance through the kitchen and into the family room where Frank was lounging in his recliner. "I'll go make some tea," she said and left the two of them alone.

"I didn't mean to trouble you," Tempest said.

"No problem. Take a seat."

Tempest lowered herself onto the couch, moving a crocheted cushion out of the way. "Why didn't you tell me you covered my parents' deaths?" she asked without preamble.

Frank jerked his recliner into a full sitting position. "Didn't I?"

"No, you did not."

Frank scratched his head. "Hm. I thought we talked about it that first day."

"You mentioned you knew a reporter named Ross, but you didn't seem to remember that he'd been killed in a car accident until I told you."

"I've covered thousands of stories. You can't expect me to remember every detail."

"Fair enough." She wasn't buying it. Frank Dunlop had a mind like a machine. Nothing escaped his notice.

Frank sat forward. "I'm sorry. Sensitivity has never been my strong suit. For what it's worth, I really didn't remember until you reminded me. Give an old man a break."

"Your article said nothing about my parents swerving in front of the perpetrator, either. Another article did." She eyed him expectantly.

"It was unsubstantiated," Frank said with a shrug.

Tempest worked her jaw. "I... it's just that I never heard that version of events before. Why would they have swerved in front of oncoming traffic?"

"You don't know that they did, which is why it's unsubstantiated."

"But what if they'd been arguing? What if..."

Frank reached over to pat her hand. "This is exactly why you should stick to the present, not dig into the past. Your folks died and it was a tragedy, but you're here with a full life ahead of you."

"Here's the tea." Edna entered the room with a tray laden with a teapot and three mugs. She set it on the coffee table.

"You want to stay and watch with us?" Frank gestured to the TV. "It's the season finale."

"Thanks." Tempest took a mug from Edna. "Um…"

"Unless there's more." Frank eyed Tempest with that penetrating stare he had so perfected.

Tempest glanced at Edna before continuing. "Actually… there is something else."

"Oh! How silly of me! I forgot the muffins!" Edna scurried from the room.

Frank watched his wife's retreating figure until she'd disappeared.

"She didn't have to leave," Tempest said.

"Edna doesn't like to get involved. Now go on, since she'll be back in a few minutes."

"A friend told me about an accident that his father had been in where two people were killed. He didn't have the exact dates, but it was about the same time as my parents' accident. His father was driving - under the influence - and hit another vehicle, killing both passengers. But according to him, the other car swerved right in front of him."

"What are you getting at?" Frank's gaze never wavered.

"The similarities are obvious. Maybe it was Geoff's father who hit my parents."

"Geoff? Who's Geoff?"

"Geoff Vanguard. My friend."

"The perp in your folks' case was McGowan."

"I know, but people don't always have the same last name as their parents."

"I still don't see the point. So what if your friend's dad was the person who killed your parents? Other than a cruel twist of fate, I don't see what you'll gain."

"Geoff feels like his father never got a fair trial."

"You want to dig into some old vehicular manslaughter case? That's not news."

"This isn't just about news," Tempest said, leaning forward. "It's personal. I need to know the truth."

Frank sighed. "I think you're heading down a dark path. I've seen it happen before. Reporters getting obsessed about things they can't change."

"Why do I get the feeling you know more than you're letting on?"

"Don't be ridiculous. Your folks had a terrible accident and there is no logical explanation on planet earth except bad timing." Frank looked over his shoulder. "Edna! You baking those muffins or what?"

"TEMPEST!"

Tempest looked to see a figure jogging toward her across the park. She waved, but then had to hold the dogs' leashes with two hands as Geoff approached. "Settle down! Sit!"

Geoff slowed to a walk several feet away. "Wow! I wasn't expecting a monster! That is one big dog!"

Jupiter growled. Paddy had been barking the entire time.

"Sh! Quiet!" Tempest commanded. "They're actually very friendly," she said apologetically. "When they get used to people."

Geoff tried to pat Jupiter but snatched his hand away at the rumbling sound coming from the Great Dane's throat.

"Jupiter! Be nice," Tempest scolded.

"It's okay. Most dogs don't seem to like me much."

"He can probably sense that you're afraid," Tempest said.

"Hm. I'll keep that in mind." Geoff surveyed the park. "Who would have guessed that we live in the same neighborhood?"

"I know," Tempest said. "Thanks for meeting me here instead of the coffee shop. I need to make sure the dogs get their exercise each day."

"This is much better than a coffee shop," Geoff said.

"So, do you want to walk around a bit?"

Geoff eyed Jupiter suspiciously. "Is it safe?"

Tempest laughed. "You can take Paddy. He's much easier to handle." She handed Paddy's leash to Geoff. If she'd been walking the dogs with Ryan, he would have taken Jupiter. Tempest frowned and willed that thought away. Of course Ryan would have because he was more familiar with the dogs.

"So… can I ask you a question?" Tempest began as they left the park.

"Sure," Geoff said.

"Your dad… does he have the same last name as you?"

"That's a funny question." Geoff scrunched his brow. "Why?"

"Just wondering."

"You'll have to do better than that," Geoff said with a laugh.

"Okay. I was thinking about what you told me the other day. About your dad's conviction. It sounds a lot like my parents' car accident. All except for the last name." She paused. "The man who hit my parents was John McGowan."

Geoff stumbled, causing Paddy to start barking. "Wow."

"What is it?"

"That's my father's name. My mother remarried when my dad got convicted, and my stepdad adopted me. My name at birth was McGowan."

Icy fingers travelled up her spine and Tempest shivered. No words would come.

"What are the odds?" Geoff continued. "It's like fate brought us together."

Tempest stopped in her tracks. She felt lightheaded, like she might faint. "Maybe this isn't such a good idea, after all. I don't feel very well all of a sudden. I think I should just head home."

"Oh dear! I can see this is upsetting. I'll walk you home."

"No need! It's close. I'll take Paddy now." She extended her hand to take Paddy's leash, but Geoff didn't relinquish it.

"What kind of a gentleman would I be if I didn't at least see you to the door?"

They'd reached the overgrown section of the sidewalk and instead of going single file, Geoff took Paddy onto the pavement so that they could walk side by side.

"Watch for traffic," Tempest said as she ducked under the overhanging branches.

"I know it's naive of me to suggest it, but I wish we could just pretend we never knew. I don't want this to ruin our friendship." Geoff joined her again on the widened cement.

Tempest shook her head. "No, if there's something more to this then I want to know. Like why your father said they swerved in front of him and why no one followed up on it."

"Even if it means you find something... unpleasant?" Geoff asked.

Tempest nodded without saying anything. Something was not right about any of it and the investigative reporter inside of her wanted the truth. No, the daughter inside wanted the truth.

Ryan

CHAPTER 7

*R*yan leaned back in his desk chair, a foot straddling one knee as he drummed impatient fingers on the armrest. Tempest actually thought he might be a dirty cop! It stung.

Yes, they had been experiencing some issues lately, and he was man enough to admit that most of it was his fault. But he did have a job to do and for that he couldn't apologize. Trained as a cop, now a Special Agent with the FBI, he'd reached the pinnacle of his career. He couldn't just give it all away. For a woman.

But Tempest wasn't just any woman. She was at one and the same time perceptive and naive; brave yet afraid to take a risk. Despite the fact that she was a journalist working for a hard-nosed guy like Frank Dunlop, she wasn't cut out of that same cloth. She needed to be sheltered, and he had elected himself to do it.

His fingers stilled. Who was he kidding? It was so much more than that. He loved her. That was the real bottom line. So much so that he wanted to put a ring on it.

Which was why breaking up with her was the best option. It was the only way to create some distance so that she would be out of danger. What he was involved in right now - what she had tipped him off to by telling him about those photographs - could get dangerous. Deadly, even. And he wouldn't allow her to be put in harm's way. No matter his own feelings.

Which brought him to the looming question: Who placed those photos in Frank's mailbox? With a grunt he straightened and rolled his chair forward under the desk.

Someone rapped on the glass wall that separated his office from the others. Since his return from Italy, he was one of only a few Special Agents afforded a private office, small as it was, although the glass walls gave the illusion of space.

Ryan looked up. Andrew Coates. He waved the other agent - and one of his few friends - inside.

They had worked together multiple times, most recently on a rescue operation involving Tempest's friend Cherise Hillyer, her brother Dirk, and Dirk's girlfriend Anne-Marie. Pharmaceuticals were being smuggled out of a Mexican orphanage, and somehow the three had gotten wind of it, putting their lives in peril. Tempest's friends had a knack for getting into dangerous situations. It was how he and Tempest had met in the first place.

"What's up?" Ryan asked.

"My question, exactly! You look like the grinch at Christmas. I thought I better intervene before your head exploded from too much thinking." Agent Andrew Coates was about the same age, height and build as Ryan, but totally opposite in complexion. His crisply cut red hair, freckled skin, and fringe of pale lashes were ginger all the way.

"You know how it is. If it's not one crisis, it's another."

Andy perched on Ryan's desk and folded his arms. "Really? I thought it might be something else. You pop the question, yet?"

Ryan shifted. "That didn't go as planned."

Andy's eyebrows rose. "Sorry, brother. What happened?"

"We're just taking a step back," Ryan hedged.

"Whatever you say. You'll fill me in when you're ready, I

guess."

"Thanks for understanding." Ryan gestured to the open glass door. "There is something else…"

Andy swung off the desk and closed the door. Although they had a clear view of most of the people at work in the agency, they were now in their own little private bubble. He came back and took a seat on the opposite side of Ryan's desk and waited.

"Have you ever wondered about why we were able to convict those two women from the orphanage in Mexico so quickly, but have basically come to a standstill when it comes to finding who's behind the bigger operation?"

Andy shrugged. "I assume it's because organized crime is involved. They're better at covering their tracks. At finding a scapegoat so they can continue without interruption. But we knew that already."

"True. But what about that case last summer in Italy? International agencies were involved, and although we caught the middle man smuggling the drugs into the States, we never actually pinpointed the real brains behind it all."

"Same deal. You know as well as I do how hard it is to infiltrate the mafia and bring them down. They've got resources beyond our scope - and that's just a fact of life."

"Granted." Ryan rubbed the back of his neck. "Sometimes it makes me wonder if it's even worth trying to go after them."

"You don't mean that," Andy said. "Both of those cases directly, or indirectly, involved Tempest. They've become personal, which breaks the first rule."

"Never become personally involved in a case," Ryan finished with a nod.

"Exactly."

"Fair enough, but what they did do is make me start paying attention. I've found other inconsistencies. Tip offs. Lack of proper protocol. Evidence gone missing."

"Just what are you saying?" Andy leaned forward.

"I think there's a mole in the agency. Someone playing it both ways."

"You think there's a dirty cop among us?"

"Has to be. There's no other explanation."

"And you have proof?"

"Slowly but surely I've been gathering it, yes."

Andy lowered his voice to a whisper. "Who?"

"That I don't know yet. But there is definitely something rotten in our midst, and I aim to find out."

"You can't do this alone. It could ruin your career - even put your life at risk."

"Don't you think I know that?" Ryan replied sharply.

Andy nodded in sudden realization. "So that's why you and Tempest broke up. You didn't want to put her in danger should things go south."

"Partly," Ryan admitted. "And partly because she accused *me* of being a dirty cop."

Andy's eyes widened. "What brought that on?"

Ryan sighed and rubbed a hand through his hair. "Someone is onto the fact that I'm nosing around. They sent photographs of me during a meet up to her boss Frank. You know, the journalist?"

Andy nodded. "I know him. And now you're afraid he's going to start digging and spoil everything."

"Or worse."

"Meaning?"

"I'm not sure. I just know I need to confront him. If he's dirty too, I'll never forgive myself for pointing Tempest his way."

"You're being too hard on yourself."

"Time will tell."

"Who else knows about this?" Andy glanced through the glass to the general hubbub of the agency and then back to Ryan.

"No one. I've been discreet."

"In any case, I've got your back," Andy said. "You know that."

Ryan nodded. "Thanks, bro. Right now, I don't know who else I can trust."

RYAN STEPPED across the threshold of Frank Dunlop's office without so much as a knock. He'd made sure Tempest was out before entering.

Frank looked over the tops of his reading glasses as he shifted his gaze from his computer. "O'Toole. Tempest isn't here right now if that's why you're here."

"It's not. I'm here to see you." Ryan stopped directly in front of the other man and folded his arms over his chest.

"Alright." Frank took his spectacles off and threw them on the desk. "It's not everyday such a prestigious public servant graces my humble office. What can I do for you?"

"What do you know about those photos?" Ryan asked without preamble.

Frank frowned. "Which photos would that be? I get a lot of tips in this business."

"Cut the crap. You know very well what I'm talking about. The ones of me outside Freemont Convenience Store."

Frank nodded contemplatively. "So, she told you, did she?"

"Yes, but I think you knew that already."

"You seem awfully defensive."

"Who gave them to you, and what do they want?"

"I'm assuming there's a story connected somehow, but I'm in the dark as much as you are." Frank's gaze never wavered from Ryan's.

"Maybe you planted them," Ryan suggested.

"To what purpose?" Frank asked.

"I haven't figured that out yet. But I will."

"Believe me, I have no idea who put them there or why," Frank said.

"Tempest thinks I'm dirty. Did you put that idea into her head?"

"Tempest is smarter than you give her credit for."

"In other words, you did." Ryan snorted and shook his head.

"Are you?" Frank asked point blank.

"No. A fact I'm sure you'll discover once you start digging - which by the way, I don't want you to do. It could put a lot of people - including you and Tempest - at risk, not to mention compromise a case I've put a lot of time and effort into."

"Seems to me the case is already compromised," Frank said.

"I mean it, Frank. This is one time I need you to back off."

"You expect this old hound dog to lay down without sniffing out the story? Even just a little?"

"Yes. Once I'm through, I'll give you the full story. An exclusive."

"And why should I trust you?" Frank asked. "You've been involved in some shady stuff recently. First in Italy, then down in Mexico. How do I know you're not the bad guy? From where I'm standing it's the most logical explanation."

"And if you really thought so, you wouldn't be telling me," Ryan countered.

Frank shrugged.

Ryan narrowed his eyes. "But it would be just like the real turncoat to try to implicate me to take the focus off him."

"So, you think this *is* about a mole in the agency," Frank stated. He shook his head. "I'd say you've got yourself in quite a pickle this time, boy. Not sure how you're going to wiggle out of this one."

"Thanks for the vote of confidence." Ryan squinted at Frank. "You sure you didn't plant those pictures yourself? I wouldn't put it past you."

"Trust me. I have enough leads to keep me busy for the next ten years. I wouldn't go compromising an FBI investigation just to get a story. I thought you knew me better than that."

"Just grasping at straws. What I don't understand is why they involved you?"

"Because I'm known for not compromising when it comes to the story," Frank suggested.

"Unless it's something more sinister. Maybe they made a connection between us... The little arrangement we've got going to share certain intel."

"Or they made a connection between you and Tempest, which by default, connects us, too," Frank offered.

"Do you think Tempest might still be in danger? Maybe she should move out of your apartment."

"A bit drastic, don't you think?" Frank asked. "The girl just got comfortable, and Edna likes having her around. Feels secure with someone over the garage."

"You mean, you like having her around," Ryan corrected and let a slight smile emerge. "I've seen the way you fuss over her."

Frank shrugged. "A man can't help having a soft spot."

"Even an old curmudgeon like you?"

"Even old curmudgeons, believe it or not."

"Still, I think she might be safer if she cut all ties. To both of us."

Frank raised his eyebrows.

"You look surprised. I thought maybe she'd shared that, too." Ryan cleared his throat. "We broke up."

"I'm sorry. I thought you were good for each other."

"Thanks. Hopefully it's not permanent, but for now it's safest, I think."

"So, this is serious," Frank said with a nod of his head. "You're not just playing around, are you?"

"No, I'm not." Ryan held Frank's gaze. "Which is why I need you to take a step back. Do not pursue this story. You got it?"

Frank took in a deep breath and then exhaled. "Well, I hate to admit it, but I think you're right - this time."

"Good. You need to look out for yourself, too. It might be

wise if you and Edna went somewhere else for awhile. Took a vacation."

Frank shook his head. "No way. I'm not telling Edna anything. It would just make her worry, and she wouldn't hear of it, anyway. She's too attached to being home. Never goes out of the house as it is, so there's no way I'd convince her to take a vacation."

"Okay. Just be careful."

"You know me," Frank said.

"I know. That's what worries me."

Ryan turned and left the office. Did he trust Frank? On the one hand, yes. He believed him when he said he hadn't planted the photos himself, and he also believed that he had a genuine interest in Tempest's well fair. But there was something else. Frank was hiding something and he couldn't put his finger on it… which wouldn't stop him from finding out.

As soon as Ryan put the binoculars up to his eyes, a twinge of guilt surfaced. What kind of man spied on his own girlfriend? Make that ex-girlfriend, but that was only temporary… hopefully. Besides, it was for her own protection.

He slowly panned the street, coming back to Frank's bungalow to rest.

Tempest emerged into the sunlight from under the breezeway between the house and the garage, her two dogs in tow. Jupiter led the way, pulling slightly on his leash, while Paddy trotted obediently by his mistress's side. Ryan could see Tempest's lips moving and he smiled. She was always talking to the dogs as if they could understand what she said.

He watched her head down the street, ducking under the low hanging branches along part of the sidewalk, until she was out of sight. He knew where she was going. Should he follow her to the park? He would have to be careful since it was more open there. He'd parked his vehicle a block away, so he could skirt the park and then double back to retrieve it.

Keeping his distance, Ryan treaded softly about a block behind the trio. Tempest was so busy chatting that she wouldn't have heard his footfalls anyway, but it was best to be cautious. He found cover in some bushes and watched as she took a seat at her usual bench, but she didn't unleash the dogs for a game of catch, as she normally did.

Instead, she waited for a few minutes, talking and petting each dog in turn, until she perked up and waved at someone. Ryan lowered the binoculars and squinted at the approaching figure. He didn't recognize the man, so he put the binoculars back up to his eyes.

Male. Late twenties, early thirties. Brown hair and beard. Glasses. Wool coat and a trailing scarf slung over one shoulder. He looked vaguely familiar, but Ryan couldn't place him.

Ryan followed the mystery man to Tempest's bench where he stopped, hands safely in his pockets. Both dogs were barking, seemingly agitated, and Tempest shushed them. Then she handed Paddy's leash to the newcomer and they started walking together toward the street.

Ryan slowly lowered the binoculars. A burning sensation churned in the pit of his stomach. Jealousy? It wasn't a feeling he was that familiar with. Not since Dirk Hillyer had been vying for Tempest's affections. That hadn't turned out well for Hillyer, but who knew who this new guy was?

Was that why she had been so quick to accuse him of being a dirty cop? She'd already found someone else and needed a reason to dump him?

He shook his head. Tempest wasn't like that, but she *was* easily influenced. No matter the personal outcome, he would always be there to look out for her.

CHAPTER 8

*R*yan drummed his fingers on the desktop as he read the article on the computer screen. It was from the archives of one of the big newspapers - a piece about a drug bust where some of the 'evidence', as in product, had gone missing. It was written by none other than Frank Dunlop. Ryan scrolled further down and stopped drumming to rub the stubble on his chin.

Frank had covered a lot in his forty-some years as a newsman. His was and had always been the crime beat - everything from trials to politics to shady business deals, which was no surprise seeing as he had strong ties to the various policing entities in the city. Frank was a valuable asset in terms of his contacts and the intel he could provide. The funny thing was, Ryan had never noticed before how Frank seemed to have reported on many of the cases that were throwing up red flags. Was he just that good at his job, or was there more to it than that?

The photographs that had showed up in Frank's mailbox were definitely a warning, but on which side the older man landed was yet to be determined. All the more reason to protect Tempest.

Somehow he had to convince her to get out from under Frank's influence.

"It's too early in the morning for such concentration," Andy said as he entered Ryan's office. He held a mug aloft. "I haven't even finished my first coffee yet."

Ryan sat back and smiled. "I'm one up on you, there. On cup number three already."

"Don't you know too much caffeine isn't good for you?" Andy propped himself against Ryan's desk.

"So I've been told."

Andy glanced at the open glass door. "I had some thoughts about what we talked about yesterday," he said in a lowered voice.

Ryan raised a brow but waited.

"Something you said got me to thinking about the case from the Mexican orphanage."

"Go on."

Andy took a sip of coffee before continuing. "You stuck your neck out on a hunch. Acted without clearance, and even though it turned out you were right, the details of the operation remained classified."

"As I recall, you came along - with or without said clearance."

"Not my point," Andy said with a grin. "The other day, one of the agent trainees mentioned something about it. How we were lucky not to have our badges taken away, even though the agency sanctioned the move after the fact."

"Who?" Ryan asked.

"Leming. You know - the new guy."

"He said that to you?" Ryan shook his head. "Ball-sie - especially for a trainee."

"He wasn't saying it in an accusing way," Andy clarified. "I think he was wondering if and when it's appropriate to break the rules. More out of curiosity than anything, I think."

"What did you say?"

Andy shrugged. "When I asked him who told him, he said it

was common knowledge. I told him he got his facts wrong - that it was sanctioned all along. But the point remains, someone leaked the information."

Ryan frowned. "Who else knew about it? Other than the Assistant Director?"

"No one, as far as I know."

"Someone from his staff?" Ryan suggested.

"The most likely scenario," Andy agreed.

Ryan sighed heavily. "Well, I suppose the fallout won't be that great. The A.D. can deal with the gossip."

"You don't think this is connected to your mole?" Andy asked.

"Hard to tell. A simple leak from inside Reynold's staff could hardly pull off some of the shady stuff I've uncovered."

"So, it goes higher up?"

"Maybe."

Andy shook his head. "You're scaring me, man." He laughed but he didn't sound amused.

"Don't worry. I'm being careful."

Someone rapped on the glass wall, and both men looked up. Jeremy Leming, the agent trainee they'd been talking about, stood just outside Ryan's door. "Assistant Director Reynolds wants to see you in his office ASAP."

Ryan stood. "Why didn't he call me himself?"

Leming shrugged. "You'll have to ask him."

Jeremy Leming was fairly short, probably only about five foot six, but he was solidly built and carried himself with confidence. He had dark hair and an olive complexion, probably of Hispanic descent. Ryan didn't know much about him, except now that Andy had brought him to his attention, he would be keeping a closer eye on the younger man.

"Lead the way, then," Andy said and swung off the desk.

"Oh, not you, Coates," Leming directed at Andy. "Just O'Toole."

Ryan and Andy exchanged a glance before Andy shrugged. "Whatever." He nodded at Ryan before leaving the office.

Leming waited for Ryan and then got into step behind him as they wound their way through the maze of cubicles that comprised most of the floor. Ryan rapped on the Assistant Director's glass door.

"Come in, O'Toole." Assistant Director Clifford Reynolds sat behind his desk, hands clasped on the desktop. He was a man of about fifty with salt and pepper hair and chiseled features who exuded exactly the air of authority that one would expect from someone of his stature within the agency. As Ryan entered the office, Reynolds held up his hand. "Just wait outside for a moment, Leming."

The young agent trainee nodded and shut the door, taking up sentry duty on the other side of the glass.

Ryan turned to his boss, his brows raised. "What's going on, Sir?"

Reynolds gestured to an empty chair on the other side of his desk. "Take a seat."

Ryan lowered himself slowly into the chair. "The new assignment, I take it? I wondered when I'd finally get the details. All you said so far was be prepared for the long haul."

"Yes, yes. We'll get to that." Reynolds rubbed his chin and then scrutinized Ryan closely. "You're a liability, you know that O'Toole?"

Ryan shifted in his seat. "Beg your pardon, Sir?"

"You heard me. A vigilante. Smuggling prisoners across the border from Mexico without my authorization. Nearly getting a French field agent killed in Italy. Somewhere you weren't supposed to be at the time, need I remind you."

"Both of those turned out to be major breaks for the department," Ryan said calmly.

Reynolds nodded. "Exactly. You go where your hunches lead, not something that can be taught in any academy."

"Yes, I've gone with my gut on occasion, but I assure you, I don't take unnecessary risks. Everything is weighed out. You can rely on that, Sir."

"Relax!" Reynolds waved a dismissive hand. "I'm not here to reprimand you. I gave you your own office, for goodness sake."

Ryan blinked. "Then…?"

"You're exactly the man I need for this next assignment."

Ryan's eyes widened. "Sir?"

"I need the kind of agent who can think on his feet. Adapt under pressure. Someone who isn't afraid to bend the rules as long as the outcome is favorable."

"Ah." Ryan nodded. "And that man is me, I take it?"

"Darn straight." Reynolds looked him in the eye. "You've proved your adaptability, O'Toole, on more than one occasion. You've got a sixth sense."

"I'm not comfortable bending the rules too far," Ryan said. "What exactly are you asking of me?"

"A diamond smuggling operation that probably fuels other criminal activity. International."

"International? Where abouts are we talking? Africa?"

"Canada. The arctic, to be exact. You'll be posing as an inspector at a diamond mine."

"I don't know a lot about diamonds." Except for the one he'd picked out for Tempest…

"I'll be sending all the details, so make sure you study up. You'll be shipping out in two days."

"The arctic in the middle of winter," Ryan said under his breath. "Great."

"Don't worry. You'll have all the cold weather gear you'll need."

Ryan glanced sideways to where Leming still stood on the other side of the glass. "What about him? What's his part in all this?"

"He's going with you," Reynolds stated.

"If it's as sensitive as you say, why risk a newbie tagging along?"

"He's got potential, and I want him learning from the best."

"Thanks for the compliment, but I work better alone. You know that. Especially if you're giving me license to... follow my gut. I don't need a freshman blowing the whistle."

"It's a two man job. I'm sending Leming."

Ryan leaned forward. "Why not Coates? He and I work well together. We trust each other."

Reynolds shook his head. "Coates is needed here. Expect the full briefing within the half hour."

A moment passed.

Ryan looked the Assistant Director squarely in the eye. "Is that all, then?"

"Yes. Dismissed."

Ryan stood and gave Reynolds a nod before exiting his office. He nodded at Leming on his way by, too. It was strange that Reynolds hadn't briefed them both at the same time. Maybe his boss didn't want to extend the same leeway to the younger agent that he had to Ryan. Whatever the case, he had two days to be ready and much to do - not only in preparation for his assignment, but to make sure Tempest was safe.

RYAN CHECKED HIS WATCH, readjusted his dark glasses, and then crossed his arms as he settled back against the rough stucco of the building. He spotted his contact as soon as the man emerged from under the awning at Freemont Convenience Store. Just like clockwork. If ever a man needed to adjust his habits, Lenny Demarco was him.

Ryan pushed off from the building. Traffic was light at this time of night, so he jogged across the street and tailed Demarco for half a block until the other man slipped into an alley. Ryan picked up his pace and followed. "Hey!" Ryan called out in a staged whisper.

Without even looking over his shoulder, Demarco took off running. With an oath, Ryan sprinted after him. Lenny Demarco was an easy catch. His limping gate, caused from who knew what, made it easy for Ryan to gain the upper hand. With a final dive, he tackled him to the ground with an "Oomph!"

"Police brutality!" Demarco called out.

"Sh! Shush up!" Ryan hissed into Demarco's ear. "It's me!" Breathing heavily, Ryan hauled himself off of the smaller man and extended a hand so that Demarco could stand also.

"O'Toole? Why didn't you just say so? I could have shot you back there."

"You don't own a piece," Ryan said.

"Well, I could have pulled a knife, then."

"Why so jumpy?" Ryan asked. "You been shoplifting again?"

Demarco shrugged. "A man's got to eat."

Ryan grunted. "More like, a man's got to feed his bad habits."

Demarco shifted from one foot to the other. He was scrawny and of indeterminate age, with blackened teeth and leathery skin. The streets could do that to a person. Make them old beyond their years. Demarco spent his days between petty crimes and running errands for one of the gangs. He also made money on the side as a snitch.

"We need to talk." Ryan pulled Demarco to one side, up against the relative shelter of the brick wall.

"I don't have any more information for you. I told you everything I know about that Mexico deal."

"That's not why I'm here." Ryan stopped and looked into the man's eyes. They shifted from side to side. "Someone is on to our meetings."

The fear on Demarco's face ramped into high gear. "Who? I could get my head blown off!"

"I don't know, but I'm looking into it. Someone took photographs of us together and left them with a reporter."

"A reporter?"

"Yes. Frank Dunlop. Does that name mean anything to you?"

Demarco's lashes blinked rapidly and he quickly shook his head. "Um. No. Never heard of him."

Ryan squinted and surveyed Demarco more closely. "You're not a very good liar. What aren't you telling me?"

Demarco's head swiveled from side to side. "Okay, yeah, I've heard of him. He comes around here sometimes, looking for information. Like you."

Ryan took a deep breath. "Okay, look. You need to lay low for awhile. Get off the streets."

Demarco laughed uneasily. "Easy for you to say. I live on the streets."

"I mean it. Stay safe. Take extra precautions. Whatever."

Demarco nodded mutely.

Ryan slapped a hand on his shoulder. "I won't be around to check in on you, either. Just lay low."

"Where you going?" Demarco asked.

Ryan smiled and pointed a finger at Demarco's face. "Nice try." He stepped away from the other man, for all intents releasing him. "Stay safe, you hear?"

Demarco nodded then loped in the opposite direction from which they'd entered the alley.

Ryan watched him until he disappeared around another corner. "Stay safe," he repeated under his breath.

CHAPTER 9

*R*yan took a reverse step to peruse the evidence board he'd been constructing on his dining room wall. It represented several weeks of clandestine visits to the evidence locker, reading countless files, and meeting shady informants whose versions of events changed with the amount of cash on hand. Not to mention spying on his girlfriend. That one made him wince, not only because he felt guilty about doing it, but because what he'd seen so far didn't please him. Tempest was seeing someone else.

Geoff Vanguard. It was so easy these days to dig into anyone's personal life. Social media had made that a breeze. But Geoff seemed like a stand-up guy. Degree in finance, office job, still lived with his mother… and he went to the same church! That's probably where Ryan had seen him before. And also where Geoff and Tempest had met. In the two days since he'd seen them together, he couldn't come up with anything untoward about the guy. Except for the fact that he was clearly honing in on his girl… but he couldn't hold that against him. Who wouldn't love a woman like Tempest?

Ryan closed his eyes for a moment.

He thought about the first time they'd met in Boston. She was pretending to be her friend Cherise, accompanied by that scoundrel Dirk Hillyer, Cherise's brother. There was something compelling about her, even then. Even when he'd thought she was involved in smuggling drugs for Cherise's brother.

If the truth were told, she wasn't very good at espionage. He knew she wasn't Cherise almost instantly - which threw up huge red flags at the time - but she'd bravely kept up the charade. Then she'd moved to Los Angeles and it was an easy thing to arrange a second meeting on the beach. She walked her dogs faithfully everyday. The fact that she was living in an upscale beach house near the boardwalk and drove an expensive car were two more red flags. That lifestyle didn't come cheap. He'd had his work cut out for him. But it hadn't been all bad, he remembered with a smile...

～

RYAN WALKED PURPOSEFULLY TOWARD HER, gaging his footsteps so that they would collide at just the right moment.

"Oh!" She let out a small squeal. "Sorry about that!"

"Cherise Hillyer?" Ryan asked. Of course, he knew the answer. "I almost didn't recognize you with glasses on."

"Oh. Right. I left my contacts in the house." Tempest touched the frames.

"What are you doing out here? In California, I mean? Besides walking one heck of a big dog." Ryan pointed to the Great Dane.

She introduced him to the dogs and they engaged in a bit of small talk. Then he dropped the bomb. "How are your parents? And your brother?"

She blinked, apparently confused by the question, as he knew she would be. Lying was hard work and she wasn't very good at it. Finally, she answered. "My brother? Oh, Dirk. Of course. He's fine. They all are. He was here visiting and just left - today."

Ryan looked out over the waves to his left. "Very scenic down here." He turned and offered a smile. "What are the odds that we'd run into each other like this, eh?"

"Yeah. What are the odds," she repeated.

"Well, now that we've run into each other - literally - we should get together sometime." Ryan smiled in what he hoped was an encouraging and non-threatening way.

"I doubt it. I mean, I'm not staying. I mean, I'm busy most of the time. Listen, I've got to go." Her voice came out in a rush and she turned on her heel, tangling herself in the leashes. The Yorkshire Terrier started yelping, setting off a baritone response from the giant Great Dane.

Ryan took a step back and let her pass. Tomorrow was another day. If he could get her to trust him, she might inadvertently leak some important intel. It shouldn't be too hard. The woman was terrible at impersonations. He already knew exactly who she was, but he hadn't figured out yet what her game was or what part she had to play in the whole operation. He was going to enjoy finding out, of that much he was sure. There was something about her...

The next afternoon he 'arranged' a second meeting and then another. The routine carried on for several more days until it was time to swoop in for the kill. "I was thinking," Ryan said as they walked. "We should go out for dinner while we're both still in town. That is, if you're free?"

"Oh. Yes."

A twinge of guilt stuck in Ryan's craw, but only for a moment. She looked so alarmed by his suggestion. He knew her bravado was being stretched to the limit. Still, he had a job to do. "How about tonight?"

"Tonight?" Tempest raised her eyebrows.

"I may have to leave tomorrow," Ryan added. That part wasn't exactly true, but...

"Okay. Tonight would be perfect."

He had to give it to her. She was putting on a brave front. If the truth be told, he was looking forward to this 'date' for more than just practical reasons.

They went to an upscale restaurant. Small talk wasn't at all difficult. Tempest - as Cherise - seemed quite open and talkative. She was finally letting her guard down. He almost felt himself buying into the charade.

Then the evening was over and Ryan was standing at the bottom of the steps that led up to her terrace. "Thanks for a wonderful time," he said. He was looking into her eyes and the way the moonlight was reflected in hers made him wish this weren't just another case.

"I'd invite you in, but my friends might not appreciate it," she said.

He was glad of the excuse. He was a Christian, but he was human, too. "That's fine. I'd better be going anyway. I'm leaving in the morning."

Nobody had said anything about stealing a kiss, though. He leaned in and gently kissed her on the mouth. It was quick and meaningless, except it rocked him unlike anything he had expected.

∿

FROM THAT MOMENT on his heart had been captured, although it took much longer for Tempest to let her guard down. She had abandonment issues, he knew that much, stemming from her parents' death when she was a child. He wondered if there was more to it than that. She never talked about past relationships, which they agreed was for the best, but sometimes he wondered at the wisdom of such a decision. If one was to truly share a life with someone else, perhaps they needed to be an open book.

For his part, he harbored no shame about his past. His youthful indiscretions had been washed away by the blood of Jesus and had no bearing over his present freedom in Christ.

He'd been raised a Catholic by loving parents, an only child of their old age - a miracle baby, or so he'd been told. When he accepted Jesus as an adult, his parents continued to support his choices even if it meant he didn't attend mass regularly, make confession to a priest, or use a rosary. They seemed to understand that God couldn't be contained by tradition, although they clung to theirs. He'd lost them a few years ago, so he knew some of what Tempest was feeling, but he did have a large extended family back in Philly.

He had no trouble sharing any of this, but for Tempest, past relationships seemed taboo. Her secrets had left deep scars, he was sure of it. He would just have to respect her choice to keep them inside until she was ready - if that ever happened. The only relationship of hers he did know about was Dirk Hillyer, and as far as he could tell, the feelings were all one-sided. Besides, the guy had apparently turned his life around, although Ryan still had his doubts.

With a sigh, Ryan turned his gaze once more to the scrawled sticky notes plastered all over his dining room wall. Thinking too much about the past was a useless endeavor.

So far, the only thread connecting all the pieces of the puzzle was Frank Dunlop, the intrepid reporter. Ryan ran a hand through his hair. "Lord, what am I missing here?" he murmured.

TEMPEST IS THE KEY.

Ryan spun, startled by the clarity with which the thought entered his head. It had not been an audible voice, but the words still echoed in his mind. What did that mean, exactly? Was he to trust her with the information he'd already found? Bring her in on the investigation even when he wouldn't be there to oversee it?

He shook his head. That idea was too dangerous. It's why he'd broken up with her. He didn't want there to be any connection between them should things go south. If Tempest was the key, then he needed to protect her, even if it meant doing it without her knowledge.

CHAPTER 10

"So? Any thoughts?" Ryan waited for his friend to answer. Andy stood perusing Ryan's dining room wall, arms folded, chin in hand. "If you ask me, it's pretty simple. Frank Dunlop is taking bribes from someone in the department." He turned to Ryan. "Who from our agency deals regularly with Frank?"

"Any number of people," Ryan replied. "You and me included."

"But there has to be a common denominator."

"So far, I haven't found one." Ryan sighed and ran a hand through his hair. "I don't want to believe Frank is involved, but you may be right."

"It seems clear to me," Andy said. "Frank just happens to have reported on most of these cases. Plus, Lenny Demarco knows Frank. What else do you need?"

"Just because Frank also gets information from Lenny Demarco doesn't mean he's up to no good. He's been a valuable asset for decades."

Andy slowly rubbed his chin, staring at the wall again. "Ever wonder how Frank manages as a freelancer? He seems to be doing well enough."

"He has a good reputation in this city."

"If Frank is guilty, Tempest could also be in danger." Andy glanced at Ryan.

"Don't you think I know that? It's why you're here," Ryan said. "I need you to take over for me while I'm away, and more importantly, to watch out for Tempest."

"Why not just tell her?" Andy asked.

Ryan shook his head. "I can't. I… we…" He stopped and took a breath. "We broke up, actually."

Andy's eyes widened. "Oh man! When you said you were taking it slow, I didn't expect this."

"It's for the best. It's exactly for this reason that I broke it off."

"*You* broke it off?" Andy's brows rose even further.

Ryan nodded. "For her safety. I don't want anyone coming after her because they think they can use her to get to me. If they think we broke up, then hopefully they'll leave her alone."

"Except she works - and lives - with Frank Dunlop, our only suspect so far."

"I warned her," Ryan said. "I sent her a text earlier suggesting she find a different job and place to live."

"You sent her a text…" Andy repeated. He shook his head. "Man, that is just cruel. Couldn't you have phoned at least?"

"I tried. She wouldn't pick up." Ryan smiled sheepishly. "And now you know why I need your help."

"Help with the ladies, you mean?" Andy quipped with a grin.

"Help protecting her. I know she won't listen to me. She likes Frank, and frankly - no pun intended - I did too, until this."

"I've got your back. You know it."

"Thanks. I need you to follow every lead and keep me in the loop. But most importantly, keep Tempest safe. If anything - and I mean anything - happens that you think might put her in danger, you contact me. Got it?"

Andy gave an affirmative nod.

"Oh, and one more thing," Ryan added.

"What's that?"

"She, um… she seems to have found a new boyfriend." Ryan rubbed the back of his neck.

"That was quick," Andy said. "Keep an eye on him, too, I take it?"

Ryan nodded. "His name is Geoff Vanguard. So far I don't think there's a correlation between him and the case, so there's nothing to worry about…"

"Except you hate the guy's guts, so naturally he's a person of interest." Andy smiled and shook his head. "I'd say, you're a sucker for punishment."

"Whatever. Can you do it?"

Andy nodded. "Anything for you, bro."

RYAN STARED AT HIS CELLPHONE. Should he try calling Tempest one more time? With a deep breath, he hit her number and waited. To his surprise, she answered.

"Hello! I wasn't expecting you to answer," he said in a rush.

"Disappointed?" Tempest asked.

"Of course not."

"I got your text."

"About that. I was serious when I said you should look for another job and place to live."

"And why should I?"

"I have some concerns about Frank."

"What kind of concerns?"

"I can't say."

"There you go again! More secrets! If you can't tell me, then why even bother saying anything?"

"It's for your own good."

"My good isn't your concern anymore," she said. "You made that perfectly clear."

"Tempest…" Ryan's tone softened. "Tempest, I'm so sorry for the way it ended between us. But it doesn't mean I don't care." He swallowed.

"You have a fine way of showing it," she said.

"I'm sorry."

A moment of silence crackled between them.

"Ryan… I'm sorry, too, for what it's worth."

Ryan felt his insides melting. He wanted to hang up and go to her. Take her in his arms and never let go.

Except that would put her in harm's way.

He worked his jaw before speaking. "You're the one who wanted to break up," he said in a clipped tone.

"I… I said I was confused." Her voice sounded small. Hurt.

He grimaced and continued. "It appears you've figured it out, though, haven't you?"

"What do you mean?"

"Just that it didn't take long for you to replace me."

"I don't know what you're talking about."

"Geoff Vanguard," Ryan stated. "You claimed you were worried that I wasn't telling you the truth about other women, that I cheated on you when on assignment - which never happened by the way - when all along you were just waiting to dump me so you could take up with him."

"That isn't true!" Tempest cried. "We're just friends. And… who told you about Geoff, anyway?"

"No one. I saw it for myself."

"When?"

"The other day at the park."

"You were spying on me?" she asked, her tone rising.

"Hardly spying. It's a public park."

"But, still…"

"I also did a search on him," Ryan stated calmly. "And you'll be happy to know he looks clean."

"How dare you!"

"How dare I what? Look out for you because you can't seem to do that for yourself?"

"What exactly is that supposed to mean?"

"I don't know, Tempest. You tell me. You're not that smart when it comes to judging character. Look at Dirk Hillyer. I can only imagine the mess you made of your other relationships."

There was a moment of silence before Tempest spoke again. "What do you know about my other relationships?"

"Exactly nothing, which is the point. You never trusted me enough to tell me anything about your past. If I hadn't been on the case myself, you probably wouldn't have told me about Dirk or any of the trouble you got yourself into by trying to impersonate your pin-headed friend. And not very well, I might add."

"I… oh!"

The line went dead.

Ryan let the phone slip to his lap as he lowered his head into his hands.

There. Now she believed the break up was real. It was for her own good.

CHAPTER 11

*R*yan skimmed through Agent Trainee Jeremy Leming's records. If he was going to have to work closely with the young man, then he needed to know all he could before they found themselves in the field.

So far, everything looked to be in order. Leming's physical fitness was peak, and he showed above average ability in most other areas, including gunmanship, problem solving, and mental stamina. He was on the cusp of being promoted to agent proper, but that didn't explain why Reynolds had insisted on assigning him to the diamond smuggling case.

"You wanted to see me?" Jeremy Leming stood in the entrance to Ryan's office.

Ryan looked up and gestured for the younger man to enter. "Come in and shut the door."

Leming did as he was bid and then took a standing position on the opposite side of Ryan's desk.

"Might as well sit down," Ryan said. "I thought we could go over some of the details of the operation before we have to leave."

"Assistant Director Reynolds has gone over all the logistics with me already, Sir," Leming said.

Ryan blinked, his brows rising slightly. "Is that so? Did he also mention that I'm the senior agent on this case?"

"I know that, Sir."

Ryan narrowed his eyes at the agent trainee, who remained standing at ease like a soldier. The young man had a chip on his shoulder, if Ryan wasn't mistaken. Typical 'small man' syndrome… or was it something else? He was solidly built despite his stature.

"Listen. This isn't the military. For starters, quit calling me Sir. Second, get your behind in that chair." Ryan pointed to the empty chair.

"Yes, Sir." The younger agent sat.

Ryan leaned forward across his desk. "Now, as the senior agent assigned to this case, may I remind you that I call the shots. Once we get out there in the field, things might not always go as planned. Sometimes we have to adapt, which is why Reynolds put me - the *experienced* field agent - in charge. Not you."

"I'm not disputing that, Sir."

Ryan raised his brows meaningfully in Leming's direction.

"I mean, Agent O'Toole."

"Ryan will do."

"Yes, Sir."

Ryan took a calming breath before continuing. "Good. As long as we're both clear on that point. So, when I say I want to go over a few things, then we're going to go over a few things. Got it?"

Leming nodded.

Ryan shook his head. "I have to be honest. I'm not sure why Reynolds feels you're the man to assist me on this, but for whatever reason he does, and I have to respect that." He perused the younger man. "Any idea why he insisted you be put on this case? I would have preferred working solo, or at least with someone I trust. I don't know you from Adam."

Leming shrugged. "I suppose he has his reasons, as you said."

"Care to enlighten me?" Ryan waited. When Jeremy remained silent, Ryan inhaled deeply again and then let the air out slowly. "Look, if we're going to be working together, we have to trust each other. I don't like feeling as if I'm being kept out of the loop."

"I have no idea why he chose me other than my record."

"Your record? Explain."

"I don't like losing. And I'm not afraid of a fight."

Ryan glanced down at the records on his desk. "It says here you were the boxing champ in your weight division three years running. Exactly what kind of fight is Reynolds expecting?"

"I'm not sure. But he knows I'm tough and I don't back down."

Ryan nodded slowly. "I can see that. Still doesn't explain why you're tagging along."

Leming cleared his throat. "I, uh, might have some insight into the local culture."

"Okay. And why is that?" Ryan clasped his hands on top of his desk.

Leming shifted slightly. "My biological father was from the North West Territories. Dene."

Ryan nodded. "Now we're getting somewhere. Do you still have family there?"

"Yes…" Leming shifted again, clearly uncomfortable.

Ryan narrowed his eyes. "What aren't you telling me?"

Leming's bravado suddenly deflated like a balloon. "Assistant Director Reynolds is my uncle."

Ryan rocketed out of his chair. "You stay put!" he barked, pointing a finger at Leming.

Without another word he stalked from the office.

RYAN JERKED OPEN the Assistant Director's office door without so much as a warning knock and marched inside. "We need to talk."

Reynolds glanced up, telephone still to his ear. "Um… can I

call you back?" Once he'd placed the receiver in its cradle, his tone wasn't as calm. "What do you think you're doing, barging into my office like this?"

Ryan pointed an accusing finger. "Why didn't you tell me Leming was your nephew?"

Reynolds stood. "Now hold on! And would you shut the door, for goodness sake?".

Ryan pivoted and shut the door, rattling the glass. Then he turned back to his boss. "You have no right putting an inexperienced boy on such a big case just to advance his career! You're putting lives at risk. Mine and his!"

"He's not inexperienced, and he's not a boy. He's shown great potential."

Ryan ran a frustrated hand through his hair. "Fine! Yes! I read his records, but still… He's your nephew! Do you know how that looks?"

"Exactly why I didn't tell you. Now, if you'll give me the courtesy of an explanation?" Reynolds gestured to the chair on the other side of his desk.

With a sigh, Ryan flopped into it and waited.

"I know it looks like I'm trying to advance my own nephew's career, but I assure you, there's more to it than that."

"He said his father is from the area. Is that true?"

Reynolds nodded. "Yes. My sister worked for a time in the NWT and took up with a local. She left before Jeremy was born, but he's always had a curiosity about his native ancestry."

"And you're giving him the chance to explore his roots. How kind." The sarcastic edge to Ryan's voice was unmistakable.

"No. He's been free to explore that part of his heritage on his own time. In fact, he made contact with his biological grandmother a couple of years ago and has been there to visit. He's learned many things about their culture that could be useful. It's one reason why I think he's the best support for you. He blends in. And he's a good agent."

"Agent trainee," Ryan clarified. "Why didn't you just tell me?"

"I was trying to avoid just such a scene!"

Ryan sighed. "Right. Sorry about that."

"I'm the one in charge here, and I don't appreciate being questioned. It's your job to do as you're told." Reynolds picked up the telephone. "Now get out of my office before I can your sorry arse all together!"

~

"Hope you have a warm coat packed," Andy said. "I hear forty below is picnic weather up there." He was perched in his usual spot on the edge of Ryan's desk.

"The arctic in winter." Ryan shook his head. "Not the most pleasant prospect, I'll admit. But, I've been issued everything I should need. Make that what 'we' should need."

Andy grinned. "You and Leming make a cute couple."

"I'm going to pretend I didn't hear that," Ryan warned, half smiling himself. "Leming's a good kid. I think he'll do alright." He clicked his laptop shut and leaned back in his desk chair.

"I heard you made a little scene earlier."

Ryan shrugged. "It wasn't a scene, exactly. Just needed to clarify a few things."

"It's a crazy case. Glad I'm not on it." Andy cocked his head to one side. "Quite the cover. A diamond inspector! If that doesn't beat all!"

"A nice change from drug dealer," Ryan said with a laugh.

"But just as dangerous. Be careful. Don't go trying to sell ice to an Eskimo or anything."

"The proper term is 'Inuit'. If I didn't know you better, I'd say that sounded racist."

"My bad. On a different note, I came across a bit of information today about Frank Dunlop that you might be interested in."

Ryan rocked forward. "I'm listening."

"He has a regular flow of cash coming in each month which then goes out just as mysteriously. I haven't been able to trace the source yet, nor where he's spending it. Could be funneled through an offshore account. I'm still looking into it."

"You hacked into Frank's bank account? That was fast."

"Hey! You asked me to do some follow up, so I'm following up."

"Just don't get caught," Ryan advised.

"And another thing…"

Ryan waited.

"Tempest stayed out pretty late last night." Andy hesitated. "She wasn't alone."

"Geoff Vanguard?"

"Yes."

It stung, but what had he expected? "As long as she's safe."

"I'll keep my eye on Vanguard, too," Andy said.

Ryan looked at his watch and stood. "Well, it's that time. Thanks for everything you're doing." He stuffed the laptop into its carrying case.

"No problem. You sure you're ready for this?"

"Ready as I'll ever be."

Ryan was thankful for Andy's friendship and for all he was doing. Where he was going, he might not see another familiar face for awhile.

CHAPTER 12

*R*yan glanced out the window of the airplane at the harsh landscape below. Rocky outcrops and giant boulders jutted against the starkness of snow packed drifts. Stunted evergreens dotted the terrain, twisted and bent in their fight against mother nature. Next to these, the white expanse of Great Slave Lake stretched past the horizon, its surface swirling with little white furies whipped up by the wind. This was the backdrop for a cluster of civilization gathered in defiance against the elements. Yellowknife, capital city of the North West Territories.

The direct flight from LA to Edmonton, Alberta, was of no consequence. Ryan and Jeremy sat together, but the younger man had had his earbuds in the entire time so there was no chatting. Not that they would have been able to discuss the case openly anyway. After a short stop-over, they flew more than 600 miles straight north from Edmonton to Yellowknife on a smaller commercial jet. Tomorrow it was off on a charter to Paragon Diamond Mine. One leg left on their journey to no-man's land.

Once the jet was grounded and secure, passengers began to file off the airplane. Ryan glanced behind him as he stood up and saw Jeremy not far behind, separated by several other travelers. He nodded an acknowledgment and then turned his gaze ahead, following at a snail's pace behind a woman with two small children plus all their carry-ons.

He ducked through the exit and maneuvered down a short ramp into the tunnel that connected the plane to the airport terminal. The thin walls could not muffle the moan of the wind as it sought to penetrate each crack.

Ryan hefted his computer briefcase onto his shoulder and took up his place beside the baggage claim, waiting for the mechanism to grind into motion. A moment later, Jeremy Leming joined him.

"You checked your bags?" Jeremy asked. "I thought someone as experienced as you would know how to travel light."

Ryan glanced at Jeremy, a solitary duffel bag slung across his body. "I brought equipment not allowed on the plane," he replied.

"Ah. Of course," Jeremy stated. "I'm just a lowly worker bee, so I didn't know."

"Careful. We shouldn't talk too much here."

"Gotcha."

"We'll go over the game plan once we get to the hotel."

Gears groaned and the baggage belt started up with a jerk. After a few minutes, Ryan's titanium suitcase appeared followed by a metal box marked 'fragile'. "Grab that end," he threw over his shoulder as he reached for one of the handles.

They each took an end of the box and hoisted it off the belt onto a cart that Ryan had secured earlier.

"Share a cab to the hotel?" Jeremy asked.

"Sounds good."

The instant he exited the terminal, the wind whisked Ryan's breath away. He gasped and hunkered deeper into his jacket, bending forward as he pushed the cart toward a cab waiting by the curb. Biting in its intensity, this cold was like nothing he'd ever felt before and he fumbled to get his belongings into the minivan.

"Wow. That was intense," Ryan said once inside the cab.

The driver just laughed and asked for directions to their destination.

Ryan gave the name of their hotel and then sat back to enjoy the rugged scenery between the airport and the city proper. The main road into town finally descended through roughhewn rock until it emerged near the downtown core. The cabby dropped them off at a modern high rise hotel - two worlds colliding in this unorthodox place.

"Check it out." Jeremy pointed to a large stuffed polar bear in the lobby.

"Hopefully that will be the closest I get to one of those fellas," Ryan said. "I read that there are restrictions about going outside at the mine, though, for just that reason."

A pretty First Nations woman behind the front desk gave them their room access cards and they headed to the elevator.

The elevator doors opened and Ryan stopped in his tracks. "What in -? What are *you* doing here?" he blurted.

Dirk Hillyer. In Yellowknife?

"I COULD BE ASKING you the same question," Dirk replied.

The elevator doors swished shut; all three men remained on the main floor.

Ryan felt like he'd been gut-punched. Not that Dirk posed a threat. And apparently, he had become a Christian, so Ryan knew he had to cut the guy some slack. Still, there was something about him that rubbed the wrong way. Even in these harsh conditions he looked like he'd just walked off a movie set with his windswept hair, fashionable overcoat, and scarf slung around his neck with just the right amount of swag.

Ryan drew himself to his full height. "I'm here for work," he said in his most business like tone. He gestured to Jeremy. "My associate, Jeremy Leming."

Dirk extended a hand to Jeremy. "Pleased to meet you. On a case, I take it?"

Ryan cleared his throat. "Could be."

Dirk nodded. "Got it. I'll pretend I didn't run into you."

"And how do you two know each other?" Jeremy asked.

"We go way back," Dirk said with a grin. "Ryan and I have worked together before. More than once."

"You're with law enforcement?"

Ryan let out a guffaw. "Hardly."

"No, not exactly," Dirk said to Jeremy with a smile.

"Not ever," Ryan clarified.

Dirk shrugged. "Anyway, fancy meeting you here - in hell. At least that's my definition, cause I think hell just froze over."

"You never told me what you're doing here, Hillyer," Ryan said.

"Oh? Well, not that it's your business, but I'm here to find my girlfriend. You remember Anne-Marie? You met her after the Mexico thing."

"Of course. Is she lost? You said you were here to find her."

"Wait a minute," Jeremy interrupted. "Now I know who you are! You're the civilian that got shot in the drug bust in Italy and then tipped Agent O'Toole here about the pharmaceuticals being smuggled from that Mexican orphanage."

"How do you know so much?" Ryan turned a steely glare on Jeremy.

"I do my research," Jeremy said with a shrug.

"That's me. How's Tempest?" Dirk asked.

"Fine," Ryan clipped. "Now, about Anne-Marie?"

"She moved up here right after Christmas. Was going to work at a nursing station in some remote community." Dirk gave a small laugh. "I think it filled a gap after leaving the orphanage. You know Anne-Marie. Once a missionary, always a missionary."

"That's good, I guess," Ryan said. "Long distance relationships can be tough, though." Didn't he know it.

"I hear you. Except…" Dirk hesitated. "We've been taking a little break, if I can put it that way."

Ryan cleared his throat. "Sorry to hear it." There was no way he was admitting the same about himself and Tempest.

"I hear she might have relocated to some diamond mine, though." Dirk shook his head. "Enough is enough. I miss her, and I don't want to do this anymore. I'm here to try and meet her on her next trip in or out. Try and convince her it's time to come home before she freezes to death."

"A diamond mine?" Ryan asked.

"Paramore… Paragon… Something like that."

"Interesting."

"Anyway…" Dirk shifted, hands in pockets.

"We shouldn't keep you," Ryan said. He wasn't about to add it had been nice seeing him.

But fate - or was it providence, seemed to keep putting them in each other's path. It remained to be seen what would come of it.

Anne-Marie

 *wo months earlier...*

ANNE-MARIE HUNG the last glass ornament on the tree, releasing her fingers slowly as she backed away to survey her handiwork. "There. The tree looks beautiful," she said with a satisfied smile.

The rest of her family - mother Linda, father Bill, and brother Tyler - had gathered in her parents' family room for their annual Christmas tree decorating ritual. It marked the kick off to the season's festivities.

The Fletcher family room was decked for the holidays with greenery above each window, garland along the fireplace, and red gingham bows for a touch of country whimsy. Candles and other seasonal knick-knacks graced each surface, with the centerpiece of it all being the huge tree that stood in front of the large bay window. The sunken family room, still visible from the kitchen and dining area, was always the hub of the home, but Christmas was truly its time to shine.

"I'm just so grateful you're here with us this year, honey,"

Linda said to Anne-Marie. "I was totally prepared for you not being able to come home this year, but I'm so glad you did."

"Me, too." Anne-Marie leaned over to squeeze her mother's hand.

"Not like she had much choice," Tyler put in as he rummaged in an open shoe box used to house decorations.

"Well, technically I could have tried to get back on at the orphanage in Mexico. I didn't do anything wrong. But after what happened, there was just such uncertainty about everything. I felt better coming home."

"I'm glad you did," her father Bill said from his easy chair. "The thought of you going back down there after the ordeal you went through..." He shook his head. "I'm glad you're safe and sound. I never did like the idea of you being away for such a long period of time."

Tyler slapped his thighs and stood. "Well, looks like the tree is done. What's next on the agenda?"

"You know, silly!" Linda turned to her son. "We still have to have hot chocolate and do the Christmas calendar. Goodness! What's the rush?"

Tyler shrugged and sat down. "Nothing."

Anne-Marie smiled. She felt for her younger brother. At twenty-two he probably had somewhere else he'd rather be, but he was being a good sport. Christmas was so important to their mom.

"Now, get the rest of the ornaments on the tree," Linda scolded good-naturedly. "No hot chocolate until it's finished."

"The tree is already full. We don't need to put *every* ornament on it." Tyler held up an oversized cardboard star sprinkled with garish sequins. It sported a piece of red wool for a hanger.

"Tyler Fletcher!" Linda looked aghast. "It's tradition! Every single ornament is going on that tree and that's final."

Anne-Marie laughed. "Maybe we could forego the ones we made as kids. Some of them are a bit tacky."

"You calling my Kindergarten creation tacky?" Tyler's lopsided grin matched the ornament. Tyler had a baby face, but his size made up for it. He wasn't fat, but he was broad and husky. It ran in the family.

"They're the best ones," Linda declared.

"No point arguing with your mother," Bill said. "She's the boss of Christmas around here."

"Find a spot at the back of the tree," Anne-Marie advised.

Her father's statement was true. As long as Anne-Marie could remember, her family had taken Christmas very seriously, thanks to her mom. They had so many traditions that it was getting more difficult each year to juggle them all now that she and Tyler were adults and had their own events to squeeze in.

"Bill, can you get the hot chocolate? It's in the carafe on the counter."

"Just like it is every year," Bill said under his breath as he hoisted himself from the depths of his chair.

"Anne-Marie, you can get the cookies," Linda continued. "And Tyler, you can bring the Christmas calendar. I'll finish up here."

Anne-Marie nodded and did as she was bid while Tyler dutifully retrieved the calendar from its spot on the side of the kitchen refrigerator. It was a large magnetic affair that had been trimmed with festive stick-ons.

They all arrived back in the family room and gathered by the coffee table for the next phase of their ritual.

"I've already slotted in the dates that can't be altered." Linda pointed to the calendar as Bill poured the hot chocolate. "Community caroling, sleigh rides at the greenhouse, the Sunday School Christmas pageant, our work parties, and of course, the Church cookie exchange."

"I vote you skip the cookie exchange," Tyler said. "Even *I* don't like most of the baking that comes out of that."

"But it's tradition!" Linda exclaimed.

"I'm with Tyler on that one," Bill said. "I like your cookies best, not Miss Mumford's. They're so dry."

"If I recall, they're always the last ones on the plate," Anne-Marie offered.

"You should go ahead and bake all the stuff we like, but just don't give it away," Tyler said. Everyone but Linda laughed.

"I will do no such thing." She put a check mark beside the cookie exchange.

Bill squinted at the calendar. "Can we skip your office party? People always get so tipsy. It makes me uncomfortable."

"I know, but that doesn't mean we aren't going," Linda replied. "We have to represent. Show people that we can be sociable and celebrate without overindulging in alcohol."

"Well, we could skip mine, then," he suggested.

"Bill! You're the owner of the construction company! You can't *not* put on a party for your own employees."

"We could just give them a nice gift. A turkey or one of those baskets with cheese and crackers."

Anne-Marie smiled. It was the same argument every year. Her dad wanted to skip the office parties and her mom always forced him into it.

"I've already got the party plans well under way." Linda turned to Tyler and Anne-Marie. "Of course you children will attend your dad's party, but mine is a chance for you to fit in something of your own."

"Our one free night," Tyler said sarcastically. "Thanks."

"Tyler!"

"Why should I have to go to Dad's Christmas party? I don't work for him."

"But you're a member of this family."

"Your office party might not line up with Tyler's other events," Anne-Marie said in defense of her brother.

"What other events?" Linda blinked rapidly, as if the thought that her children might have other plans had never occurred to her.

Tyler just sighed.

"Now, one thing where we do have some flexibility is our games night. We can fill that in when the rest of the dates are set. Which brings me to our dinner with Auntie Pam and Uncle Bruce. I'll have to phone her first thing tomorrow and find out what date works for everyone."

"I won't be able to make it," Tyler said.

Linda looked up with wide eyes. "What do you mean? You don't even know the date yet."

"I don't need to know the date to know I don't want to be there. Once Uncle Bruce starts talking you're trapped!"

"You could be like Dad and just fall asleep while he's talking," Anne-Marie said with a grin. She gestured to where her dad was nodding in his chair.

"Children! They're family!"

"Don't tell me you don't find it annoying just as much as the rest of us," Tyler said. "I've witnessed you suddenly changing the topic whenever Uncle Bruce starts a story."

"I won't have you talk like that about my only sister's husband."

"Whatever. Well, if that covers it, I'm going to see if I can still catch the guys." Tyler stood.

"Where? What guys?" Linda asked.

"Oh, just some guys from my hockey team. They were meeting for a beer."

"Tyler! You know I don't like it when you drink."

"M-o-t-h-e-r," Tyler stretched out the word. "I'm not 'drinking'. Just having a beer with the guys. Geez. I'm an adult for crying out loud."

Linda tilted her head. "And I don't like it when you say 'Geez'. It's too close to taking the Lord's name in vain."

Tyler shook his head with a grin and then kissed his mother on the cheek before leaving the room.

"Don't be too hard on him," Anne-Marie said as they watched Tyler disappear around the corner.

"It's like he doesn't even want to be part of this family anymore."

"I don't think that's true. But he's an adult now, and has his own life. His own interests. You can't expect him to want to spend all his time at home."

"You did."

"Did I?"

"Well, until you ran away to Mexico."

"I didn't run away! I was working."

"You probably wish you were away this year." Linda looked down at the now empty mug in her hands.

"Mom, don't do this."

"What?"

"The guilt trip thing."

"I don't do any guilt trip thing!" Linda declared.

Anne-Marie placed a hand over her mother's. "I know you mean well, but you have to let go just a bit. As much as I love all of the memories, sometimes it's a bit too much, you know?"

"Well…" Linda sniffed and stood up. "I'll put this back on the fridge where we can all see it." She exited with the calendar.

Bill stirred and opened his eyes. "Did I miss anything?" he asked.

"Not really." Anne-Marie lowered her voice and looked over at where her mother was busy straightening the calendar on the side of the refrigerator. "Just a bit of drama."

"Oh?" Bill glanced at his wife. She moved from the refrigerator to the sink and started filling it with water.

"Mom is being Mom. She can't seem to wrap her head around the fact that Tyler and I might not want to participate in all the same traditions that we did as kids."

"You know Christmas is important to her. She overcompensates because she wasn't allowed to have Christmas when she was a kid."

"I know that. Just because they were raised Jehovah's Witnesses, both she and Aunt Pam go overboard. I get it."

"She just wants to make it extra special for you and your brother."

"Except we aren't little kids anymore," Anne-Marie reminded.

"I can still hear you," Linda called from the kitchen as she turned off the tap.

"Then come and join us," Anne-Marie called back. "There's something else I want to talk to you about."

Linda dried her hands and descended the two steps from the kitchen-dining area to the family room.

Anne-Marie waited until her mother was seated before she continued. "So… there's something I haven't been exactly honest about since coming back from Mexico."

"Oh?" Linda clasped her hands in her lap and straightened her spine. "No matter what, you children can tell us anything."

"Sometimes I wonder…" Anne-Marie said with a nervous titter.

"Not productive," Bill commented under his breath.

"Sorry." Anne-Marie sighed and then took a deep breath. "Remember the people who helped uncover the drug smuggling operation at the orphanage?"

"A brother and sister who were also working down there," Linda said with a nod.

"Right. Dirk and Cherise Hillyer."

"From Boston, you said?" Bill asked.

"Yes, that's right. Anyway, Dirk and I… we were more than just colleagues…"

Linda gasped and put her hand to her heart. "You're pregnant!"

"No! I'm not pregnant!" Anne-Marie cried. "Just listen! We

never slept together so there is no way I'm pregnant! But we were dating. He wants to come for a visit at Christmas and… I haven't told him whether he can come yet or not."

Linda blinked rapidly. "Why not? Are you embarrassed of us?"

"No! But… you can be pretty intense at this time of year."

"Why didn't you tell us about him sooner?" Bill sat forward.

Anne-Marie shrugged. "I don't know. Sometimes I don't believe it myself. What he sees in me, I mean."

"I don't know why you'd say such a thing," Linda said. "You are beautiful and smart and -"

"Large," Anne-Marie finished.

"You are not large!" Linda exclaimed. "I have no idea where you got such an idea!"

"Maybe the hints about dieting I've gotten my whole life?" Anne-Marie suggested.

"Only for health purposes! You kids both take after me in that department, I know, but I only want you to be healthy." Linda sniffed.

"Well, I have to agree with your mother on this one," Bill said.

"Oh, really?"

"Yes. You *are* beautiful and you're *not* fat."

Anne-Marie laughed. "Thanks, Dad, but you were never a good liar."

"I mean it. Besides, if he loves you he won't mind." Bill squeezed his wife's hand. "Maybe he even likes a little meat on the bones."

Anne-Marie closed her eyes for a second and took another deep breath. "Be that as it may, there's more." She looked from one parent to the next. "He's actually quite… rich. As in very wealthy."

Bill raised his brows but didn't comment.

"And?" Linda asked.

"I'm not sure how he'll take it," Anne-Marie gestured to the room in general. "This. It's one thing to be in an environment like the orphanage. There is poverty everywhere in that community, and we offered hope and a better life. Everyone was in the same boat - neutral ground, so to speak." She paused and gave a small laugh. "Although, Dirk was definitely out of his element there at times. But he did a good job of adapting."

"So you *are* embarrassed," Linda cut in. "About the fact that we're ordinary."

"No, not embarrassed. Just apprehensive. I'm proud of who I am and where I come from. You did a good job of raising us, if I do say so. But it makes me wonder once he sees the real me, in my own environment. He might decide I'm not for him after all."

"All the better to find that out now, I'd say," Bill said.

"Exactly," Linda agreed. "Now, just let me know what day he's arriving so that I can add it to the calendar. We could have a special family dinner, or, if you prefer, we can schedule the cousins' dinner to coincide with that date."

Anne-Marie threw up her hands. "Mom! This is why I wasn't sure letting him come was a good idea! I don't want special dinners, or having his whole time here planned out for us. What if we just want to spend time together? Alone?"

"How alone?" Bill asked.

"Dad! I'm twenty-six years old!"

"Well, we don't have to decide an agenda now." Linda stood and gathered the empty mugs from the coffee table.

"I think you should tell him to come," Bill said. "I'd like to meet the man that swept my baby girl off her feet."

"Dad..." Anne-Marie exclaimed less forcefully. She looked down at her toes.

Had Dirk Hillyer swept her off her feet? Maybe, if not being able to get him out of her head was any indication. Still, there were so many reasons to question the wisdom of such a relationship. Praying hadn't helped, so maybe the answer was letting him come so that he could see for himself the inequities that stood in their way.

CHAPTER 14

*A*nne-Marie busied herself rolling out a lump of cookie dough while her mother slid the next batch into the built-in eye level oven. The kitchen smelled of gingerbread and all things Christmas. Anne-Marie inhaled deeply and let out a sigh. "I do love Christmas baking."

"At least there's one tradition not getting thrown out the window." Linda shut the oven door and set the timer.

"What are you talking about?" Aunt Pam asked as she mixed up some colored icing.

"Oh, just that my children are too busy for family time during the holidays," Linda said.

"What?" Aunt Pam's voice sounded alarmed.

"Not exactly true." Anne-Marie put a little more 'oomph' behind the rolling pin. "I'm here, aren't I?"

"Yes, but you like baking. You just said so."

"Don't worry, Anne-Marie. Mom and I had this very same conversation a couple of years ago when Serge and I got married." Anne-Marie's cousin Daphne bounced her baby on one hip. She broke a small piece off one of the fresh gingerbread cookies and popped it into little Ava's mouth. "You can't expect us to do all the same things we did as kids. We have our own lives to lead."

"Exactly. Thank you." Anne-Marie nodded in Daphne's direction.

"Especially once you get married and have a baby," Daphne added. "That changes everything."

Anne-Marie kept rolling. Of course, Daphne would have to put it that way.

Anne-Marie loved her cousin Daphne. They were only one year apart in age so had grown up together, and Daphne was nice in her way. She liked to hear herself talk, though - a trait she probably got from her father, Uncle Bruce. But sometimes it came across as bragging or showing off. She was always one-up; been-there-and-done-that. Anne-Marie knew that Daphne didn't mean to sound like a know-it-all, but for her whole life, Anne-Marie felt like she never quite measured up to her talented, pretty, *skinny* cousin.

"Speaking of getting married, Anne-Marie is -"

Anne-Marie cut her mother off in mid-sentence. "Hey, remember those horrible Christmas dresses we had to wear every year from Great Aunt Marie? That is one tradition nobody misses! Remember, Daph?" She smiled at Daphne encouragingly, hoping her change-the-subject tactics had worked. The last thing she wanted was an inquisition about Dirk

Daphne looked off into the distance. "I used to love the dresses that Great Aunt Marie picked out. Always so pretty. I felt like a princess."

"But they were so uncomfortable! And we had to wear them all day. She dressed us up like her own personal dolls."

"That's because Aunt Marie never had any children of her own. You were the closest thing she had to children and she liked to spoil you," Linda said.

"She had expensive taste, too," Pam added. "We certainly never got anything as pretty as children. You should be grateful."

Anne-Marie sympathized with her mother and Aunt Pam. Their own mother, Great Aunt Marie's sister, had become a Jehovah's Witness after marrying. Christmases and birthdays became taboo. Anne-Marie had never received a card or gift from her own grandmother in the years that she was alive. It made Linda and Pamela even more determined to celebrate each event to the max.

As if sensing her nieces' need to make up for lost time, Great Aunt Marie sent lavish gifts to her great nieces and nephew, including matching Christmas dresses for the girls. They were opulent affairs with flounces, ruffles, ribbon, and lace. Anne-Marie and Daphne were forced to wear them the entire day.

As a youngster, it wasn't such a bad thing. What little girl didn't want to dress like a princess? Plus, she had been named for Great Aunt Marie and wanted to please her. But as the years went by, it became increasingly difficult to don the dress and still keep smiling.

For one thing, the dresses were always 'matching', made from the same stiff material and loaded with puffs and gathers. The situation wasn't so bad for Daphne with her much slimmer build, but it made Anne-Marie feel as wide as she was tall.

"I cannot believe you didn't like the dresses, Anne-Marie," Daphne exclaimed. "I certainly loved mine. I wish we could have kept them instead of donating them the next year."

"It was her wish," Linda said. "Part of the bargain."

"And one didn't cross dear Aunt Marie," Pam added fondly.

"At least yours always fit," Anne-Marie said with a laugh. "I usually had to squeeze into the thing and hope the zipper didn't pop."

"That only happened once," Linda said.

"One time too many," Anne-Marie said wryly.

Daphne cocked her pretty blonde head to one side. "You've lost a ton of weight, Anne-Marie! Mexico must have suited you. Were you dieting or was the food bad?"

"Neither. The food was just plain."

"Serge and I are doing that new cleansing diet. I have so much more energy now! You should try it. It's super easy and super good for you, too. It really doesn't cost any more than buying regular groceries, either." Daphne popped the last of the cookie in her own mouth.

"Are gingerbread cookies part of it?" Anne-Marie raised a brow.

Daphne shrugged. "No, but you're allowed to cheat once a week, and that was such a small bite it doesn't count."

Linda shook her head. "As if you need to diet anyway, my dear. Just look at you! After being pregnant and giving birth, you still have the figure of a model. Not fair!"

"I worked hard to get my figure back. I can't go to the gym anymore now that Ava's here. It's just not practical, but we bought one of those home gyms. So far I've used it at least twice a week, if not more. You should come over and try it sometime, Anne-Marie. Maybe you'll like it and want to buy one of your own."

"Um, I'll think about it." Anne-Marie started cutting out gingerbread men.

"Can we make extra of these?" Daphne pointed to the cookies. "I think Ava really likes them, and it's a shame they're all going to the cookie exchange."

"You mean *you* like them." Anne-Marie said.

"I think we can make a few more," Linda agreed.

"One can always use a few more good men," Pam added and both of the older ladies laughed. "Which reminds me," she continued. "Your mother tells me you have a new man in your life. Someone you met in Mexico. Is it serious?"

Anne-Marie stopped, the metal man-shaped cookie cutter in midair. So much for changing the subject.

"Really?" Daphne's eyes were wide. "Is he foreign? Why is this the first I'm hearing about it?"

"Well..."

"I was just about to tell you all about it when we started talking about Christmas dresses," Linda supplied. "He's not foreign exactly. Well, he is but he's American, so that doesn't really count. And apparently, he's very wealthy!"

"Oh!" Both Pam and Daphne gasped.

"Yes! And he's coming for Christmas!" Linda smiled broadly.

"I said he *might* be coming for Christmas." Anne-Marie deliberately cut another cookie, keeping her eyes on the task at hand.

"Tell us more!" Daphne exclaimed, then without missing a beat continued. "Oh! I remember the first time I brought Serge home for Christmas! Do you remember? It was family dinner but it was our year so Mom was hosting at our house. He was so nervous! He said afterward he felt like everyone was either asking too many questions or just staring! Poor guy! Fortunately for me he still asked me to marry him, so I'm sure it won't be that bad. If he's the one, that is."

"It's a little early to be talking marriage." Anne-Marie pressed the cookie cutter into the dough.

"How did you meet? What does he do? Is he really rich?" Daphne bounced Ava more vigorously on her hip. "Oh, I can hardly wait to tell Serge all about it tonight when he gets home!"

"We know very little about him," Linda said. "Anne-Marie has been very secretive about the whole thing."

Anne-Marie slammed the cookie cutter down, spoiling a couple of the gingerbread men. "Stop! Just stop!" Linda, Daphne and Pam stood statuesque for a moment as Anne-Marie caught her breath. "Sorry. I didn't mean to yell, but..." She sighed and looked ceilingward. "I just need a bit of air."

She wiped her hands on a nearby towel and left the kitchen without looking back.

She loved her family. Truly she did. But their stifling cocoon of concern was smothering her. She needed air. Like a salt sea wind blowing in from the Baja coastline through a small Mexican village. Like the stillness of the night that enhanced the chirp of cicadas, or the stiff rustle of Macadamia leaves in the breeze. Like the whisper of a man who had no right to be so beautiful, telling her he loved her…

~

IT SEEMED like yesterday that she was stitching up Dirk's finger in a little Mexican clinic. It felt like a lifetime since he'd kissed her last. They had been through so much in their brief time together, it was almost hard to reconcile.

The first time they'd met, when Dirk had come into the emergency room with a sliced finger, of course she had taken note of his good looks and charm. But she was on the job. Practical and efficient as all good nurses should be with every patient, she hadn't even considered vying for his attention. Besides, a man who looked like that would never be interested in a woman like her, so why even go there? But then, gradually, when they kept running into one another at church, her insides started to do a little salsa every time she saw him. She now knew that Dirk had orchestrated these happenstance meetings. He was good, she'd give him that.

One thing led to another, and they'd started taking moonlit walks after the services. It was then that she'd fallen. She should have known better; kept her guard intact. Except Dirk Hillyer made her want to let her guard down. She'd confided in him. Told him things about herself that she'd never admitted to other boyfriends - not that there had ever been anyone serious. Things like her insecurities about being overweight - which he had instantly dismissed as false. Oh, how she wished she could believe it!

Dirk had a lot of questions in those early weeks, too, and now she knew why. He wasn't even a Christian then, although he had kept that fact hidden quite convincingly. She had to cut him some slack because she wasn't sure he even knew he was hiding anything until after the fact. He had no background in a life of faith. However, now that he did know Jesus, was he still hiding? He was a good actor.

He had a whole list of attributes that set him out of her league. Beyond his physical looks, he was wealthy and privileged. And he had lived a far more dangerous and adventurous life than she. He'd inevitably tire of her hum-drum existence.

Before she even knew Dirk, he had helped crack a drug smuggling operation in Europe. He'd even taken a bullet, and he wore the scar like a badge of honor. Perhaps that experience had enhanced his sleuthing abilities. When he'd first had suspicions about something shady going on at the orphanage in Mexico, she had balked at the idea, but it had turned out to be true - and not without some danger involved.

From clandestine meetings in the dark while gathering evidence, to being arrested, falsely accused, and even spending a night in jail, her adventures with Dirk had never been dull. The most frightening had to be the ride in the back of an armored van to the US border. They'd been handcuffed and thrown inside with little ceremony, not sure if the police officers who'd incarcerated them were dirty or not. In the end, one of Dirk's FBI connections came to the rescue and they'd made it back to the States without further incident.

The real perpetrators were caught - at least the scapegoats at the bottom of the heap. One was Linda Gallagher, the wife of the orphanage administrator. The other was a fellow nurse named Franchesca. Anne-Marie could hardly believe it still. She and Franchesca had been friends. How could she have been so wrong about someone?

She'd always thought she was a good judge of character, but that theory got blown out the window. Perhaps she was too trusting, which was why she now had huge questions when it came to Dirk. What kind of wealthy socialite worked at an orphanage for kicks? Yes, he had proved himself in many ways. He'd worked hard, stayed longer than necessary, and brought the entire pharmaceutical fiasco to the forefront at great personal risk. He was even helping by contributing to the orphanage's finances since its fall from grace. Her trusting side wanted to believe it was all genuine.

Thinking back to her own carefree and open commitment to God, it was difficult to know when the fear and doubt had crept in. Her faith had led her to Mexico in the first place. She loved God with all her heart and wanted to serve Him. She'd always dreamed of being a missionary and nursing seemed like a perfect avenue to fulfill those dreams. But somewhere insecurity had taken root. How could a man like Dirk Hillyer possibly find her anything other than a novelty?

They'd had words about it when they were back in LA, after being rescued. He'd insisted on buying her a new outfit, paying for her room, taking her on extravagant dinners. She didn't like taking handouts. Call it pride, but she was used to being independent. Not only that, but he wanted to control where she lived and what she did, too.

Perhaps 'control' was a bit strong. He'd called it wanting to look after her, but it caused more than a little tension. Dirk didn't know what it was like to be an ordinary person; to have to support yourself or to take pride in your work. For her part, she would never be satisfied with being a kept woman. Her self-worth came from the fact that she was a good nurse - that she was helping people. She needed to feel useful. And he didn't get that.

Which brought her right back to her present dilemma. If Dirk came for Christmas he would likely start talking about her visiting Boston next, which she wasn't ready to do. Once she got there and he saw how she didn't fit into his environment, he might send her packing, minus her heart.

"Where's that confident woman I met in Mexico? The one who trusts God?" he'd asked her once.

She wasn't sure. Maybe she'd always been an imaginary character in her own stage-play. And here she was, on the brink of starting the charade all over again.

CHAPTER 15

*A*nne-Marie checked her watch and then peered toward the escalator where arrivals descended near the baggage claim area at the Edmonton International Airport. Butterflies fluttered in her stomach, so she took a deep breath and let the air out slowly through her mouth. Yes, she was excited to see Dirk again. And nervous, too.

She spotted him at the top of the steps and he started waving. She waved back and then inadvertently adjusted the bulky coat she was wearing. It added at least ten pounds, but it was the dead of winter so she didn't have much choice.

He looked polished and fit in his stylish wool coat and scarf ensemble. There was something else different beyond the clothing, too. His hair was clean cut and much shorter than she was used to. He'd shed the shaggy surfer persona for a man-about-town. She, on the other hand, felt like a frump. She should have braved the cold without the puffy down-filled jacket.

Dirk bounded from the final step, a huge smile on his face, and bolted toward where she was waiting. "At last!"

All of her fears exploded into thin air with the whoosh of his

127

body colliding with hers. He enveloped her in his arms, and they rocked back and forth for a few minutes, not speaking.

"You have no idea how much I've missed you!" Dirk said, still clutching her close.

"I missed you, too." Her words were muffled by the wool of his jacket.

He pulled away, still holding her by the shoulders, and just looked at her, letting his eyes roam her face.

Anne-Marie smiled tentatively. "You clean up nice."

His smile was broad. "Thanks. And you are just as gorgeous as I remember."

Anne-Marie waved a dismissive hand. "Whatever. Come on." She took his hand to lead him closer to the conveyor designated for his flight.

"Wait a second." Dirk held back. When she turned to look at him he pulled her forward, like in a dance, and drew her close. "You haven't even kissed me yet."

Her gaze skittered sideways. "People are watching."

"So?" He bent his head and captured her mouth with his own.

All her insecurities were replaced with the headiness of emotion that kissing him invoked. What had she been worried about again? Who knew and who cared.

"This is it." Anne-Marie slowed down and pointed to the house on her left. The yard was decked with blinking colored lights and moving contraptions depicting Santa's workshop. Under a large tree, also outfitted with twinkling lights, an illuminated nativity scene took centerstage. Every available architectural feature of the home was outlined with lights as well, from the roofline to the windows, shutters and eavestroughs. Santa's sleigh, complete with reindeer, topped the roof.

"You weren't kidding when you said your folks went in for Christmas," Dirk said, leaning forward to get a better view.

The headlights of her older model Volkswagen Golf cast circles of light on the garage doors as Anne-Marie pulled into the driveway of her family home, then winked out when she cut the engine. She jerked the emergency brake into place with its typical grinding protest and turned to Dirk. "You ready?" She gave him her best reassuring smile, not sure if he could see past her nervousness.

"I'm still impressed with the fact that you can drive a standard and got us here in one piece." Dirk took her gloved hand and kissed it.

She laughed. "You had doubts?"

"I've just never driven anywhere with you before."

"I grew up in this city, and my dad forced me to learn on a stick. He said it was a skill everyone should know, just in case."

"Smart." He unbuckled his seatbelt. "Well, speaking of firsts, let's go meet your parents."

"Right." Anne-Marie took a deep breath and let it out again.

"Relax. You're more nervous than I am."

"I warned you already. I love my parents, and they're nice people, but my mom can get a bit overwhelming. If she asks any awkward questions…"

"Deflect them by commenting on the food or the decorations or anything else festive," Dirk supplied.

"Exactly. My mom is a Christmas nut-case, as you can see, so if you make it seem like you love Christmas, too, she'll forget her tendency to interrogate."

Dirk rubbed his thumb over her knuckles. "You worry too much. I'm not intimidated by your parents' need to make sure I'm genuine. I think it's natural and healthy."

"You haven't met them yet," Anne-Marie said with a grin.

"So, let's do it!"

They both emerged from the car, and when Dirk came

around to meet her on the sidewalk leading to the front door, they took one another's hand.

"Here goes." Anne-Marie led him up the candy-cane lined steps.

Before she could open the front door, it swung wide. "Welcome to our home." Linda waved them into the house. "Bill! Tyler! They're here," she called over her shoulder.

Still holding Dirk's hand, Anne-Marie stepped over the threshold. Her father appeared around the corner followed shortly by Tyler, while her mother busied herself by taking their coats.

"Mom, Dad, Tyler, this is Dirk Hillyer. Dirk, my parents Linda and Bill and my brother Tyler."

Dirk shook hands with her father first and then Tyler. "Pleased to meet you."

"Come this way." Linda pointed toward the back of the house. "Dinner is just about ready, but we might as well sit in the family room for a bit until it is."

They filed down a hallway that joined the front foyer to the family room, by-passing the formal living room, kitchen and dining area.

"Anne-Marie tells me you've done some construction work." Bill lowered himself into his easy chair.

Dirk sat next to Anne-Marie on the sofa. "While I was in Mexico at the orphanage," he replied. "I didn't know much when I first started, but I found I enjoyed getting my hands dirty, so to speak, once I got the hang of it."

"You didn't do that kind of work in Boston, then, I take it?" Linda perched on the arm of her husband's chair.

Dirk smiled. "No, I didn't."

"What kind of work did you do?" Linda asked. "Or should I say, do you do, since you're back there now."

Dirk cleared his throat. "Investments."

"Mom, did you say you needed help in the kitchen?" Anne-Marie asked brightly.

Linda shook her head. "No. As soon as the timer rings everything will be ready."

"Investments," Bill repeated, nodding his head thoughtfully.

"Sounds like code for something," Tyler said with a grin.

"Tyler!" Anne-Marie glared at her brother.

Dirk let out a small laugh. "I watch to make sure any investments I've made are growing and not the other way around." He paused. "Anne-Marie may have already told you that I come from a fairly well-off background, so technically, I inherited most of my money. I know it doesn't sound as honorable as working for a living, but it's who I am. But I'm trying to be a good steward these days."

"He invested in the orphanage in Mexico," Anne-Marie put in.

"So you said," Bill replied.

"I admire people who work hard and who know what they want from life." Dirk took Anne-Marie's hand. "It's one of the things I admire most about your daughter. The fact that she loves being a nurse and wants to help people is one of the things that drew me to her in the first place."

"Tyler is studying to be an engineer," Linda said.

"An engineer and a nurse. You must be proud," Dirk said.

"Do you have family?" Linda asked.

"My parents live in Boston, of course, and my sister recently got married. She and her husband are traveling right now."

"Traveling? Where?"

Dirk shrugged. "Around. I don't really know unless I check Social Media. They eloped, so I suppose you could call it an extended honeymoon."

"Is that the one who was with you during that horrible ordeal?" Linda directed at Anne-Marie.

"Yes. Her name is Cherise, Dirk's sister."

Linda clucked her tongue. "I'm just glad you got out of there in one piece. I can't imagine!"

"Your daughter is very brave," Dirk said. "She kept a cool head through the whole thing and without her, we never would have found the evidence."

"More thanks go to you," Anne-Marie countered. She looked at her parents. "If it weren't for Dirk, I never would have clued into the fact that there was a problem, let alone believed it. Plus, it was his FBI contact that got us out of there safely."

"So, you're the one to blame for putting my girl's life in danger," Bill said, not cracking a smile.

Anne-Marie noted how Dirk's eyes widened. "I... well..."

"Bill!" Linda scolded.

Tyler was chuckling to himself.

Dirk pointed to the tree in front of the bay window. "That Christmas tree is spectacular!"

Anne-Marie smiled and squeezed his hand.

ANNE-MARIE SURVEYED THE BASEMENT 'REC ROOM' with its dark paneling, eclectic mix of mismatched furniture, and long forgotten memorabilia, landing on the pull-out couch that had been made into a bed. "I'm sorry about the sleeping arrangements. I assumed you'd be upstairs in the spare bedroom, but Mom says we need to keep it free in case my cousin's baby Ava needs to nap when they visit."

Dirk sat on the springy mattress and bounced a few times. "This is fine. I've never slept on a pull-out couch before. It'll be an adventure."

Anne-Marie lowered herself into a nearby gold upholstered rocking chair, its mechanism creaking when she rested her weight on it. "It's probably Mom's way of making sure we aren't sleeping too close together. She's big on appearances."

"It's fine," Dirk repeated.

"Tyler could have given you his room," Anne-Marie continued. "He took over the basement bedroom when he was a teenager, so it would have been perfect as far as distance goes."

"Why should he do that?" Dirk asked. "There's no point in displacing him. He'd have to come in every morning to get his things anyway, so this makes more sense."

Anne-Marie smiled. "You're pretty adaptable for someone who is used to being pampered."

"I'm learning." He smiled back.

"I apologize for the way my parents are behaving. I expected them to be curious, but they really gave you the third degree earlier."

"At least they're interested." Dirk looked around at his surroundings.

"Unlike your parents, you mean?"

"I suppose."

Anne-Marie cocked her head to one side. "You don't talk about your parents much. Or your growing up years."

"Don't I?"

"No, you don't."

"I can't really complain, can I? I mean, I had everything money could buy and then some."

"Everything except what you really wanted?" Anne-Marie persisted.

"You're very perceptive."

"Tell me more."

Dirk shrugged. "They were both just very busy. Meetings, clubs, philanthropic projects. I guess they didn't take into account that they also had a couple of kids who needed some attention. Of course, I went to boarding school, so that got them off the hook for the majority of the year, but even when I was home, they didn't have a lot of time - or interest - in what I was doing."

"I'm sorry."

"I could have spoken up, but I didn't know any different. I thought that's how all families operated."

"What about now? Could you try to improve your relationship with them now that you're an adult?"

"I suppose." Dirk sighed. "I'd probably fair better with my father than my mother. She's an alcoholic, you know." He glanced at Anne-Marie. "Of course, in her mind, nobody knows, and my father pretends there's no problem. He just leaves her to her own devices and goes off to his study or keeps busy at the men's club so he doesn't have to deal with it."

"I'm sorry."

"You said that already, and there's no reason for you to be sorry. It's not your fault."

"I know, but I still feel bad. It makes me feel guilty for complaining about my own parents. They can be a bit over protective, but at least I know they care."

"Come sit by me." Dirk patted the springy mattress.

"Hm. Not sure my dad would approve." She got up and moved to sit beside Dirk on the make-shift bed.

Dirk laughed. "I was expecting your mom to give me the third degree, but you never said anything about watching out for your dad!"

"He's normally harmless."

"Except when it comes to his little girl," Dirk replied dryly.

"I guess he's never been in this situation before. Sorry."

"What do you mean?"

Anne-Marie lifted a shoulder. "Bringing home boys."

"Because you've never been in a serious relationship before," Dirk stated.

"Right." Anne-Marie straightened her spine.

Dirk reached for her hand. "Call me crazy, but that makes me happy."

Anne-Marie glanced over at him but didn't say anything.

There were no words to express her feelings. He was so gentlemanly. So genuine. So beautiful in a manly sort of way. Could she really trust him with her heart?

"I half expected him to ask me about my intentions." Dirk examined her hand in his. "I wouldn't be opposed, you know."

Anne-Marie's breath caught. "Opposed to what?"

"Making my intentions known." Dirk captured her gaze with his own.

Anne-Marie's eyelashes fluttered down. The tension was too much and she broke contact by retrieving her hand and clasping it with the other in her own lap. "You're getting ahead of yourself," she said with a nervous laugh.

"Am I? My bad."

Anne-Marie stood up and went to a nearby shelf cluttered with curling trophies, a collection from past bonspiels now gathering dust. "Let's not spoil things by getting too serious, okay?" She picked up one of the trophies, a small statue of a man stretched out while throwing a curling rock. "We have lots of Christmas cheer to get through, you know."

"I know, and I'm ready."

Anne-Marie set the figurine back on the shelf. "Oh, I don't think you do! There's caroling, sleigh rides, and of course, the big family dinner. That will take an enormous amount of fortitude on your part."

"So you've said." Dirk stood and took a few steps to stand beside her. "What if I don't care about caroling or sleigh rides? I'm here to get to know you better."

"Well, this is part of it." She gestured to the clutter. "This is the real me."

He picked up a curling trophy and examined it before putting it down again. "I hardly think so. What is this for, anyway?"

"Curling, silly! Don't tell me you don't know what curling is?"

He shrugged. "Vaguely."

"We used to participate in a family bonspiel every year. As you can see, we cleaned house."

"Nice. Another item to add to my inventory of information."

"You're keeping an inventory?" She laughed.

"Sure. Let's see… you like the 'Sound of Music', Eighties Rock Bands, and cheese pizza." He grinned.

Anne-Marie's eyes widened. "How did you know that?"

"You told me once. Did you forget?"

Anne-Marie shook her head. "I guess I just didn't pay that much attention. I'm surprised you remembered, though."

"I remember everything about you, woman."

"Oh yeah? What's my favorite color?"

"Green."

She screwed up her forehead. "Okay. Favorite author?"

"Hm… don't tell me… Tom Clancey?" he asked hopefully.

"Wrong. Jane Austen."

"I'm not a machine," he said with a laugh and then sobered. "But I want to get to know everything about you." He took a strand of her hair and rubbed it between his fingertips.

"There you go again." She brushed his hand away, striving to keep things light.

"I can't help it. You know how I feel about you."

She stepped away and ran a finger along another shelf, gathering a small film of dust on her fingertip. She examined it and then wiped it on her pant leg. "You keep forgetting that there are… complications."

"Like what?"

"Like the fact that I live here and you live in Boston." She turned to look at him and crossed her arms.

"That can change."

"Not right away."

"If it's time you need, then I'll give you time. Although I don't see why. I love you, and that's not going to change. I know that, and I thought you felt the same way about me."

"What if love isn't enough?" She lifted her chin.

He took a step toward her. "How will we know if we don't try?"

She held up her hands. "I already told you I won't be a kept woman."

"I know that. Nobody said you have to give up nursing. And nobody said you have to move to Boston. I'd move here, if that's what you want."

Her eyes widened. "You'd do that?"

"Of course." He took the final step and grasped her shoulders. "I told you. I love you, and I'm in it for the long haul."

She blinked rapidly. "I've been putting out resumes," she blurted. "Some of them up north." She held her breath for a response.

"Up north?" He laughed. "We're already on Santa's doorstep."

"Hardly." She let out a small chuckle and relaxed as she moved to sit in the creaky old rocker again. "There's a whole lot of real estate between here and the North Pole."

He frowned and followed suit by taking up his spot on the pull-out once again. "Tell me more."

"Well, I have some friends who've done some nursing in the North West Territories. Many of the communities are remote and only have nursing stations, no actual hospitals. Nurses often stay for longer shifts - say a month at a time. According to my contacts, they're always looking for nurses. It's isolated and can be difficult work."

"Right up your alley," Dirk said. "Kind of like being a missionary."

"Yes. Kind of like that." She looked at her hands. "I'm sorry I didn't mention it sooner. On the phone or something."

"Why didn't you?" he asked.

"I thought you'd try to talk me out of it. Try to convince me to come to Boston instead."

"Maybe I would have. Not that you listen to me, anyway." Dirk grinned.

"So you're not mad?"

"Why would I be mad?"

"That I might not be available to visit you in Boston, like we talked about."

Dirk narrowed his eyes. "I'm assuming this isn't a permanent situation?"

"Who knows? I only just applied."

Someone cleared his throat, and they both swiveled to the sound.

Tyler was standing at the bottom of the basement steps, a few feet away. His sturdy silhouette blocked the light coming from the upper level. He waved a hand in greeting. "Just heading to my room," he offered.

"Okay. I suppose Mom is wondering what I'm doing down here so long," Anne-Marie said.

"She may have sent me down to check." A corner of Tyler's mouth lifted. "Well, good night." He waved again and retreated down the short hallway that led to his domain.

"I better get going." Anne-Marie stood up.

"Not without a good night kiss." Dirk stood also.

They each took a step, reducing the space between them, and Anne-Marie tilted her head for the kiss she knew was to follow. It was lingering and gentle, but still ignited her senses, making her crave more. With resolve, she stepped back, out of the flame that threatened to become a raging wildfire.

If she was like most modern women, they would have already been lovers, and she would have insisted Dirk share her room, no matter her parents' moral standing. But she was a believer first and foremost, and was glad that tonight she had the ingrained code of her upbringing to keep her on a steady course.

"See you tomorrow," she said. "And don't forget your Christmas cheer, because you're going to need it."

CHAPTER 16

*A*nne-Marie took a sip of coffee as she perused the Christmas calendar on the side of the fridge. She glanced at her brother Tyler when he entered the kitchen.

"Coffee! I need coffee!"

"You know where the mugs are," Linda stated, mixing pancake batter at the counter.

Anne-Marie smiled, noting the stubble on Tyler's usually clean shaven face and the rooster tail at the back of his head.

"Is Dirk up yet?" Linda asked.

"How should I know?" Tyler poured himself a cup.

"I assume you had to walk right by him," Linda said.

"He's in the shower I think." Tyler sat down at the kitchen island. He took a swig of coffee and let out a satisfied sigh.

"That explains it," Anne-Marie teased.

"Explains what?"

"Why you look like you just rolled out of bed."

"I did! Where's Dad?" Tyler asked.

"He had to go into work this morning. Can you believe it?" Linda sighed and beat the batter a little more vigorously. "Hopefully he can meet us later at the greenhouse."

"I guess it's to be expected when you own the company," Anne-Marie offered.

"Good morning."

All heads swiveled to Dirk. The smell of fresh shampoo or after shave or both wafted from where he stood in the doorway. Anne-Marie's heart did a little flip. He looked as handsome and put together as ever in casual jeans and a sweater. "Good morning," she said.

"How did you sleep?" Linda asked.

"Fine." Dirk walked to where Anne-Marie still stood by the fridge and positioned himself behind her. "What's this?" he asked.

His tone was friendly, like he was making small talk with an acquaintance, but the intimate look in his eyes spoke so much more.

Anne-Marie cleared her throat, striving to sound casual as well. "It's the Christmas calendar. It's our way of keeping track of all the festivities."

Dirk leaned in a bit closer, his breath warm on her neck. "So, what's on the agenda for today?"

Before Anne-Marie could answer, Linda spoke from her spot in front of the stove where she was pouring batter on the griddle. "Sleigh rides at Morrow Farms. It's this lovely greenhouse and tree farm out of town. I like to go early to beat the line ups, and of course, I always like to pick up a few more poinsettias when I go, or maybe another wreath. They do the fresh ones up so beautifully!"

"I know what you're thinking." Anne-Marie glanced back at Dirk. "Where could she possibly put more decorations?"

"No, I was thinking that you could never have too many wreaths. Or poinsettias." He grinned.

"Exactly!" Linda exclaimed.

"I have some shopping to do this morning," Tyler said. "So, I probably won't make it to Morrow's."

"Tyler!" Linda turned to look directly at her son, pancake flipper in hand. "How many times have I told you not to leave your shopping till the last minute!"

"Hm. I've been known to leave my shopping until Christmas Eve," Dirk said. "I take it that's frowned upon?"

"Yikes!" Anne-Marie laughed. "You're taking your life in your hands to admit to that."

Dirk reached across Anne-Marie and pointed to the calendar. "What's this?"

"Family dinner. Tonight." Anne-Marie lowered her voice. "Be prepared."

"I usually like to have it earlier in the month, but it just didn't work out this year," Linda said as she busied herself flipping the first batch of pancakes. "Two days before Christmas is so late for family dinner!"

"She postponed it especially for you," Anne-Marie whispered.

Dirk nodded. "Ah…"

"We go to church on Christmas Eve and then come home to open one present before going to bed early," Linda continued. "Santa won't come if you stay up too late on Christmas Eve!"

"We always get the same thing," Tyler said in a staged whisper. "New pajamas."

"Tyler!"

"It's not like I don't know," he protested with a laugh. He went to the sink with his mug, kissing his mother on the cheek on the way by. "Oh, and for the record, I know who really fills our stockings, too."

"Brat!" Linda swatted at Tyler with the flipper.

He laughed again, dodging the implement, and turned to leave.

"Where do you think you're going?" Linda asked. "Breakfast is almost ready."

"For a shower."

"Good idea," Anne-Marie said. "You smell."

Tyler sniffed his armpit and made a face.

"Oh, for heaven's sake!" Linda exclaimed. "Well, just hurry up about it. I'll keep some warm for you."

Still grinning, Tyler exited the kitchen.

"Hm. I might need to do some shopping myself. Do you think your brother would mind if I caught a ride?" Dirk asked.

"I can take you," Anne-Marie offered.

Dirk shook his head. "Not this time."

"Oh dear! If we wait to go out to Morrow's too late in the day, it'll be such a rush preparing for tonight's dinner," Linda said.

"We could just skip the sleigh rides this year," Anne-Marie suggested.

"Absolutely not!" Linda looked like she was on the brink of tears.

"I agree with your mother," Dirk interjected. "I for one have been looking forward to going on a real sleigh ride. Why don't we go this morning, and I can take a cab later to do some shopping while you help your mom prepare for tonight?"

Linda's countenance visibly lifted. "That sounds like a wonderful plan. You are just such a smart and helpful young man!"

Anne-Marie smiled and shook her head. Dirk was doing his best to win her mother over, and by the looks of it, he was succeeding. Now he just had to work on her dad.

MORROW FARMS WAS a short drive northwest of the city. Anne-Marie let Dirk sit in the front seat of her mother's minivan so that he could have a better view during the trip. As they neared the farm, straight rows of evergreen trees lined the highway for several acres leading up to a large sign marking the entrance to the property. She had to admit that this was one tradition she actually still looked forward to each year. There was something about the fresh air, smell of pine, and festive atmosphere that gave the whole experience a nostalgic feel.

They pulled into a large parking area and got out of the van. Dirk immediately took her mitted hand in his. "So, this is where Christmas trees come from," he said, looking around.

"Some of them," Anne-Marie responded with a smile.

"Shall we look at the tree displays first?" Linda asked. "They do such a nice job every year."

They walked toward a large barn style structure whose doors were currently open to the outdoors. Inside, the place was full of trees decorated in various themes. A large crowd of people was already milling about looking at the displays.

Linda sucked in her breath. "Oh! Isn't it just lovely!"

"How can they think of so many different ways to decorate a tree?" Dirk asked.

"It's a competition," Anne-Marie explained. "Businesses and organizations pay to enter, and Morrow's supplies the trees. It brings lots of people out every year and winning is kind of a big deal around here."

Linda pointed. "Over there are the wreaths, and there are more displays in another building. Table centerpieces, garland for fireplace mantels, etc."

"I'm not sure how you're supposed to take it all in at one time," Dirk said. "This could take hours."

"Oh, we come more than once during the season," Anne-Marie said with a laugh. "Trust me on that! But we save our sleigh ride day for closer to Christmas because that way Mom can see who actually won the competition."

Dirk nodded. "I see."

"This way!" Linda waved them toward a large sign near the middle of the room. On it were the names of the winners in each category as well as their location on the floor.

"Why don't you go ahead and check out the winners while

Dirk and I browse a bit? We'll meet you back here in, say, half an hour?" Anne-Marie suggested.

Linda looked at her watch. "That should do. Your father texted and said he was able to get away, so he should be here in about that time, and then we can go on our sleigh ride together."

"Sounds like a plan."

Anne-Marie and Dirk strolled for a few minutes, hand in hand, just looking at the trees.

Dirk inhaled deeply. "The smell in here is beyond divine. I'm beginning to get why your mom is so into Christmas."

Anne-Marie let out a small chuckle. "Sure you're not just trying to gain points with her?"

"No, I mean it. This is so… down to earth. I don't know how else to explain it. The servants always looked after decorating our tree. It was beautiful, no doubt, but it always looked very… professionally done."

"Oh, I'm sorry," Anne-Marie said. "I like down to earth. I think I gravitate to the country look, myself." She pointed to a tree with lots of gingham and raffia.

"Nice." They walked a bit more without talking before Dirk spoke again. "Um, about our conversation last night…"

Anne-Marie caught her breath. "Yes?"

"I would never stop you from following your dreams. If being a missionary nurse is what you want, then I fully support that choice."

"But…?"

"But I just hope there's room for me in your plans, too."

"There is. It's just -" Anne-Marie sidestepped to avoid bumping shoulders with someone, then stopped suddenly. "Dad?" she called to the person whom she'd just passed.

Bill Fletcher turned around, and a smile lit up his face. "There you are! I got away earlier than expected, but wasn't sure how I was going to find you in this crowd."

"Mom will be so happy."

"Where is she?"

"Checking on the winners."

"Bill, you made it!"

They all turned to Linda, who was rushing to join their group. She and Bill exchanged a quick kiss before Linda put her hand on Dirk's arm. "Come with me, young man. You seem to have a good eye, and I want you to take a look at something before we go on our sleigh ride."

"What am I? Chopped liver?" Bill asked.

"You always have the same opinion," Linda responded. "'What do we need that for? We have enough decorations!'" she said in a false baritone.

They all laughed.

"Well? It's true," Bill defended. "Besides, you never listen anyway."

"Never mind. We'll just be a minute."

Anne-Marie caught Dirk's look of surprise before he was led away by her mother. She smiled.

"Looks like you think pretty highly of that young man," Bill said.

Anne-Marie blinked and turned back to her father. "Oh. Yes, I suppose."

"I wonder. Do you think you line up?"

"What do you mean?"

"Your worlds. Do you think they line up?"

"He is a Christian, Dad."

"So you say, but there's more to it than that. It just seems like you come from very different places. Have different ambitions and so on."

"If you mean the fact that he comes from a wealthy background, then yes, I have thought about that, and I know it's a hurdle, but it shouldn't keep us apart. Not if we're meant to be together."

"Now there's a phrase that I've always had an issue with."

"What? We're meant to be together?" Anne-Marie screwed up her brow.

Bill nodded. "I believe in God's providence, don't get me wrong, but there's more to marriage than that. That kind of commitment is a choice. It can be hard sometimes, to love the other person like Christ loved the church. To put their needs above your own. Somedays, love is a choice, no matter how much we want to believe in fuzzy feelings."

"Are you saying you don't think Dirk and I are ready for that kind of commitment?"

"I didn't say that," Bill responded. "And I'm not saying you aren't good for each other or that you won't be able to work out your differences. Heck, I like the guy, despite my best efforts to find fault with him."

Anne-Marie laughed. "Last night's interrogations."

"You're my only daughter. It's my job to look out for you," Bill said with a lopsided grin.

"But...?"

"There are no 'buts', really. Just your old man's caution to make sure he's willing to make those kinds of sacrifices for you when the time comes, and to know that you're willing to make sacrifices for him, if need be. It's what marriage is about. Give and take."

Anne-Marie blew a dismissive breath through her teeth. "Dad! We're not ready for marriage, anyway."

"No? I know a man in love, and that young man is definitely smitten."

"It's too soon for that. We're still just getting to know one another."

"I wouldn't be surprised if he doesn't see it differently."

"Good thing he's only here for a few days, then." She flipped her long braid over her shoulder.

Bill squinted as he searched Anne-Marie's face, and she had to look down under his penetrating gaze. "What's really going on, my girl? You seem confused. Don't you like him after all?"

Anne-Marie shook her head. "No, I like him alright."

"Then what is it?"

Anne-Marie let out a frustrated sigh. "What if he... what if he gets tired of me? What if I'm just a novelty and he goes back to pursuing skinny bathing suit models?"

"Is that what this is about? You feeling insecure? Honey, you are the most beautiful woman alive - inside and out."

"Says my dad!" Anne-Marie sniffed and looked to the side.

"I mean it, girl! You've got to get over this sense of insecurity you carry around. You wear it like a security blanket. Now, I'm not saying everything is going to work out, and you'll live happily ever after. But you cutting yourself down all the time is never a good thing. No matter what happens."

"Look at what I found!" Linda called from several yards away.

Anne-Marie and her father both looked in her direction. Dirk was trailing a bit behind her, carrying two large wreaths.

"Where are you going to put those?" Bill asked.

"On the garage doors," Linda said without missing a beat. "You two go get into the line-up for sleigh rides before the rush starts, and Dirk and I will take these out to the van."

"I don't know if they'll fit in the van," Bill mumbled as he watched them continue toward the exit.

"Come on." Anne-Marie took her father's arm. "We better get in that line-up."

ANNE-MARIE SPRINKLED some parsley on top of the casserole dish and smiled at Dirk as he sat down across from her at the kitchen island. "You survived your shopping trip, I see."

"I did."

"Was the mall crowded?"

Dirk nodded. "I'd say so, but I managed to find what I wanted."

"I was beginning to worry you wouldn't make it back in time," she said.

Dirk's eyebrows rose. "Am I late?"

"No. Just under the wire."

"Sleigh rides, crowds of shoppers… I don't know when I've had so much Christmas cheer all in one day."

"And it ain't over yet," Anne-Marie said with a grin. She glanced past him toward the adjoining sunken family room where the rest of the family had gathered including her Aunt Pam, Uncle Bruce, cousin Daphne, husband Serge, and little Ava. "The minute one of them spots you, be prepared for twenty questions."

Dirk turned to look over his shoulder. As if on cue, Daphne waved. Both she and Aunt Pam got up from their spots and scurried up the steps into the kitchen.

"Hello! You must be Anne-Marie's friend." Daphne extended her free hand. Ava was on her other hip. "I've been dying to finally meet you. Anne-Marie's told us so much about you!"

"Hardly," Aunt Pam put in. "She's been very secretive."

Anne-Marie cleared her throat. "Everyone, this is my friend Dirk Hillyer. My cousin Daphne and her daughter Ava, Aunt Pam…" She gestured to the family room. "Uncle Bruce, Serge - Daphne's husband, and you know Dad and Tyler already."

Dirk waved. "Hi, everyone."

"Dirk, dear," Linda said from across the kitchen as she donned some oven mitts. "Can you help Anne-Marie bring the food to the table so we can all get seated? All I have left is to get this pie out of the oven."

"I can do that," Pam responded before Dirk could say anything. "Why didn't you say you needed help?"

"Dirk doesn't mind, do you?" Linda said, looking directly at him.

"Of course not." Dirk picked up a large salad bowl filled with greens.

"The rest of you go get seated," Linda directed.

"Wow. You *are* special. She never lets company help," Anne-Marie said in a near whisper.

"I'm trying," Dirk said near Anne-Marie's ear as he passed.

Anne-Marie followed him with the large casserole dish.

~

"I can't believe Anne-Marie kept you a secret all this time!" Daphne said to Dirk before lifting a forkful of casserole to her lips. "Mm, this is so good, Aunt Linda!" She held her hand up to her lips to cover the fact that she was talking with food in her mouth. "I've tried Mom's recipe, but it never tastes the same. It's a good thing you make it every year for family dinner. I crave it sometimes, but it just isn't the same. Is it Serge?"

Daphne's husband, Serge, just shook his head and then wiped a bit of food from his daughter's chin. As an RCMP officer, he had a well-muscled physique and kept his dark hair cleanly cut. Their daughter Ava was sitting between them, but Serge seemed to be attending to her needs more than her mother.

"It's in the way you layer the ingredients," Linda explained. "Your mother always mixes them together."

"I don't mix them together!" Pam defended herself. "You add something to Grandma's recipe that you won't tell the rest of us."

"Oo… the secret ingredient," Tyler said in a conspiratorial tone.

"It is very good," Dirk offered. "I've never had anything like it. My family usually has turkey at Christmas."

"We do, too, of course, but not until Christmas Day!" Linda said.

"Oh, if course. May I ask what's in it? Not the entire recipe, of course." Dirk smiled and took another bite.

"Oh, you're good!" Tyler teased, pointing his fork at Dirk. "You think just because you've gotten on her good side, she'll let loose with the secret ingredient?"

"It's just a family favorite passed down from my grandmother." Linda lifted her chin.

"Don't expect more than that," Anne-Marie whispered.

"She's very territorial," Pam added. "One would think she invented it, for heaven's sake."

Uncle Bruce dabbed at his mouth with a napkin. "The tradition of keeping family recipes a secret dates way back to Roman times, I believe. I just read a fascinating story about -"

"The sleigh rides were lovely," Linda interrupted her brother-in-law. "Weren't they, Bill? I'm surprised you didn't take Ava this year, Daphne."

"She screams every time she sees an animal," Daphne said. "I don't know what's gotten into her. We're thinking about getting a pet, aren't we honey? But right now I'm not sure it's a good idea."

"There's plenty of time," Pam added.

"The psychological reasons for childhood fears usually have a root in some kind of trauma. Your neighbor has a big dog, if I recall. Perhaps he scared her one day." Uncle Bruce took a breath. "In fact, I read an article about -"

"You enjoyed the sleigh ride, Dirk?" Tyler asked, cutting Uncle Bruce off again.

"Yes. It was lovely, as your mother said."

"I've never been much for animals myself, come to think of it." Daphne tilted her head in thought. "Maybe that's where Ava gets it. Oh! Remember that time we snuck into the stables at the rodeo, Anne-Marie? You were so scared we'd get caught, but then that nice looking cowboy helped us sneak out the back door."

"I wasn't the only one scared," Anne-Marie said. "And it was your idea in the first place. I never would have done such a thing on my own."

"This is the first I'm hearing of it," Bill said.

"Where was I?" Tyler asked.

"Who knows!" Daphne waved a dismissive hand. "We wanted to talk to the rodeo cowboys, so you weren't invited."

"*You* wanted to talk to the cowboys," Anne-Marie clarified.

"Quit pretending you didn't want to, just as much."

"I'm intrigued. Tell me more," Dirk said, leaning forward.

"We were teenagers. There's nothing to tell." Anne-Marie sat up straighter. "Pass the butter, please."

"Too much butter isn't good for your figure," Linda scolded as she passed the butter dish to her left.

Anne-Marie blinked, but kept her mouth clamped tight.

"Experts are now saying that butter isn't as bad for you as some people might think. In fact, recent studies show that the fat in butter is more easily digested that modified vegetable fat." Uncle Bruce took a bite of food before anyone could interrupt him again. "It's true," he added and kept chewing.

The butter dish arrived at Dirk's elbow and he handed it to Anne-Marie. "Here you go."

"Actually, I changed my mind."

"Stop worrying about your weight," Daphne said. "It's Christmas! If there's one time a person should be able to eat what they want, it's the holidays."

"So, I can go off that diet you've had me on?" Serge asked.

Everyone laughed and Anne-Marie was glad for the way Serge had so unwittingly diffused what was sure to have escalated into an embarrassing exchange.

"You're so silly!" Daphne gave her husband a little shove. "I never said you had to go on a diet. You wanted to do the cleanse as much as I did. And we both felt so much better!"

"Whatever you say," Serge responded with a shrug.

"Leave poor Anne-Marie alone," Pam said. "She can't help

how she's built. Besides, remember when you got back from Thailand after that trip with your friend? You were as skinny as a rail! I'd never seen you so slim."

"It's true," Linda added.

"Right!" Daphne said. "And you bought all those cheap clothes. Too bad they don't fit anymore."

Anne-Marie could feel her cheeks heating up, and she clutched the napkin that was in her lap. This was exactly the type of scene she had expected, so it wasn't like it was a surprise or that anyone had actually intended to hurt her feelings. It was just how they operated.

Ever so softly, she felt Dirk's hand enveloping hers as he clasped it under the table. She glanced over, and he offered a slight smile. She smiled back and willed herself to let the negative emotions run off.

"I had a friend who went to Thailand once," Bruce began. "He -"

"You went with that other nurse. What was her name?" Daphne interrupted her father this time.

"Monica," Anne-Marie supplied.

"Yes! Everyone had suspicions about her... well, that she was, you know..."

"A lesbian?" Anne-Marie supplied cooly.

"Oh!" Daphne covered her mouth. "Well, not that I would care, but you know, we were worried that you might be influenced, if you know what I mean."

"She is and I wasn't."

"I think that's enough about Thailand," Bill piped up. "What's for dessert?"

"I'll get it," Anne-Marie pushed her chair back. "Mom, you stay put for a change."

"The small serving plates are in the side cupboard!" Linda called.

"I know, right where they always are," Anne-Marie said under her breath. She proceeded to the kitchen and yanked open the door to an upper cabinet.

"You okay?" Dirk asked in a whisper.

Anne-Marie whirled around. She hadn't known he'd followed her.

"Fine. Yes. Just getting the small serving plates for the pie, as ordered."

"I'll help."

"Okay."

"They're blunt, I'll give them that," Dirk said as he took a small stack of plates from Anne-Marie and set them on the counter.

"Is that what you call it?" Anne-Marie let out a frustrated laugh. "I was leaning toward unfeeling, but blunt it is. And for the record, all family gatherings are usually just as awkward, which is why I warned you to brace yourself."

Dirk put his hand on her arm as she reached to shut the cabinet door. "For the record, they're wrong. You are absolutely perfect just the way you are."

"Thanks." Anne-Marie took a deep breath. "Just don't make me cry by being so darn nice, okay?"

"I'm not saying it to be nice."

"Okay, fine. You bring the plates, I'll bring the pie."

Anne-Marie grabbed the pie from off the cooling rack and marched toward the dining area. She stopped when she heard her cousin speak.

"I'm just surprised, that's all. He looks like a model!" Daphne exclaimed.

Those same words had echoed in her own brain ever since Dirk had told her how he felt about her.

A sob caught in her throat and she spun around. "I can't do this anymore." She rushed for the island counter and deposited the pie with a clatter and then ran for the hallway. She could hear Dirk and others - perhaps her mother - calling after her as she bounded up the stairs to her old bedroom, but she didn't stop until she'd shut and locked the door.

This is why she'd retreated to Mexico. This is why she needed to get to the Arctic. She was tired of playing the ugly duckling in a family where bluntness, as Dirk called it, was considered a virtue.

CHAPTER 17

a grown woman couldn't stay locked in her room forever, so Anne-Marie steadied herself for the next day's bustle. Christmas Eve was always a busy day, with meal preparations for the morrow, last minute wrapping, and a flurry of other activities, not the least of which was the Christmas Eve church service. Her family always went to an Anglican service in a large cathedral near downtown, even though they attended an evangelical church on a regular basis. There was something special about the solemnity of the liturgy, enhanced by the classic architecture, that made the occasion special, her mother always said. Anne-Marie couldn't disagree.

Somehow she managed to get through the rest of the day, feigning a sudden stomach bug last night. Dirk knew differently, but he played along. She managed to avoid alone time with him, too. The last thing she wanted was more sympathy. If she could just get through this holiday season, she'd be okay. She and Dirk did much better as a couple on neutral ground.

Thankfully, it was a clear, though somewhat crisp evening as the family walked the two blocks from where they'd parked to the cathedral. The street was lined with elm trees on either side, providing shelter over the sidewalk. Mini lights had been wrapped around many of their trunks, adding a fairytale quality to the night. Anne-Marie's mom and dad walked in front along the sidewalk, Linda clutching Bill's arm through his dress coat. Tyler walked next, also wearing his Sunday best. He looked handsome in his suit and tie, although the winter jacket he wore overtop took away from the effect. She and Dirk brought up the rear, hand in hand. Dirk always looked good, no matter what he wore. She wished she had another coat other than the puffy down-filled one she had to wear over her dress. It would have been impossible to go out without a jacket, so she'd resigned herself to wearing it. One of the first things she was going to do once she started making money again was buy a new winter coat.

A crowd of people were gathered on the front steps as they waited to enter the cathedral. Anticipation began to fill Anne-Marie's chest. This was possibly her favorite tradition of all. There was a sense of awe and reverence that enveloped her each Christmas Eve that was almost magical. This was the true meaning of Christmas - that Jesus Christ came as a tiny baby to be the Savior of the world. Her Savior.

Inside, dimly lit sconces welcomed all with a warm embrace, casting shadows up into the far reaches of the soaring arches. Traditional greenery decked with twinkling lights and a host of candles flickering near the front added to the ambiance. They found a long pew with enough room for all, and slid into a lineup of others waiting in anticipation for the service to begin.

Somehow the prayer of the minister as it echoed along marble and stone became even more reverent. Then the choir sang - soaring, reaching, filling the place with a feast of sound resonating into every nook and cranny, and straight into Anne-Marie's heart.

She glanced at Dirk and noted the look of awe on his face. One couldn't be here and not feel the presence of Almighty God.

She took his hand and smiled, closing her eyes to allow the music to envelop her completely.

The service was not long - only about forty-five minutes - and they soon found themselves back on the street walking to her parents' van.

"So? Did you like it?" Anne-Marie asked.

Dirk smiled. "Indeed, I did. It brought back memories of going to church at the orphanage. There was something powerful about those services, and I felt the same thing tonight."

"The Holy Spirit," Anne-Marie said.

"Not that I haven't been going to church back in Boston. But it hasn't been quite the same." Dirk glanced over at Anne-Marie. "Perhaps there's another ingredient missing." He stopped walking and pulled her to a stop as well. "There's something I want to ask you."

Anne-Marie glanced ahead to her family. "Okay…"

"I was going to wait until we got back to the house, but this just feels right. The atmosphere… the air… everything. I talked to your dad earlier today and…"

Her sense of wellbeing fled as another emotion - fear - wrestled for dominance. "You talked to my dad? Why?"

"I'm getting to that." He cleared his throat and then slowly got down on one knee right there on the sidewalk. "Anne-Marie Fletcher, I love you with all my heart. Will you do me the honor of becoming my wife?"

Anne-Marie's eyes widened. Her voice had disappeared. She stared at Dirk's upturned, expectant, and very handsome face. Her gaze darted up to where her parents and brother were now standing watching, about half a block away.

"I…"

"This is what I went shopping for yesterday." Dirk held up the engagement ring, an obscenely large diamond encircled by a cluster of smaller gems.

"Dirk, stand up!" Anne-Marie glanced wildly from side to side. "People are staring."

Indeed, there were several people standing statuesque on either side of the street observing the ritual. A few even clapped and someone whistled.

"So what? I'm proposing. Although, it isn't going quite the way I'd hoped."

Anne-Marie grabbed his arm and yanked him to his feet.

"Is that a no?" Dirk asked. He pocketed the ring.

"No." Anne-Marie let out a frustrated groan. "I mean, no, it's not necessarily a 'no', but here and now is not the time. I need to think."

She started to march toward her parents, hands jammed in her pockets.

Dirk jogged to catch up, and waved to the few passers-by who were still watching. "G'night folks! All is well!" he called out.

Anne-Marie avoided her father's gaze and her mother's query about what was happening and just kept walking.

The ride home was made in complete, utter, and awkward silence.

"I don't know what more I can do or say to convince you." Dirk ran a hand through his hair as he paced the small space beside his pull-out couch.

"Sh. Keep your voice down," Anne-Marie said. "Even though they're giving us some privacy, sound still travels upstairs."

"Who cares? I don't care if they hear me. I love you! And I thought you loved me, too."

"I do. But this is just too soon. We need more time."

"Why?"

"I… just because!"

"We had time, and it sucked!"

"Not enough time."

"You just want more time to convince yourself that we aren't meant to be together."

"Now that you've seen me in my own environment, you must see that we come from very different worlds."

Dirk pointed a finger in her direction. "You've convinced yourself you're not good enough. That you won't fit into 'my world'. But you haven't given it a chance. You haven't given us a chance."

"I have and I know. It would never work."

"You do not know!" Dirk stopped pacing and inhaled a few deep breaths. "Obviously, if you did, you'd know that I mean what I say."

"Just look at me!" Anne-Marie gestured to her body.

"I am looking at you, for goodness sake! I can't stop looking at you because you're the sexiest woman I've ever laid eyes on, and if you don't marry me I'll go stark raving mad."

"That's ridiculous. I'm a novelty. You'll get tired of me."

"I am so sick of you saying that! You don't have much faith in me if that's what you think."

"When I get fat, you'll change your mind."

"You are not fat!"

"It'll happen. I've always struggled with my weight; been on one diet or another. During high school I was really large. I mean overweight for real. It could happen again."

"And if it did, I'd still love you because you're you. I'm not just in love with the outside, although I admit I find it pretty appealing."

"You're being naive."

"Haven't you been listening? Argh! You are very frustrating, do you know that?" He held up his fingers to count off his next points. "So, other than your fear of me rejecting you because of your weight, judgment because I don't have a real job, and general lack of trust because you think I'm the stereotypic rich playboy, what other excuses do you have?"

"I never judged you for not having a job."

"Could have fooled me." He turned away and ran a hand through his hair again.

"We just have different aspirations in life. I want to be a missionary. You're just a brand new Christian."

"There. You're judging me."

"No, I'm not. I'm being realistic. I told you that I applied to be a nurse up north. How would that work if we got married?"

"We'd figure it out."

"Maybe we would, but I'm not ready for that."

Dirk sank down onto the pull-out, the springs squeaking as he did so.

Anne-Marie came near and sat in the chair opposite. "I'm not saying 'no' forever. I just think we need time to work some things out, and if I'm feeling this way, then there's no point rushing."

"That's a copout. An excuse for your fear of rejection - which won't happen, by the way."

"No, it isn't. It's real life." She sighed and stood. "Now, let's go upstairs. Mom and Dad are waiting so that we can open our one gift before bedtime."

"The pajamas," he stated.

Anne-Marie smiled. "Yes, the pajamas."

"You go ahead. I'm packing up and moving to a hotel. I'll get the first available flight back to Boston tomorrow." Dirk stood up.

"What? But -"

"Say thanks for the hospitality, and tell them sorry I couldn't stay." He retrieved the suitcase he'd tucked between the couch and the wall and threw it onto the bed.

"You don't have to leave. Not yet. Tomorrow is Christmas."

"I can't stick around and pretend I'm not hurt." He turned to look at her. "I think you're right, though, in saying you need time.

You need time to learn to love and accept yourself. Until you do, you won't let anybody in."

She watched him for a moment as he threw some of his belongings into the suitcase. Then she turned and headed up the stairs, her feet like lead.

Maybe Dirk was right, but at this moment in time, loving herself felt like an impossible feat. She was fat, ugly, and stupid, because she'd just rejected the perfect man. But better she do it to him than the other way around, because that scenario was inevitable.

CHAPTER 18

*A*nne-Marie hunkered into her puffy down-filled coat, pulling the collar more closely around her neck as she prepared to descend the narrow steps from the Twin Otter onto the tarmac. The Yellowknife airport was a now familiar stopping off point between her many other destinations in the far north.

In the two months since she'd been flying around the arctic to various remote indigenous communities as a short-term respite nurse, she was glad she'd kept the coat. Practicality was what mattered most when faced with such harsh temperatures.

Her work had been eye-opening. The relative isolation of most places didn't stop outside influences from creeping in. Popular culture lived alongside traditional means of survival like hunting, trapping, and fishing. Unfortunately, so did substance abuse and poverty which inevitably lead to violence or neglect. Beyond common illnesses and accidents, it meant expending an above average amount of energy treating the aftermath. It was heartbreaking.

Yet, she had also grown to love the people. Generosity and genuine openness were hallmarks wherever she went. Many communities had either a Catholic or Anglican church, often without regular services, but still a presence in the village. The people as a whole were very spiritual. Often there was either a small mission station or home group, and she made a point to meet with other believers, seeking them out even if she knew she was only going to be there for a short time. She'd grown as much spiritually as she had healed emotionally. Putting others above yourself had that effect.

She would miss that aspect of the job, but not the pain caused from social dysfunction, deeply rooted in residential school syndrome and other atrocities. The people had suffered much, but they were proud and resilient. She prayed that somehow, sometime, equilibrium and restoration would reign.

The agency that had hired her had only guaranteed a two-month position. So now she was embarking on a different adventure working as a nurse at a fly in Diamond Mine. By rights she should have taken some time off in between, but she had no desire to go back to Edmonton just yet.

Memories of the disaster that was Christmas were still too close. "Why didn't you snap him up?" her mother had asked more than once, as if an offer of marriage might never come her way again. Maybe it wouldn't. In retrospect, her entire family's reaction was very Jane Austen, which was ironic since Anne-Marie loved the classic author's books, but she preferred reading them, not living them.

She'd set her mind to her work, trying to forget about Dirk Hillyer and the reasons for her insecurities when it came to him. Despite her best efforts, he did come to mind often, but the pain was lessening. Sometimes she wondered why she'd refused him, but decided that, "all things worked together for the good of those that loved the Lord," and focused on her relationship with God, instead.

Dirk's words when they had parted rang true. Before she

could commit to a relationship with another human, she had to learn to love and accept herself - something she thought she had already done, but apparently hadn't. It had taken Dirk's attentions to make her false sense of self acceptance come crashing down. Now, she was trying to build her self-esteem back up, minus the tendency to compare herself to others that had always contaminated her perception.

The wind whisked her breath away and tried to pull her in the opposite direction as Anne-Marie leaned forward. Thankfully, it was a short walk from the airplane to the terminal. The blowing snow swirled in front of the automatic doors, piling up along the edges of the building.

The glass doors opened with a swish, and Anne-Marie stomped the snow off her boots in the vestibule before the next set of doors opened as well. She headed directly to the luggage area, one of only a few people with more than a carry-on bag. She wouldn't have to wait long, she knew. There were few line ups here. Once she did get her bag, she'd be spending the night at a local hotel before taking the chartered flight to Paragon Diamond Mine tomorrow.

A few minutes later, her bag appeared on the squeaking belt. When she went to grab it, she bumped into the only other man who was on the same mission. "Sorry," she said automatically. She judged him to be in his forties, obviously in the northern city on business. He was wearing an overcoat over a three-piece suit, but his shoes seemed frightfully inadequate for the conditions outside.

"Ladies first," he said, gesturing to the mechanical round-about.

"Thanks." She hoisted her suitcase from the belt and set it on the floor.

Once he retrieved his own bag, he nodded and went on his way.

With a sigh, she rolled her suitcase to the terminal exit, hunkering into her outerwear once again in preparation for the frigid onslaught she knew was coming. Tomorrow would be the beginning of the next chapter in her northern adventure. Make that the next chapter in her solo adventure. If she kept it up long enough, Dirk Hillyer would be no more than a dream.

Trio

*T*empest checked her watch as she waited on the sidewalk in front of the park. Geoff was picking her up, and since he lived not far away, it wasn't *really* an inconvenience. She just didn't want Frank to know.

She'd told her employer that she was doing some research and wouldn't be able to make it into the office. It was true. He just didn't know *what* she was researching. He'd already left for the day, but she didn't want to take the chance that Edna might tell him, so she'd walked the short distance to where she normally took the dogs.

The fact that Frank had written about her parents' death after it happened but never told her about it, still stung. He claimed he'd forgotten or some such thing, but she wasn't buying it. He was covering something up. She could feel it. She just had to figure out what, without him knowing.

Geoff's dad's account was the logical place to start. "*Although Mr. John McGowan's blood alcohol was close to the legal limit, it was not over. His claim that the other vehicle drove directly into his path was unsubstantiated.*" How could something so vital - so pivotal - have been dismissed?

Geoff pulled up along the curb, and Tempest waved.

"Hi. You look nice today," Geoff said as she got into the vehicle.

Tempest glanced down at her cotton sundress. Perhaps a little too summery for March, but this was California. She'd thrown a light sweater overtop just in case. "Thanks. And thank you for doing this. For taking me to see your Dad. I know it can't be easy."

"I offered, so there's no need to apologize. If I were in your shoes, I'd want to do the same." He shoulder checked for traffic and then accelerated.

"I appreciate it. I know that you two don't always get along."

"It's more awkward than anything," Geoff said. "He distanced himself after he got out of jail, as if he was ashamed - which I suppose he was. Mom had remarried, and he just faded into the background. We hardly saw one another."

"He didn't mind that your stepdad adopted you? That you changed your name?" Tempest glanced at Geoff's profile.

Geoff shrugged his shoulders. "I was too young to have a say in the matter, and frankly, I didn't like being associated with him."

"I'm so sorry." She blinked and focused on her hands.

"No family is perfect. I've tried to connect with him a bit more now that I'm an adult, but he's not always receptive. I'm actually surprised he agreed to meet you today."

"Oh? Did you explain who I was?"

"Yes. He doesn't usually like visitors, but I got the feeling he wanted the opportunity to talk to you."

"I'm glad." Was she? Really? She was about to meet her parents' killer. Tempest swallowed and watched out her window as they merged onto the freeway.

Half an hour later they turned off and drove more slowly through a run-down neighborhood that Tempest had not visited before. Another left found them in a dusty trailer park, and Geoff slowed to a mere crawl, affording plenty of time for inspection. The mobile homes were a mash-up of well kept dwellings along-side those in disrepair. Geoff pulled into a gravel driveway and came to a stop. "Well. Here we are."

A shiver ran down Tempest's spine. Geoff's father's home appeared to be one of the latter. The trailer's aluminum siding was pock marked, and there was a drunken wooden fence cordoning off the backyard. There were no weeds or garbage, though. She wasn't sure if it was a good sign or not.

"Just a warning. He can be... unpredictable." Geoff said as he got out of the car.

Tempest followed, and they picked their way along the gravel and up the lopsided wooden steps attached to the entrance. A large dog started to bark, jumping at the back fence. "He's a dog lover?" Tempest asked brightly. Inside, her stomach was clenching and unclenching, making it hard to breath.

"That's one way to put it," Geoff said. "Quiet down!" he yelled and then continued in a normal voice. "I think Dad keeps him as a guard dog. I've certainly never tried to pet him." Geoff knocked and then he waited, hands in pockets.

Tempest closed her eyes for a moment, trying to settle her nerves. She quickly opened them at the sound of shuffling feet. The door was yanked open, the screech of wood on wood making her cringe.

She blinked and let out a soft sigh. She wasn't sure what she had expected, but it certainly wasn't the rather unremarkable man on the other side of the entrance. John McGowan looked to be a regular, clean cut man of fifty or so. He had a full head of brown hair with some grey around the temples, a trim physique, and was wearing a plaid shirt and jeans. Not the monster of her dreams who had willfully taken her parents away without remorse or regret.

"Hi." Geoff lifted a hand while the other remained in his jeans' pocket. "Thanks for letting us come over."

John just nodded and stepped aside to let them enter.

"This is Tempest. The one I told you about."

"I figured. Sorry for the mess. Coffee?" John offered.

"No thank you." Tempest looked around the compact quarters. As far as she could see, the place was spotless, if not shabby. She wasn't sure what he was apologizing about.

"I'll just grab one for myself and then we can sit." John went to the kitchen counter and busied himself with pouring coffee into a large travel mug. He added several scoops of sugar, some powdered cream, and then carefully placed the lid on the mug. Finally, he directed them to the adjoining living room. "Take a seat."

Geoff led Tempest to a faded flowered couch, and they both sat down. John followed and lowered himself into a worn upholstered chair, its stuffing peeking out at the arms.

"Geoff tells me you have some questions about what happened the night your parents were killed," John began without preamble.

"Um, yes. And, thank you for taking the time to talk to me. I know it must be hard."

"What's done is done. No one feels worse than I do, but there's no undoing it." John took a sip of coffee.

Tempest swallowed hard. It was a reasonable viewpoint, but there was no real apology attached. Her gaze faltered down to her lap. This man had killed her parents, yet he didn't even say he was sorry.

"I'm sure you already read everything, so what is it you want to ask?" John continued.

"If this is too difficult, we can come another time," Geoff said quietly.

Tempest shook her head and straightened her spine. "You said that they swerved right in front of you. Why do you suppose they did that?"

"I've asked myself that over and over again." John furrowed his brow in thought. "Suicide came to mind first."

Tempest gasped.

"But then I got to thinking maybe the driver had a heart attack or some such thing," John finished. "Either way, they definitely swerved right in front of me. I had no time to get out of the way."

Tempest just blinked. She didn't know how to respond. Neither option sat well.

"Don't worry. I ruled both those out, even though I don't think either were investigated. Anyway, I had lots of time to think about it afterward. In the clink."

"Yes. Sorry," Tempest said.

"I got my hands on some of the witness statements. Don't ask me how." John hesitated momentarily, his eyes shifting from Geoff to Tempest. "In those days I was more determined than I am now. Anyway, I read that someone was seen running from the scene. As far as I know that line was never followed - seeing as they got the man who did it. And I'm not denying it. I did hit them, and I had been drinking. Still, I wondered about that for a long time afterward. Who was running and why?"

"Ever come up with any theories?" Geoff asked.

John shook his head. "Oh, I have theories, alright, but nothing I can prove."

"Such as?" Geoff prompted.

There was a moment of silence and John frowned. "Dirty government sons-of... They're on the verge of a take over, you know." His eyes had glazed over and his tone had shifted from quietly factual to a barking, stilted cadence. "One world government, that's what's coming. We'll all be wearing the mark of the beast before long if we don't watch out. Mark my words."

Geoff flashed Tempest a look that said 'I told you so'.

"Keep your voice down. They could be listening. Always listening." John lowered his voice. "And watching."

Geoff stood up. "Yes. Okay. Well, thanks, Dad. We have to go now."

John held up his hand, looking past them into the distance. "I'm going to have to ask you to leave now. It's not secure here."

"Right. Well, bye." Geoff took Tempest's arm and maneuvered her to the exit. John shut the door emphatically behind them and locked the deadbolt with a click. He could still be heard mumbling on the other side.

"What just happened?" Tempest turned wide eyes to Geoff. He hadn't let go of her arm and was leading her down the steps and to the car.

"I told you. My dad can be unpredictable. One minute you think he's the most normal man you ever met, and then he just goes into crazy mode. At least he didn't accuse you of being a spy."

"He's mentally ill?" Tempest asked as she got into the car.

"And then some!"

"Has he seen a doctor?"

Geoff backed out of the driveway. "Yes… He doesn't always take his meds, though. I should have known asking questions would bring on his conspiracy theories."

"That's so sad. And he lives all alone. Can't someone - a neighbor - make sure he takes his medication? Surely there's something that can be done."

Geoff sighed, gripping the wheel more firmly as he drove onto the main street. "I wasn't completely honest with you about my Dad, okay?"

"What do you mean?"

"He wasn't considered a reliable witness. It's one of the reasons his testimony was dismissed. He might have dreamt that your parents swerved in front of him. Or that he saw someone running. His testimony can't be relied on. I'm sorry. I should have told you."

Tempest took this in. She should probably just let it rest. But something inside couldn't do that… Not quite yet.

TEMPEST GLANCED toward the office entrance one more time before scooting to the filing cabinet along the wall. Frank was out that morning so it might be her only chance to peruse some of his old files.

The metal screeched as she opened the ancient filing cabinet. These days, even Frank filed most things online, but her parents' death was long enough ago that he might have saved something relevant the old way. Despite the fact that Frank looked haphazard on the outside, she'd come to realize he was meticulous about recording and keeping everything. He cultivated the absent minded persona because it encouraged people to let their guard down. It's why she couldn't believe he'd simply forgotten about covering her parents' accident.

She flipped through the old tabbed system until she came to a section labelled 'traffic accidents'. She pulled the drawer open just a bit more to afford a better look. There it was: 'Ross'.

She looked over her shoulder, a nervous reflex more than a necessity, and then pulled the file from its resting spot. The manila folder was yellowed around the edges. It probably hadn't been out in the daylight for a decade. The drawer squealed as she pushed it shut. Then she slipped to her desk with the file and sat down.

She'd just started reading when she heard Frank's footsteps on the stairs leading up to the office. Her heart began to pound and she quickly tucked the file into the large tote bag she used as a briefcase. Further investigation would have to wait.

TEMPEST SAT cross-legged on her futon, file folder open beside her. Paddy sat nearby, and as usual, Jupiter was on the floor, his head resting on the seat cushion.

The first piece of paper contained Frank's handwritten notes. There was a big question mark beside a scrawled account of John McGowan's version of events. Mr. McGowan claimed, as he'd told Tempest yesterday, that her parents swerved in front of him. However, he hadn't explained just how forceful or sudden that movement apparently had been. According to John, the car literally careened across the meridian almost like someone else had grabbed the wheel by force.

Tempest let her gaze wander. Could it have been a heart attack, as John had suggested? If so, why hadn't an autopsy been done? She shook her head. Suicide was out of the question, but what about an argument? Her parents had always seemed level headed and very in love, but maybe that had been her own juvenile projection.

Tempest closed her eyes momentarily and took a deep breath. She had to distance herself from her own feelings if she was ever going to get at the truth.

She went to the next document, a Xeroxed copy of an eye witness account that Frank had somehow obtained from the police. A garbage truck driver said he saw someone running in the opposite direction right after the crash. Just as John had said. She flipped to the next and then the next. Two more eye witnesses, a cab driver and a prostitute, both said the same thing. She set them aside and moved on.

Next in the file was a copy of the article Frank had written. She'd read it before, but skimmed it again just to make sure. It was short and to the point and did not mention any of the details she had uncovered. It was unlike Frank to put such a bland spin on the story when there was obviously more to it. He'd made a name for himself by stirring the pot, not playing it safe.

And that was it. There was nothing else to look at. Feeling

somewhat deflated, she slipped the newspaper clipping back into the file folder, flipped the manila cover over, and tossed it on the floor at her feet.

Jupiter lifted his head. "Sorry, boy. Did I startle you?" She scratched behind his ear and he laid back down. Then her eye picked up on a scrap of paper that had floated free of the folder and was lying on the floor next to Jupiter's leg. "How'd I miss that?" she asked out loud and bent to pick it up.

It was a sheet torn from a small notepad - the kind synonymous with old school reporters, and it was in Frank's distinctive scrawl. It listed the make and model of a handgun with the words, "Found in dumpster one block away."

A shiver went through Tempest's body. Things had just gotten serious.

CHAPTER 20

*R*yan took a moment to secure his heavy mittens and hood before exiting the airport terminal. There were no fancy tunnels connecting Paragon's chartered airplane to the terminal. It was straight through the exit and out onto the tarmac, no matter how far below zero the temperature had fallen.

Wind whipped against the exposed skin of Ryan's face as he leaned forward to counter the wind that wanted to throw him off balance. This wasn't like in the movies where tourists wore high heels and nothing on their heads. Survival in the arctic was real - a brutal reality of the extreme temperatures that locals endured on a daily basis for more than half the year. He had new respect for those who chose to live here year round.

His friend and colleague Andy Coates had called last night, after the unexpected meeting with Dirk Hillyer. Apparently, Tempest had been spending more time with Geoff Vanguard. Ryan felt a tightening in his chest at the thought, but shoved it aside. He was doing what he had to do at the moment.

"She also asked me for a favor," Andy had said.

"She contacted you?"

"I was just as surprised to hear from her, believe me."

"What did she want?"

"She asked me if I was able to access information from an old vehicular manslaughter case." Andy had paused. "She's investigating her parents' death. I don't know to what purpose, but I thought you should know."

Ryan's intuition gave him a bad feeling about this. Even if she was just doing it for personal closure, she could end up getting hurt. He should be there for her right now. Instead, he was boarding an airplane in the middle of the next ice age.

There was little room to spare on the flight, a fact that surprised Ryan, but he supposed shift changes meant high volumes of traffic in and out of the mine. He and Jeremy did not sit together. He was posing as an independent inspector while Jeremy would be working as a laborer in the processing plant. Their communication from here on in would be clandestine. By coming at the problem from both ends of the spectrum, they would hopefully be able to piece together how the diamond smuggling took place and who was behind it.

A man in a business suit sat down in the seat next to Ryan. They nodded mutual acknowledgement before the newcomer belted himself in. Once he was settled, he spoke. "So, what takes you to Paragon? Work, I presume?"

Ryan cleared his throat before speaking. "I've been hired by an investor to do some independent inspections. Make sure the diamonds are being sourced responsibly and that quality can be assured."

The man nodded. "I heard you were coming." He extended his hand. "Richard Camry. Director of Operations for Paragon."

They shook hands. "Ryan Grant. Pleased to meet you." If the man knew he was coming, was he privy to the fact that Ryan was actually working undercover? Ryan knew there would be an inside man, but for security purposes, he didn't know who it was.

"I visit once a month," Richard went on. "I suppose I'll be seeing you around this week while I'm here."

"Looking forward to it." Ryan nodded and turned to look out the window. He wouldn't pry too deeply into exactly what the man knew or didn't know. There would be time for that later. For now he needed to be cautious and not draw undue attention.

Although the mine was a few hundred miles north of Yellowknife, it seemed like the chartered jet had just gained cruising altitude when it was time to start descending again. The land was a mixture of dark green forest and snow covered tundra, basically unmarked by human activity, and vast in its scope. Ryan squinted out the small window. There was movement on the otherwise white stillness of the surface. Several animals were running, caribou if he wasn't mistaken, creating a written trail of footprints in the otherwise pristine snow.

Then in the distance he saw a formation that didn't quite fit. The angular white clearing gradually got larger as the plane approached. His eyebrows lifted at the sight of two gigantic circular craters spiraling down into the earth. The topography was unlike anything Ryan had seen before.

"Welcome to Paragon," Richard said.

"Thanks." Ryan felt a lot like Alice at the moment, about to jump down one of those giant spiraling holes, not quite sure what was waiting on the other side.

THE PASSENGERS DISEMBARKED and were transported to the main administrative building, a large structure clad in metal siding, as all the buildings were. Ryan was directed to the housing department where he was assigned his room. A maze of corridors attached all the housing units, long trailers strung together in rows. The mine could house up to 800 people at any given time, so in some ways it was like a small community. He strode down the long hallway to his room with his luggage in tow. Inside, the room was comfortable enough, much like a low grade hotel room.

After that he met with other newcomers for a health and safety meeting and tour of sorts, all part of the orientation package. He noted Jeremy among the twenty or so others, but didn't make any move to acknowledge him.

They were not taken to the mine site itself, but watched a video describing the production process. The diamonds were found in a rock called Kimberlite, originally formed in the magma under the earth's core, but thrust upward during some kind of volcanic activity in the past. The ore was extracted using explosives and then hauled to the processing plant in huge trucks. The size of the excavation equipment and the precision of the blast patterns were impressive, creating the gigantic spiral shaped depressions he had seen from the air. There was also some mining done underground. It sounded dangerous, but modern mining methods relied on precise calculations that seemingly kept the workers safe.

In the plant, several cleaning and extraction processes separated the rough diamonds from the Kimberlite. Millions of tons of ore were processed each year in order to get to a relatively small number of raw diamonds. The rough diamonds were then sorted individually by color, clarity, and size before being sold to clients worldwide.

Most of it was information Ryan already knew from preparing for the mission. His focus would have to be on finding the breech in security since the company stressed that part of the operation in the video. As far as they were concerned, there was no way for someone to slip a diamond into their pocket and walk away. Still, it was happening.

A coffee break after the video afforded Ryan a moment to talk to Jeremy. "So? Thoughts?"

"I think it really comes down to keeping my eyes and ears open once I actually get to work," Jeremy said.

"Agreed. Security throughout the entire operation seems extremely tight. The perp must have an inside track."

After the break, they went on an actual tour of the plant. It was a large building, several stories high with crisscrossing trellises and steel walkways high above conveyer belts that carried the raw material, crushing, shaking, and washing it to finally leave only the diamonds. Everyone wore a hardhat, and the woman conducting the tour had to shout to be heard above the loud machinery.

"At this stage, the product never goes through human hands," she shouted. "It's one of our most important security measures. Limited human contact. Of course, once sifted out, the diamonds drop into a pipe which transports them to a sealed off collection area where they are sorted, inspected and graded in preparation for market."

The final stop on the tour was the camp itself and all its amenities. Living in a remote location far from family and friends for long periods of time could take its toll, so the company made every effort to provide everything that a person could need. There was a gym, work out rooms, theater and TV areas, and of course a large dining facility. Working out might be a good option, Ryan decided, but most of his free time he hoped to spend tracking security.

By early evening it was time to hit the cafeteria. So far he had more questions than answers, but it was only his first day. He got into the long line that had formed and grabbed a tray. He glanced behind him and his eyes widened. Anne-Marie Fletcher.

"I wondered if I would run into you," he said.

Anne-Marie blinked, not registering at first that he was talking to her. Then recognition dawned on her face. "Ryan, isn't it? What are you doing here?"

"Working." He widened his eyes slightly in hopes she would understand his meaning.

"Ah." She nodded.

He looked around to see who could hear them. "Let's sit together and catch up."

She nodded. "Okay."

They moved forward in the line-up. "By the way, I saw someone in Yellowknife you might be interested in knowing about," he said.

"Oh?"

"Dirk Hillyer." Ryan noted her intake of breath.

"Dirk was in Yellowknife?" she asked. Ryan could tell she was trying to sound unaffected by the news.

Ryan nodded. "Saw him in the hotel last night. He said he was looking for you."

"Oh." She glanced down at her tray. "Well, I've been here for two weeks as the camp nurse. I suppose he has his ways of finding things like that out."

"You didn't tell him, I take it?" Ryan asked.

She shook her head. "No. We've been... taking a break."

"I see. Well, it sounded like he had all the time in the world, so you might want to contact him."

"Chicken or fish?"

Ryan turned his attention to the server on the other side of the counter. "Fish." The rest of the conversation would have to wait until they got through the line-up.

Ryan waited for Anne-Marie and they found a table together that was far enough away from others that they couldn't be heard.

"By working you mean...?" Anne-Marie trailed off.

"Exactly." Ryan glanced to the side and then back at Anne-Marie. "The name is Ryan Grant, by the way."

She nodded. "Got it. Anything else you can tell me?"

"Probably not wise," Ryan said.

"Fair enough. And what about you and Tempest?" Anne-Marie asked.

He hadn't expected the question and blinked before answering. "Taking a break, as you say."

"Oh. Sorry to hear that."

"I guess we're in similar situations, then," he said.

Anne-Marie smiled wistfully. "It's strange how God keeps circling around, bringing me back to the same people."

"Agreed."

"Maybe He's trying to teach me something, and I've just been too dense to learn it the first time."

"I feel exactly the same way," Ryan said before taking a bite of his fish.

What are you trying to teach me this time, Lord?

CHAPTER 21

*I*magine meeting Ryan O'Toole at a remote Diamond Mine at the top of the world? Anne-Marie hadn't recognized him at first, when she'd gotten in line behind him. Why would she? They'd only met a few times, starting with the terrible ordeal in Mexico when she, Dirk and Cherise had been arrested in the drug smuggling case, and then afterwards when Ryan had rescued them and helped to absolve them of any blame.

Of course, he was also Tempest's new boyfriend, a fact that had given her some comfort then, since Dirk had had feelings for the other woman. Finding out that Ryan and Tempest were no longer together did little to comfort her now, though. Perhaps it freed both Tempest and Dirk to get back together...

Such thinking was ridiculous and totally unproductive. She, herself, had discouraged Dirk's advances - had sent him packing. All because of her own insecurities. Now that she'd had some space, she saw how her fears had been unfounded, but perhaps now it was too late.

Or maybe not. Ryan had said that Dirk was in Yellowknife, waiting for her next time out of camp. If he had come all this way to see her on such an off chance, maybe there was still hope for them after all.

Anne-Marie continued stocking the first aid cupboards. There were several nurses on staff at the small clinic at any given time since the mine ran its operations twenty-four seven. A doctor visited at scheduled intervals, but in the case of emergencies, patients were flown out to Yellowknife by air ambulance.

Someone rang the bell in the waiting area and Anne-Marie immediately stopped what she was doing and went to see who it was. "Hi. What can I do for you?"

The young man shrugged. "I don't really think it's necessary, but the foreman insisted." He looked to be of First Nations' descent, judging from his dark hair and eyes. He was obviously embarrassed to be there.

"Okay. Can you tell me what happened?"

"I slipped on some ice just outside the load up. My hardhat flew off and I hit my head. I don't think it's a big deal, but apparently I have to check in to make sure."

"It's always best to be safe. They have very strict protocols around here, so don't feel too badly. Now, come around and have a seat," Anne-Marie directed. "Are you dizzy? Headache? Did you black out at all?"

"No."

She shone a small light in his eyes, directing him to follow it as she moved it slowly from side to side. "You're sure?"

"I don't think so."

"Hm." She felt the back of his head. "There is a goose egg forming. You should stick around for concussion protocol just in case."

"Seriously?" He didn't sound pleased.

"I'll get you set up on a bed where you'll be more comfortable, and then I have a bit of paperwork to do."

"I really don't think that's necessary."

Anne-Marie smiled. "While I admire your desire to get back to work, enjoy this little respite, hm?"

"I only just started. I can't be off the job yet."

"Is that so?" Anne-Marie sat down at the nearby desk and started filling out the required forms. "Now, I have a few questions for you. Name?"

"Jeremy. Uh, George."

"Jeremy George…" Anne-Marie repeated as she typed the name into the computer. "Ah, there you are. Okay, so all your other medical information is already here, but I do have to verify your identity. You understand."

"Yes."

They went through a series of questions. "It says here you currently live in Yellowknife?" she asked.

The young man cleared his throat. "That's right."

"Were you born and raised there?" she asked. "Just curious. That part isn't on the form."

"Not exactly. I'm from… south."

"Me, too. Although you probably assumed that. Edmonton, to be exact."

"I've been to Edmonton. But my grandmother is from the NWT, so I came here a few times to visit. Then I got this job, so I figured it would be a way to see her more often."

"Family is so important," Anne-Marie said. She finished the last of the paperwork and clicked enter on the keyboard. "Let's hope this goes through," she said under her breath. "These electronic forms make a lot more sense, but sometimes the connection here isn't the best, and they don't always send. Part of the joys of living in the north, I suppose."

"I wonder if it's really done that much to improve the lives of the people. I mean, having internet and access to the outside world is great, but when you're packed like sardines into a broken down house, I wonder which is more important?"

"Good question. I worked as a respite nurse in several

communities before getting this job, and I saw some very disheartening things, including some of the terrible living conditions you're referring to. Does your grandmother live in one of the communities?"

"Yes. Fort George."

"Really? I worked there! Maybe I met her." Anne-Marie glanced his way and noted the way he'd closed his mouth into a set line, like he was unhappy about something. "Was the place named after an ancestor?"

He cleared his throat. "Not sure. Possibly."

"I met some Georges while I was there. There was this little house church in one of the elder's homes - Beatrice George. Such a nice lady! Are you related?"

"That's my grandmother," he said.

"Really! What a small world! She told me she had a grandson down in the States. When you said 'south' I didn't realize you meant that far south."

"Yeah, well, I think I'm feeling fine, so I'd like to go back to work now." Jeremy sat up and swung his legs off the bed.

"Not so fast. One more set of vitals, mister," Anne-Marie said with a laugh. Jeremy sat still while she wrapped the blood pressure cuff onto his arm and pumped it up. "As a matter of fact, Beatrice told me her grandson worked for the FBI. She was very proud." She noted how Jeremy became very still. "I assume you are here with Ryan O'Toole? Or should I say Ryan Grant."

He let out a breath, like a deflating balloon. "I'm in trouble if he finds out."

"Don't worry. He and I are old friends and I know he's here undercover working a case, so I presume you're his partner."

"I saw you two talking last night in the cafeteria," Jeremy said. "And I put two and two together, but I didn't think it wise to blow my cover just in case."

"What do you mean you put two and two together?" Anne-Marie folded the cuff and hung it on the machine.

"We ran into your boyfriend, or whoever he was, in Yellowknife, so Agent... I mean, Ryan, filled me in."

"I see. So, we've both had our covers blown."

"I suppose, if you want to put it that way. I'd appreciate it if you didn't let on to Ryan."

"Why should it matter? I'm no threat."

"Well... It's my first big assignment and I want to do things right. You understand?" He turned hopeful eyes her way.

"Deal." She held out her hand to shake on it. "Is Beatrice George really your grandmother?"

He nodded. "I decided to use her last name for my cover. I guess it wasn't such a bright idea. Hopefully, no one else figures it out."

"Would it be that bad if they did?"

"This operation is potentially dangerous."

"Oh. Well, then for her sake - and yours - I hope nobody makes the connection. When this is all over, maybe you can say hi to her for me."

"Okay. I will." Jeremy stood. "Nice to meet you."

Anne-Marie watched him leave the small clinic. Knowing Ryan, she'd already surmised that the operation he was working would have an element of danger, but meeting Beatrice George's young grandson made her see it in a different light. She just prayed that everyone involved would be safe.

Anne-Marie made eye contact with both Ryan and Jeremy at the evening meal, but chose not to sit with either of them in order to keep their association discreet. To her surprise, another man she recognized hovered near her table with his tray. She'd already heard through the grapevine that he was Richard Camry, Paragon's Director of Operations, whatever that meant. He was also the man she'd bumped into at the airport a few weeks ago when she was on her way to the camp for the first time.

"May I sit here?" he asked.

"Go ahead."

He sat down and started rearranging the food on his tray. "I hear you're one of the new nurses on staff. I thought I should introduce myself. Richard Camry, Director of Operations."

"I know," Anne-Marie said.

"Of course. It's one of the ways I'm at a disadvantage. People know who I am, but it's not always the other way around."

"Anne-Marie Fletcher," she supplied. "I've only been here a couple of weeks, so it's no wonder."

"I like to meet as many of the staff as possible," Richard said.

"We actually bumped into one another at the airport in Yellowknife a couple of weeks ago."

"Oh?" Richard raised his eyebrows. "My apologies if I was in a hurry or rude."

"Oh, no, not at all. It was mutual, I think."

He nodded. "Good, good. So, how do you like it so far?"

She shrugged. "I'm liking it fine. I've been nursing in the communities for a few months, so I'm used to the travel and the temperatures. I'm still on my first rotation, but so far, so good. The clinic is well equipped."

"We try to provide the best for our workers." Richard smiled.

"I can see that."

"Do you have plans for your time off?" he asked.

"Um, I was thinking of going to the Snow King Festival in Yellowknife. I hear it's kind of a big deal, and it sounds fun."

"Do you know, in all the time I've been traveling here, I have never gone to it myself? Always just fly back to Toronto. But one of these years I should probably check it out for myself."

"I hear the snow castle is amazing - almost unbelievable. I'm excited to see it."

He nodded. "Made entirely out of snow and ice. You can even

rent rooms! And they have live concerts inside, among other things. Will you be meeting anyone there?"

"I'm not sure." She wasn't sure what else to say, so took a bite of her meal instead. She was thinking… hoping… to meet Dirk, but hadn't quite settled it in her mind yet.

"Have you seen the aurora borealis?"

She blinked and looked up, jerked from her own thoughts. "Pardon me?"

"I said, have you seen the aurora borealis yet? You know. The northern lights."

"Do you mean here or in general?"

"Here. I know most of us have seen them at one time or another, but they are really quite spectacular the farther north you go."

"I've seen some pretty nice ones outside of Edmonton, in the country, but nothing like what I saw while in the communities. I suppose they'll be just as nice here."

"Spectacular. Every color of the rainbow. Pinks, greens… even red. We could check it out later, if you like."

"I didn't think we were supposed to venture outside," Anne-Marie said. "Do polar bears really come into camp?"

He looked at her intently over his fork, poised in mid-air. "Of course. This is their natural habitat. It's dangerous out there without security present."

"I know people go out on the fire escapes to smoke, but…"

"Not the fire escape!" He laughed. "I mean out farther, away from the lights of the camp. Out there is where you can really see a light show."

"That sounds dangerous."

"Oh, the danger is real," Richard said. "But you forget who you're talking to. I'm in charge around here. Well, second in command next to old Herschel, the CEO. But, I have my ways."

"Um…" She glanced around the cafeteria, suddenly feeling flustered. Was Richard Camry interested in her, or was he just being friendly? He wasn't unpleasant to look at, Anne-Marie decided. Probably in his mid-forties, with a trim physique and a few strands of grey woven through his hair. Not that she cared.

"There's nothing to be nervous about," he said. "It's true that you're not supposed to go out without security present, but we'll be in a vehicle. One of the company trucks. I often borrow one when I'm here and drive out to the edge of camp just in case there's a good display of northern lights. I've taken all the shareholders out when they've visited. There's absolutely nothing to worry about."

She felt herself relaxing. Of course he was just being friendly. "I'd like that, actually."

"Great. I'll meet you by the front doors in…" He checked his watch. "Half an hour? That'll give me time to let security know and have someone bring one of the trucks around. Oh, and dress warm."

"Okay. Sounds good." She just hoped it was as innocent as it sounded.

ANNE-MARIE MET Richard by the front doors. She was wearing her full winter armor. A security officer, also outfitted in winter gear and hefting a rifle, escorted them to the pick-up truck that had been brought around. Once inside, she and Richard drove a short distance to the edge of camp, facing away from the lights and the buildings.

Richard put the truck in park, but left it idling. "Come on," he said. "You can't see anything from in here." He opened his door and waved for her to follow.

"Is it safe?"

"Of course. We'll stand right by the truck. If anything comes along, we can just jump in."

Against her better judgment, Anne-Marie slipped down from

the high cab. Her boots crunched on the wind packed snow as she joined Richard in front of the grill.

"See that." He pointed. "We're just in time."

A dancing shimmer of iridescent light floated across the sky.

"Hello!" Richard called out, cupping his mouth with his mitten covered hands. As if by magic, the lights responded, shifting across the night.

Soft green and white, almost florescent in nature, they spiked and arched, like sound waves on a screen. Then they morphed into wispy shapes like smoke coming from a fire, joined by a string of soft pink highlights.

"I never get tired of this," Anne-Marie murmured. "It really is beautiful."

"I agree," Richard said.

Anne-Marie smiled and glanced his way, but then froze. He wasn't looking at the sky. Her eyelashes, already stiff from the cold, fluttered, and she looked quickly back at the light display. So. Maybe there was more to his interest than being friendly. "Oh, look at that one!" she exclaimed, to get him looking in the proper direction.

An explosion went off behind them and she jumped. It sounded like fireworks. "Oh! That scared me," she said with a nervous laugh. "Just blasting, I suppose."

"They don't blast at night," Richard said. "It probably means a polar bear or other predator was spotted nearby. Security use firecrackers to scare them away from camp."

"Oh." Anne-Marie's stomach lurched.

"We should head back. You're probably getting cold, anyway."

She was. "Um, thanks for this. I think these ones really were the nicest I've ever seen."

"My pleasure. Maybe we'll do it again sometime."

She had mixed feelings about that. It was nice to get some male attention from someone other than Dirk. It made her feel as if she wasn't as undesirable as she sometimes felt. Still, her heart belonged to Dirk, and there was no point leading another man on. "I… there's something you should know."

"What's that?" Richard asked as they slammed their doors simultaneously.

"I have a boyfriend. At least, I did have one. He's waiting for me in Yellowknife."

"So? I'm married. That doesn't mean we can't be friends."

The news hit Anne-Marie like a slap in the face. She felt her face heating up and not just from the warmth of the truck's heater. Had she imagined the come on? Or was Richard Camry a sleaze-bag with a woman in very port? Either way, she was glad she hadn't made a bigger fool out of herself.

CHAPTER 22

Tempest held her cellphone to her ear, glancing to where Geoff was tossing the ball to Paddy on the park grass. He was trying. Paddy was glad of the attention, but she had to keep Jupiter on his leash by her side. For some reason, the larger dog had not taken to Geoff.

She listened more intently as Andy Coates came back on the line. "Sorry for that interruption, Tempest," he said. "Just something I had to look after."

"I shouldn't have called you at work."

"It's fine. Now, back to that other issue." He lowered his voice. "I couldn't find anything about a gun being found at or near the scene of your parents' accident. I couldn't find the eye witness accounts you were referring to, either. Maybe they don't keep files beyond a certain year. Or maybe they got destroyed. The case was open and shut, as far as I can tell. There's nothing more I can tell you."

"Thanks for trying. I shouldn't have involved you." She looked skyward.

"Are you sure this is something you want to pursue? I mean, what are you hoping to find?"

"I'm not one hundred percent sure. All I know is, something isn't right. Maybe I'll just have to bite the bullet and ask Frank. Admit that I took the files out of his cabinet."

"I'm not sure that's such a good idea," Andy said.

"Oh? Why not?"

"Frank could be, how can I say this…" Andy hesitated and then sighed. "Frank could be up to something that isn't above board."

"What do you mean, exactly?"

"I can't go into details."

"Can't or won't?" Tempest asked.

"Maybe a bit of both. Listen." He hesitated again. "I wasn't supposed to tell you this, but… Ryan asked me to do a bit of digging, and it doesn't look good. Frank's been receiving a lot more money than would be expected from a guy in his position. That, plus the threatening photos that were left in his mailbox, and you might not be safe."

Tempest swallowed as she took this information in. "What about my parents' deaths? Frank is involved in covering something up there, too."

"I wouldn't have made that connection before, but now I'm suspicious. You should find a different job and most definitely move out of Frank's house."

"But if I ever hope to get to the truth, I need to find out about Frank's involvement."

"Is getting to the truth worth your life?"

Tempest's breath caught in her throat. "You think it's that serious?"

"I just wouldn't trust anyone right now. I know that sounds harsh, but it's the best way to stay safe."

"That sounds extreme." She glanced at Geoff, still playing with Paddy.

"Just friendly advice from someone you *can* trust. Speaking of… maybe you should be careful about hanging out with people you haven't known very long. People who aren't vetted."

Tempest's eyes narrowed. "Did Ryan ask you to spy on me?"

There was a moment of silence on the other end. "He's worried about you."

"So, he *did* ask you to spy on me. You didn't think I noticed your car lurking outside my house the other day. Well, I did."

"I just told him I'd keep an eye out."

"For your information, Geoff is a very nice Christian man. He goes to my church."

"I'm sure that's true, but -"

"I can take care of myself." She interrupted with as much confidence as she could muster. The truth was, she was at war on the inside, with indignation at the nerve of Ryan for sending Andy to spy on her and the realization that he still cared enough to do so.

"I know you can, and Ryan does, too. But this could be above your head. You don't know who you're dealing with. What you're getting into. You're opening up a can of worms that you might not be able to close."

Tempest stiffened. "You mean Frank?"

"It's bigger than that." Andy lowered his voice even more. "Ryan and I have been looking into a possible mole in the department. The fact that those photos showed up at the same time that Frank also seems to be receiving mysterious payments doesn't strike me as a coincidence. Add to that the incongruities about your parents, plus Frank's involvement in that, too, and I can't help feeling you need to distance yourself. You could be playing right into someone's hands."

Could it really be as dangerous as that? "I'll take it on advisement." She sounded a lot calmer than she felt. "I have to go, now. And no more spying!" She hung up before he could respond, just as Geoff and Paddy approached.

"Phew! This little fella has me beat!" Geoff flopped down on the bench beside Tempest.

Jupiter growled.

"Stop that!" Tempest scolded the Great Dane.

"So? What did you find out?" Geoff asked.

Tempest wasn't sure how much of the conversation she should share with Geoff, especially in the light of Andy's last warning. "No luck with any of it."

"We'll keep on trying. If that's what you want to do, that is."

Tempest took a moment before answering. It seemed everyone she knew was involved in a circle of suspicion. Frank said don't trust Ryan, Ryan said don't trust Frank, and now Andy said don't trust Geoff. Who could she trust? She turned to look at Geoff. "Why are you helping me? I mean, really."

Geoff blinked. "Because we're friends. Why else?"

"Really? That's it?"

"Well, my dad was involved, so I feel somewhat guilty about that, even though I had nothing to do with it. And I'll be honest, if there's a chance that he was telling the truth and it wasn't just that he was an irresponsible lush, I'd be happy to hear that, too."

"What about that first day you came and sat with me at church? That was a little sudden, wasn't it, especially since I had just broken up with my boyfriend?"

"I didn't know that," Geoff said with a nervous laugh. "That you had broken up with your boyfriend."

"Yet, you came and sat with me anyway."

"Wow. I can see that something has you riled." He took a breath. "Okay, I admit it. I'd noticed you on more than one occasion, and finally just got up the nerve to talk to you. I hadn't really seen you and Ryan together all that much, so I took a chance."

Tempest sighed and scratched Jupiter's head absently. "I'm really grateful for your friendship, Geoff. I am."

"But...?" he prompted.

"I'm confused. And something Andy said made me feel worried."

"What did Andy say?" Geoff asked.

"I'm either the most naive person alive or the worst judge of character. He said that Frank might be dangerous." She looked square at Geoff. "And that you might be dangerous."

"Me?" Geoff's voice went to falsetto.

"Are you dangerous, Geoff? Did you purposely introduce yourself that day because you're actually the member of some gang and have a nefarious plan to get rid of me?"

"That is the most ridiculous thing I've ever heard!" Geoff exclaimed.

"It is, isn't it?" Tempest smiled over at Geoff. "Obviously, if it were true you'd deny it, so the really ridiculous thing is that I even asked you."

"I hope that's not what you really think."

"No. Not really. But Andy has me all paranoid now. I trusted Frank. Felt a softness toward him, even, like I would for an uncle. And now to think he may be one of the bad guys… It just makes me scared."

"If you're scared, you should find a different place to live."

"That's what Andy said." She laughed. "And Ryan, too, before he left."

"Well, maybe you should."

"Where would I go?" She shook her head. "I don't want to quit working for him yet. I still need to figure out the truth about my parents, and so far he's the best lead I've got."

"Is that smart?" Geoff asked.

"Not sure. All I know is, I'm not giving up that easily. I'll just have to be more careful. You know what they say about keeping your enemies closer. If I moved out but kept working for him, that would only make Frank suspicious."

"You could always move in with me."

Tempest blinked before turning to gaze at Geoff. His eyes

were wide with innocence. "Um… I've had the feeling for a while you might want to be more than just friends, but I'm not sure I'm up for that. Not yet, anyway."

"I didn't mean it that way," Geoff said. He laughed nervously. "I still live with my mom. She has a room down in the basement that she's been talking about letting. You could move in there."

"And what would I tell Frank?"

"Well, he wouldn't have to know we're just friends."

"Hm. I'm not sure how comfortable I am with that. But thanks for the offer."

"Whenever you're ready, the offer stands."

Paddy whined and Tempest bent to pat his head. "You tired of sitting there so quietly?" Paddy barked. "Okay, let's go home." She turned to Geoff. "Thanks for being such a good friend, Geoff. I'm not sure what I would have done these past weeks without you."

"Do you want me to help you home with the dogs?" Geoff asked.

She readjusted both leashes as she stood up. "No, we're fine, aren't we boys?" Both dogs affirmed her question with a bark.

She couldn't help notice the look of relief on Geoff's face. He was doing his best and trying hard to make the dogs like him. He was a good man, even if his presence brought no spark. But that's not what she was looking for right now. She had bigger things to think about. Starting with Frank.

TEMPEST PATTED Jupiter's head where it rested on the futon beside her. Paddy was curled up nearby. She was scrolling through the digital images of the documents she'd taken from Frank's files. She'd already put them back in his filing cabinet, which was a relief beyond measure. Her next move seemed elusive, though. She was still considering asking him outright what his involvement was and why he had covered up the information about the eye witnesses. She also wanted to ask about the gun. Somehow, she just couldn't believe Frank was dirty. There had to be more to it than that.

A knock sounded on the door followed by a muffled, "It's me." Speak of the devil. It was Frank.

Both dogs immediately started barking.

"Quiet," she scolded, then called. "Just a minute."

Tempest's heart pounded as she belted her bathrobe a little more securely around her waist. The suite above Frank's garage had its advantages, but it also meant he had access to her whenever he wanted. Right now, that thought brought to mind every horror movie she'd ever seen. What if he was here to do her in and hide her body? "Don't be stupid," she said under her breath and walked as calmly as possible to the door.

Frank was standing on the other side, leaning against the bare wood walls of the interior of the garage.

"Hi. What's up?" she asked.

"Can I come in?"

Tempest blinked, her insides fluttering beyond control now. "Um, sure." She waved for him to enter, but left the door ajar. She might need it open for a quick escape. "Can I get you a tea?" she asked with as much pleasantry as possible.

"No, thanks." Frank headed straight for the futon. Fortunately, she hadn't put it down for the night yet, or she would have felt awkward about him sitting on it. Paddy scattered from its surface with a miniature bark of protest while Jupiter stood and slunk away to find a different spot in the room.

"What's up?" Tempest repeated, perching on the opposite edge of the futon.

Frank didn't answer right away but just sat there, hands clasped between his knees, staring straight ahead.

"Frank?"

He looked at her then, and she could see he was upset. His

eyes were narrowed, his mouth an angry line. She thought about bolting for the door, but her legs wouldn't move.

"I thought we had an understanding, you and I."

"We did," she stuttered. "We do."

"I took you under my wing. Gave you a job. Leads. Introduced you to quality contacts. Put a roof over your head. Heck, I treated you like my own child."

"Thank you," she managed. *Oh God! Was this the part where he pulled out a weapon?*

"Then why did you do it?" he asked.

"Do what?"

"Go sneaking around behind my back."

"Wha... what do you mean?" she whispered. She closed her eyes.

"What in tarnation! What's gotten into you?"

"I can explain. I just wanted to know -"

"No, I'm not going to listen!" he bellowed. "You wrote a piece on that art gallery and submitted it to a competitor without giving me first option. You know that's not part of our deal! I get first rights to your articles and if I don't think I can sell them, then - and only then - you are free to find another publication that will."

Tempest felt her body deflating as the tension evaporated. "I, um... you said you weren't interested in art pieces after the last one I brought to you. Too fluffy, you said."

"I know what I said, but I didn't tell you to submit them without at least letting me take a look first." He pointed an angry finger. "That's a breach of contract. I could can your hide. Send you packing."

"I know. I'm sorry. I won't do it again."

"You better not." He stood. "I own this city, you understand? You do that again and I'll blacklist you from ever publishing another article." The anger in his eyes told her he wasn't kidding.

"I'm sorry. It won't happen again."

His face softened. "Good."

Tempest waited.

Frank rubbed the back of his neck. "Sorry. I came on a bit strong with that last part. I wouldn't do that to you, and you know it."

"You have every right. It's in our contract, as you said."

"No, I overstepped. I was upset about something else entirely, and I took it out on you."

"Anything I can help with?" Tempest walked him to the still open door.

"No, just something about Johnny."

"Your son."

Frank nodded. "But it's nothing you can help with. Just parent child stuff. You know how it is."

"No, I don't, to be honest." Tempest stood with her hand holding the door while Frank hovered on the landing which led down to the garage.

"Oh. Right. That was insensitive. Seems I've been doing that a lot lately."

"Is he okay? He's overseas, right?"

"We'll figure it out. Anyway, sorry about the outburst." He stopped and caught her eye, his gaze penetrating with intensity. "Oh. And next time you want something from the filing cabinet, just ask."

Tempest watched with wide eyes as Frank descended the steps. She shut the door with a quiet click and slid the deadbolt into place. Her heart had taken up pounding in her ears again.

Like an automaton she shuffled to the futon, picked up her cellphone and dialed Geoff.

"Hi, Geoff? How does your mom feel about pets?"

CHAPTER 23

One week in and Ryan was no closer to finding out who was behind the smuggling. Security measures at the facility were strict and tight. Every step was under multi-camera surveillance with an added layer of on-duty security officers. The pipes that took the raw diamonds to the secure area were sealed off, remotely opened by a valve into containers so that the whole process could be hands free and carefully watched.

Even once the diamonds were inspected and graded, everything was done under the strictest security measures, with layers of surveillance cameras and security officials present so that no one person could be put in a vulnerable position.

Iris scans were required for those working in these highly secure areas, and searches took place when entering or exiting. In fact, the people actually handling the diamonds were required to take off their clothes and agree to a search before leaving!

Sealing and tracking procedures any time product was transported between locations, even on site, were also tight. All data was recorded more than once, both physically and on video before and after each transfer. As far as Ryan could see, smuggling would be a very difficult thing to execute and very risky, but it was still happening. He just had to figure out how. Digging for the truth would be a lot like digging for the diamonds themselves.

During his time, he'd visited the inspection area each day and then gone over the footage again and again, scouring for any inconsistencies. He just didn't see any.

It was time for supper soon, and Ryan checked his watch. Jeremy should be calling any minute with an update. As if on cue, his phone beeped and he answered it. "Anything?" he asked without preamble.

"Not sure if this qualifies," Jeremy said, "but one of the loader operators was telling a story today about a movie he saw where these diamond thieves swallowed condoms full of diamonds in order to smuggle them out of a jewelry store."

"That sounds disgusting," Ryan commented.

"Mostly everyone just laughed. Made a joke of it, you know? But one guy seemed upset. He told the other guy to shut up because that kind of talk could get him fired."

"Was he just being cautious, or do you think there's more to it than that?" Ryan asked.

"Probably just being cautious, but I thought I'd mention it anyway."

"I suppose that is one way to get the diamonds off site, but that still doesn't tell us how they're getting them out from under security in the first place."

"That's all I got," Jeremy said. "But I'll keep my nose to the ground."

"You better. After blowing your cover with the nurse, I'd say you better come up with something to redeem yourself." Ryan's tone was serious, but if Jeremy could see his face, he'd see that he was smiling. The kid was okay.

"Hey, you're the one who blew yours first," Jeremy reminded. He sounded defensive.

"I'm just kidding. Relax."

They hung up. Just as Ryan was about to head out the door toward the cafeteria, his phone rang again. He put the device to his ear without bothering to look at the display. "You forget something hotshot?"

"Is that supposed to be a compliment?"

"Andy?" Ryan held the phone out and looked at the number. "I thought you were Jeremy."

"You two still squabbling like an old married couple?" Andy asked.

"You know it," Ryan said with a laugh. "So, what's your news? I was just about to head out for supper."

"Um… it's not good, man. I can't lie."

A cold shiver ran down Ryan's spine and he sat down on his bed. "Tempest?" he managed to get out.

"Well, yes and no. She moved out of Frank's place."

"That's good."

"Yeah, but you won't like where she moved to…"

"Okay. Give it to me." Ryan steeled his jaw.

"She moved in with that guy she'd been seeing. Geoff Vanguard."

Ryan grunted, his gut literally tightening like he'd been punched.

"I'm not sure if it's, well, you know. He could just be offering a place to crash for now, but…"

Ryan still couldn't speak. Tempest. *His* Tempest, had moved in with another man? It didn't compute. She had been frank about her desire not to engage in casual sex, and he had agreed. As Christians, it was what they both believed, as hard as it had been at times. At least it had been hard for him… And now this?

"Ryan? You still there?" Andy asked.

Ryan blinked and looked at the phone. "Yeah, I'm here."

"I thought maybe we'd lost connection there for a second."

"No. Just processing."

"So… that's actually not the worst thing I have to tell you," Andy went on.

Ryan closed his eyes. Could it get worse? "Go ahead," he said, his tone clipped.

"Okay…" Andy took a deep breath and let it out. "Man, this next one really sucks."

"Spit it out already!"

"Okay. Lenny Demarco was found dead this morning."

Ryan's jaw clenched. "How?"

"Gunshot. They're saying it's gang related, which it could be since he was connected."

"Or it could be that whoever put those photos in Frank's mailbox made good on his promise."

"Exactly what I was thinking," Andy said.

"I'm glad Tempest is out of there. Even if it is with…" Ryan couldn't bring himself to say the other man's name.

"Anyway, I should let you go so you can eat. I'll let you know the minute I hear anything else."

Ryan set his cellphone down on the bed beside him. He wasn't hungry anymore, but knew he needed to make an appearance. He wasn't sure which information had him most upset. The fact that Lenny Demarco's life had come to an untimely end, or that Tempest had moved in with another man.

Lenny Demarco had lived a high risk lifestyle. Not that he had it coming, or that anyone deserved to die by another's hand, but it was probably just a matter of time before it happened. Tempest, on the other hand… Now, that was a situation he couldn't quite wrap his head around.

Despite the fact that she was capable and smart, she was also naive. Innocent. It was one of the things that had drawn him to her in the first place. Then when he'd been praying and trying to figure out the mole in the department puzzle, he'd been sure he'd heard God's voice. Well, not an audible voice, but that still small voice that popped into your head when you least expected it and for no reason. It had said that Tempest was the key... But how? Now that she was with another man, maybe he'd never find out.

RYAN'S STEEL-TOED boots clattered on the metal mesh of the catwalk. Earplugs muffled the sound of the sluicing machines below. He stopped to observe the production line, leaning against the rail as he watched a maze of belts and conveyors running crisscross throughout the huge plant.

He caught the movement of another person out of the corner of his eye and pushed off the railing. An older man, also wearing a hardhat and safety glasses, approached. He was wearing a sheepskin jacket, jeans, and an oversized safety vest of florescent orange over the entire outfit. Ryan had not seen him in the plant before, but there were a lot of workers on site, so he probably was someone's cross shift.

He expected the man to pass him on the catwalk and go about his business, but to Ryan's surprise he stopped right beside him and stuck out his hand. "Ryan Grant?" the newcomer yelled in question.

Ryan nodded. "Yes."

"Good. I was told I'd find you here. Let's go somewhere quieter to talk."

Ryan followed the man the length of the metal walkway and then down at least three levels of steps with a switch back at each level. There were still more levels to the plant, but this one connected to a quieter corridor that led to another part of the facility.

"That's better," the man said as soon as the fire-door shut behind them. The hallway was definitely quieter, although the muffled rattle of the machinery could still be heard. "So? How are you getting on?" He was not a tall man, but thin and wiry and looked to be in his sixties, at least.

"Fine..." Ryan responded hesitantly. "I'm sorry, but you have me at a disadvantage. I don't know who you are."

"My apologies!" the man blustered. "Of course you wouldn't. William Herschel." He extended his hand, and they shook a second time. The older man's handshake was surprisingly firm.

It took a second for the name to register and when it did, Ryan's eyes widened. "William Herschel? CEO of Paragon?"

"One and the same." William laughed good-naturedly.

"I'm sorry I didn't recognize you," Ryan apologized. "Very nice to meet you." The man in front of him didn't look anything like the serious businessman in the brochures.

"It's the hardhat and glasses," William said with a sweeping gesture. "Or maybe the clothes. I'm not much for suits, so whenever I can get out of wearing them, I jump all over it. Not practical for these parts."

Ryan couldn't agree more, although Richard Camry had been all about the suit. "Is there something you wanted to discuss with me?"

William looked from side to side. "Not here. I have a little office they let me use when I come up." He removed his hardhat and glasses. "Follow me."

Without the hat and glasses, Ryan could see the white haired executive, even under the casual garb. He seemed like an unpretentious sort for the head of a multi-billion dollar company.

Ryan followed William through several corridors - there were so many it was confusing at times, but all the buildings were connected so that people didn't have to go outside. Finally, they came to the offices near the main entrance.

"Hello, Francine," William greeted as he marched through the reception area. They arrived at an office tucked out of the way. William tossed his hardhat, glasses and the vest, which he'd shed enroute, onto a nearby chair. "Not very fancy, but out here serviceable is the order of the day. Make yourself at home."

Ryan removed his own protective gear and sat in one of the chairs across from William's desk.

"So," William began. "Tell me what you've found out so far."

Ryan kept his face a passive mask. "Well, my company is very pleased with the quality of the diamonds as well as the practices used to ensure the safety of the workers and the integrity of the inspection process."

"Not that!" William waved a hand. "I suppose I should be happy that you gave me the correct answer, but I *know*."

"You know?" Ryan didn't go any further, leaving it up to Mr. Herschel to tell him exactly what that meant.

"Yes! Who you really are and what you're doing here! Who do you think set it up in the first place?" When Ryan still didn't answer, William laughed. "Your poker face is good, I'll give you that." He leaned forward and lowered his voice. "I know you're undercover, sent by the FBI because they think there's a connection between the son-of-a-gun who's stealing my diamonds and some drug cartel. I just want to find out who's stealing from me."

Ryan cleared his throat. "I wasn't told who our inside man would be. I'm surprised it's you."

"Why? Because I'm old and frail?" William raised one eyebrow in a magnificent display of facial acrobatics. Then he laughed. "I'm not as frail as I look. I was out digging through the permafrost on this god-forsaken tundra forty years ago. A young starry eyed geologist with more spunk than sense. The mosquitos almost flew away with me! It took every dime I could scrape together along with calling in every favor I could think of. Ten years and a few grey hairs later, I found it. The Kimberlite I knew was buried here. The rest is history. I'm not going to lie down and let some dirty thief steal from me without a fight."

"Who else knows?" Ryan asked.

"Not a darn soul!"

"Not even Richard Camry?"

William shook his head. "Nobody but me, you, and the fly on the wall."

"I have a partner working with me," Ryan said. "A young agent posing as a local laborer."

"Whatever. I'll leave the logistics to you. Just find me that thief."

"I'm doing my best, but so far it's difficult. You run a tight ship here, much to your credit."

"I don't do much. Just swoop in every month or so to keep people on their toes. Usually unannounced." He grinned.

Ryan smiled. He liked Mr. William Herschel.

"Tell me what you need to get the job done. Let's catch the dirty bugger."

Ryan furrowed his brow. "Blueprints of the system that carries the raw diamonds to the secure area? Tubes, junctures, all the release valves… I've been combing over the surveillance video, but if I could identify any weak spots, that would be a start. After that, I might need to inspect it in person."

"Done."

"Just like that?" Ryan raised his brows.

"Well, it will take some doing, but I do own the place…" William chuckled. "I have to answer to a board of directors, but I do have some clout left."

"You'll take this to the board?" Ryan was even more confused and he was sure it showed on his face.

"Of course not! I'm not telling those old boys anything! For all I know one of them could be behind it! But I have my ways, don't you worry. I'll have what you need by tomorrow."

"Thanks."

"Say? You ever been on an ice road?" William asked. "You know the kind I mean. Only open a couple of months a year built on a river or a lake."

"Can't say that I have."

"If you're still here before the ice road goes out, you should tag along on the next fuel run to Yellowknife. Sometimes you can hear the ice cracking beneath you. It's quite the sensation."

"Sounds frightening."

"It's a thrill, for sure. Those eighteen wheelers are heavy, but the ice is thick enough. Still, they say you can't get going too fast for fear of creating a wave underneath the surface. It could start a tidal wave that could compromise the integrity of the ice."

"Hm. Not sure I'll have the pleasure of that experience," Ryan said with just a touch of sarcasm.

𝒶 nne-Marie inhaled deeply and let her breath out in a white cloud of condensation. It was an absolutely gorgeous day in Yellowknife. By this time in March, the winter darkness had given way to bright sunshine for most of the afternoon. Yes, it was still cold, and the earth was still blanketed in white, but it sparkled with cleanness and purity, the air filled with a sense of hope at the coming spring.

Just like her heart. She had contacted Dirk this morning when she got into Yellowknife and was glad to hear he was still in town waiting. He had been slightly miffed that she hadn't called sooner and that he wasn't able to meet her at the airport, but she didn't want their first meeting after so long to be in front of a group of acquaintances from Paragon. Instead, she had the perfect location in mind. A fairytale castle made of ice and snow.

An actual castle built from snow blocks complete with turrets, parapets, courtyard and yawning gates rose in sparkling white splendor on the flat expanse of Great Slave Lake. Even the window panes were made from ice cut from the lake. Anne-Marie stood back admiring the spectacle. It was almost unbelievable to think it was constructed completely out of snow and ice and would eventually melt away with the strengthening sun and disappear into the lake with the rest of the ice. She could hardly wait to see inside, but she'd told Dirk she would meet him outside by the entrance to the Snow King festival grounds.

Unfortunately, everyone in town had the same idea. The place was milling with people in brightly colored parkas and toques. The ring of children's laughter carried across the frozen air as they participated in various games and activities that had been set up, including a huge slide built out of snow that wound out from the side of the castle.

"Anne-Marie!" someone called.

Anne-Marie's stomach did a little flip and she turned to the voice. Instant disappointment made the smile on her face fade until she realized how impolite she must look, and she carefully constructed another to replace it. "Mr. Camry. You decided to take in the festival after all."

"Just Richard, please. After our talk the other night I decided it was time." He looked at the castle in the background. "Pretty impressive."

"Yes."

Richard held up a brochure. "It says here that it all started with a local who built a small fort out of snow on the lake. Now it's grown to be... well, that!" He pointed.

"I hear they have concerts every evening," Anne-Marie offered.

Richard perused the brochure again. "Auditorium, cafe, dance floor... even some rooms for rent! Live music, art displays, ice sculptures, puppet theater, film showings, family activities, ice slide, hockey games and so much more!" He looked up. "At least that's what the brochure says."

"I'm looking forward to taking it in." Anne-Marie glanced past him to where she hoped to see Dirk.

"Meeting someone?" he asked, following her gaze.

"Um, yes."

"Your boyfriend?"

"Yes, that's right."

"Well, I won't keep you then." He smiled. "And what I said the other night - about being married. I wasn't implying anything unseemly. I just meant that we could be friends. Period. I hope you didn't take it the wrong way."

Of course she had. Even now she wasn't sure she believed him. But it didn't really matter. It was best to leave it be. "It's fine."

"You're sure? I would hate for you to feel uncomfortable."

"No, really. I'm fine."

"Good. Can we hug on it?"

Her lashes fluttered, but he had his arms outstretched, and he was smiling in a friendly, if not creepy, sort of way, so what was she to do? Leave him hanging? She moved forward for a quick hug, and he embraced her lightly with a pat on the back. There. It was over in seconds.

"Well, I really should get going now," he said cheerfully. "Maybe I'll see you and your man around."

"Maybe." She raised her hand in a half hearted wave as he trudged toward the castle. The moment she turned back, she saw Dirk. Her heart lurched into her throat with both excitement and fear. Had he seen the exchange? Would he care? She took off at a brisk pace to meet him. At the same time, he started to jog.

Their bodies crashed together in a crushing embrace and he swept her off her feet as he spun around, his head buried in her neck. "I missed you!" His voice was muffled through all the clothing.

"Me too," she admitted. What had she been so afraid of all these months? Somehow, none of it mattered anymore. Dirk was here, and she was safe in his arms.

Dirk set her down and held her at arm's length. "Does this mean you've forgiven me?"

"I'm the one who should be asking for your forgiveness," she said. "For being so... indecisive and making you wait so long."

"For not letting me pick you up at the airport," he added and then grinned.

"Yes, that, too, I suppose." She smiled, drinking in the sight of him. He was wearing a puffy jacket like the one she had on, only not as long in length, a scarf and a floppy toque. He looked like a local, but somehow still managed to look like he was posing for a northern fashion shoot. She sobered. "I can't tell you how relieved I am to see you face to face. I'm so sorry, Dirk, For everything."

He gazed at her for a moment and then bent to kiss her. She sighed into his mouth and knew she had finally given in to what she knew was right all along.

After a blissful moment he broke contact and pulled away. "Should I be jealous?" he asked.

"About what?" She hoisted her backpack so it fell more comfortably on her shoulders.

"Buddy-what's-his-name I saw you hugging earlier." He was smiling, so Anne-Marie doubted he was actually worried.

"Absolutely not." She took his hand and started walking toward the castle. "He's actually some big-wig from Paragon Diamond Mines, and for some reason, thinks he's my friend." She didn't mention the sleazy parts. No point in making Dirk worried for no reason.

Dirk nodded. "Just checking. You've been away a long time. It's like you've been living in a different world."

"I have, to a degree." She looked over at his handsome profile as they walked hand in hand, their arms swinging slightly back and forth.

He looked at her and smiled. "Let's not do that anymore, 'kay?"

She gave him a withering look. "Don't tell me we're going to take up the conversation right where we left it? Me moving to

Boston, you moving to Edmonton. Can't we just enjoy being together for a bit before the drama starts again?"

"Deal," he said and then grinned. "Maybe we should just both move to Yellowknife."

She gave him a little shove but couldn't help smiling. This man really was willing to do anything, live anywhere, for her. "Maybe we could live in a castle."

"Sounds like a plan to me," Dirk said. "Come on."

They picked up their pace as they headed toward the structure, its surface sparkling in the sun, just like in a fairytale. The one she felt she was in.

THE DAY COULDN'T HAVE BEEN BETTER. Browsing the art displays hand in hand, watching an amazing show of talent as ice sculptors from around the globe showed off their skills, cheering on both sides at a hockey game at the huge open air rink on the lake. Even the hotdogs they ate tasted like a gourmet meal! It was amazing how one's perspective could change when seen through the lens of love.

Dusk had fallen, and the ice castle took on a whole new magic under the glow of the aurora borealis. Inside, candles set strategically in recessed alcoves flickered, while mini-lights and colored flood lamps brought just the right amount of ambiance. It was surprisingly warm, although not enough to melt the structure. Most people kept their coats on.

Dirk and Anne-Marie found a spot along the wall of the auditorium - a bench seat carved out of snow - where they could watch the jazz ensemble that was playing.

"Do you believe me now?" Dirk asked above the music. He reached for Anne-Marie's hand and cradled it in his.

"About what?" She knew, but she wanted to hear him say it.

"That I love you. That it's for real and not some phase I was going through."

She smiled. "I know." She would never tire of those words.

"You are the perfect woman." He kissed her hand.

"Hardly perfect," she protested with a laugh.

"The one God made especially for me," he said. "You have captured my heart, Anne-Marie Fletcher, once and for all."

"Such a smooth talker."

"Wanna dance?" Dirk stood up and pulled her with him.

"Do I have a choice?"

He bent for a lingering kiss - one of hundreds they'd stolen all day - and then wrapped his arms around her. She rested her head against his chest and they swayed in place, not bothering to actually join the others on the dance floor proper.

"I love you, too," she murmured.

Someone tapped her on the shoulder. "Excuse me."

With reluctance, she and Dirk parted. Her eyes widened when she saw two uniformed police officers. They were wearing fur hats and parkas, but the distinctive RCMP shield was on both, and they looked very official standing there in their winter uniforms. "Yes?"

"Anne-Marie Fletcher?"

"Yes," she said again.

"Open your bag, please," the older of the two said. He pointed to the backpack that lay on the snow bench beside them.

Her eyes darted from one to the other and then to Dirk for reassurance.

"What's this about?' Dirk asked. "Do you have a warrant?"

"It's okay," Anne-Marie said nervously, reaching to unzip the backpack. "I've got nothing to hide." She spread the opening apart so they could see inside.

The younger officer thrust his hand in and felt around then shook his head.

"Open the front compartment, please," the one in charge instructed.

Anne-Marie blinked and did as she was told.

"This seems irregular to me," Dirk protested again. He looked at Anne-Marie and said more quietly. "You don't have to do anything. They have no right."

"Not sure where you're from, buddy," the older officer said. "But this is Canada. We have every right to search and seize if we suspect illegal activity."

"Illegal activity?" Anne-Marie burst out.

"Found it." The younger man held up a small velvet bag.

Anne-Marie's eyes widened even further. "That's not mine! I have no idea who that belongs to!"

One of them swung her around and proceeded to handcuff her while the other one read her her rights. A horrifying wave of deja vu swept over her.

"I mean it. I don't know what that is or who it belongs to!"

"Sir, I'm afraid we'll have to search you as well."

"Absolutely not! I'm an American citizen and -"

"You're not in Kansas anymore," the older one said. "Spread 'em. Hands on your head. Unless you'd like cuffs, too?"

Dirk widened his stance and placed his hands on his head. Anne-Marie watched helplessly as the younger cop thoroughly frisked Dirk. "Nothing," he said.

"You'll have to come down to the station with us anyway, just to be sure," the other one said. "Cooperation is appreciated, but we can always use force if necessary." He gave Dirk an uncompromising stare that brooked no more argument.

"We'll figure this out," Dirk said over his shoulder as he was led forward by one of the officers.

Lord, what was happening? This was not the way their romantic evening was supposed to end.

CHAPTER 25

"Patience!" Tempest opened the back door to the house and held it aloft while both Jupiter and Paddy scooted outside under her arm. So far, her new living arrangements were working out. For the dogs at least.

Geoff's mother, Isabel, owned an older bungalow not far from Frank's neighborhood. Tempest's domain was dark and cramped with a low ceiling, like most basements in a house of that era. She had the run of the so called 'Rec room' which was little more than an old carpet thrown on the cement floor along with some mismatched furniture. Her bedroom was especially small, with one window that she'd need a chair to reach for egress. The only bathroom in the basement was a two piece, so she had to go upstairs in order to use the shower. However, the yard was large and fenced in, so the dogs thought they'd died and gone to heaven. Isabel seemed happy to have her and was charging less than what she'd paid above Frank's garage.

Tempest didn't leave the dogs unattended outdoors for fear they'd dig in Isabel's flower beds, but they played fetch, and sometimes she tied them up under a large tree so that they could enjoy the fresh air if she had other things to do. They were used to being confined indoors for part of the day, so letting them lounge outside seemed like a treat.

After both dogs had done their business and she'd cleaned up the evidence, Tempest clipped them to separate stakes, far enough apart that they couldn't get tangled, but close enough that they could get within sniffing distance. "I'm going in for breakfast now, so you behave, okay?"

Tempest went back inside the house. The backdoor opened right onto the landing for the basement stairs - convenient for letting them out in the morning, but a death trap if one should accidentally step the wrong way. Many of these older homes had a similar set up, and she wondered who had designed such an obvious flaw.

Instead of going down, Tempest went up two steps into the small kitchen where the delicious smell of bacon had traveled to the landing. Isabel was at the stove, and she nodded when she saw Tempest. "Breakfast is almost ready. Geoff is just in the shower."

"Oh, okay. You didn't have to. I could just grab some toast."

"Of course you'll eat with us! You can pour some coffees, though, if you like."

Tempest found three cups in the cabinet and took them to the table.

It was Saturday morning, and Isabel was home from work. She worked as a receptionist at a dental clinic during the week. She was about fifty, short and rounded through the middle, but feisty. Her husband, Geoff's stepdad, had died several years ago of cancer, so Geoff was her entire world.

Even though it had only been a week, they hadn't quite worked out the food situation. Tempest preferred her independence, but so far Isabel insisted she eat dinner with her and Geoff in the evenings. Apparently, Saturday morning breakfast was now added to the docket. Tempest wasn't sure how long the situation could continue, but for now, it was a safe haven, and she appreciated the older woman's generosity. As long as Isabel didn't get any ideas.

That was the real problem. She and Geoff were on the same page, at least in Tempest's mind, about their relationship. They were strictly friends, and Geoff seemed fine with that. Despite the fact that he had approached her first, he had never really come across as having expectations too far beyond that. Isabel's expectations seemed to be different, however. Twice now, she'd said something to the effect that she should let them have some alone time, as if they were a couple, and she was the third wheel.

Geoff entered the kitchen, his hair damp from his shower. "Hm. The bacon smells good."

"Take a seat, and I'll bring the pancakes." Isabel reached into the oven to retrieve a stack of pancakes.

Tempest finished pouring coffee into the three mugs and put the coffeepot back in its spot. When she turned back to the table, Isabel was blocking her usual seat as she reached across to set the food down. "Just sit by Geoff this morning," the older woman instructed.

Tempest gave a half smile. Of course.

"So, what are your plans for the day?" Geoff asked as they started to eat.

Tempest glanced at Geoff. "Um, still working on that project. You know the one?"

He nodded. "Right."

She didn't want to say more in front of Isabel. The truth was, she had been following up on Andy's tip about Frank's financial situation, but couldn't come out and say it in front of the other woman.

"It's Saturday," Isabel said. "You should take the day off and go somewhere nice together."

"I'm sure Geoff has other things to do," Tempest said.

"I can't imagine what. Most young men want to spend their free time with their special someone."

Tempest glanced at Geoff again, expecting him to set his mother straight. He seemed extremely focused on spreading jam on his piece of toast. She turned to Isabel. "Actually, I'm not sure what Geoff has told you, but -"

Geoff interrupted. "That's a great idea, Mom. I've been meaning to take Tempest to that ice cream shop you used to take me to as a kid. What's the name of it again?"

"Ye Old Ice Cream Shop," Isabel said. She smiled at Tempest. "It's at a dairy where they make their own ice cream. It's quite a drive just for ice cream, but it's divine."

Tempest tried to catch Geoff's eye, but he was purposely avoiding her, she could tell. "As wonderful as that sounds, I may have other commitments today."

"I think you'll like it," Isabel said. "It's very quaint."

Tempest didn't push it and finished her breakfast. When she offered to help clean up, Isabel insisted that she wanted to do it alone. "You two have better things to do."

"Thanks for a delicious breakfast," Tempest said. "I'm going to go see to the dogs. Um, Geoff? Can you join me for a minute?"

The moment she appeared outside, both dogs stood up from their lounging positions and started to bark. She went to them and scratched each one behind the ears. "I know, I know. It's nice, but you liked our old place, too, didn't you?"

She heard the screen door creak and waited for Geoff to join her. He stood a few feet away, out of the dogs' reach. He still hadn't quite made friends with either of them. although he was trying.

"Why didn't you say something?" she asked, still scratching.

"What do you mean?"

"You know. Your mom thinks we're dating. We're not."

He shrugged. "It just seemed easier than embarrassing her at the moment. I'll set her straight later tonight."

"You better or I will," Tempest said.

"I will, but let me handle it, okay?"

Tempest glanced over her shoulder at where he was standing. "Why lead her on?"

He sighed. "My mom wants me to find a girlfriend. It's her greatest wish."

"Well, you'll have to break it to her that it's not me. I'm not interested in being more than friends right now. I thought you understood that."

"I do. It's my mom who is having trouble with it." He laughed, the sound not quite genuine. He cleared his throat. "So, about your plans for the day? You found something new about Frank?"

"He's definitely getting money from somewhere other than writing. I'm planning a bit of a stakeout if you want to come along."

"A stakeout? Doesn't that sound exciting. But do you think it's wise? Maybe you should get that cop friend of yours to help."

"Andy?" Tempest shook her head. "I've asked for too many favors from him already. Besides." She hesitated. "It's becoming awkward."

"Because he's Ryan's friend?" Geoff asked.

She nodded.

"Well in that case, I suppose I should come along just in case you need backup." He smiled. "What do you think? Am I body-guard material?"

"I hate dragging you into my problems all the time. You're a trooper."

"I want to. It gets me out of the house. And that way, my mom will think we're out together."

Tempest frowned and gave him a sidelong look. Why was he acting so strange around his mother? It just didn't make any sense.

～

"So, how were you going to pull this off without my help again?" Geoff asked in a good-natured tone as he drove. He glanced at Tempest in the passenger seat before turning his eyes back to the street in front of them.

"I'd have thought of something," Tempest replied. Not having her own set of wheels was becoming inconvenient, especially now that she didn't have Ryan or Frank to rely on. Geoff was filling that void, but she was beginning to wonder how smart it was to keep relying on his willingness to help. He might develop expectations.

As an added precaution, she'd donned a head scarf, and both she and Geoff wore dark glasses. So far, they had managed to follow Frank for a good forty-five minutes without being seen. Geoff was good at keeping his distance, that was for sure, and Tempest was grateful. She wasn't sure how she would have done it if she'd been driving. She'd probably have blown her cover by now.

Frank and Edna's Saturday routine was like clockwork, so it was just a matter of waiting on a side street for them to pass by in the minivan. It was the only time that Edna went out of the house. Frank did all the shopping, and as far as Tempest knew, Edna didn't even go out to restaurants, preferring to cook at home. She had always been a nice woman, but there was something strange about her, too. A nervousness that made Tempest wonder if she had always been that way.

Geoff smiled across at her. "You remind me of someone from one of those old spy movies from the sixties."

Tempest glanced at herself in the little mirror on her visor and touched the head scarf. "I see what you mean. I suppose you're James Bond, then?"

"Not as nice a car, I'm afraid."

They had asked to borrow Isabel's car since it was less likely that Frank would recognize them in it should they get too close. Isabel was more than happy to comply. She was satisfied with

Geoff's excuse that he needed to check something on his own vehicle and didn't want to take it all the way out to the ice cream shop they had talked about earlier. Tempest agreed that they would go there afterwards if there was time, just so that they didn't have to lie about it to Isabel.

"I want to thank you again for everything you've been doing lately," Tempest said. "It's above and beyond. I'm not sure how I'll ever pay you back."

"I'm not looking for payback," Geoff said. "Friends help friends out. It's as simple as that."

Tempest shifted in her seat. "I hope you're not hurt about our talk earlier. I like you, Geoff, but just not in that way. But I do value your friendship. I hope you understand."

"No worries. It's my mom who has designs on you, not me." He laughed. "Of course, I don't mean *she* has designs on you! It's on my behalf."

"I knew what you meant."

"I'm sorry about that. I'll try to do better at discouraging her. I just hate to disappoint her. She's been through a lot."

"What do you mean?"

He shrugged. "My stepdad wasn't a very nice person. I think at first she was just glad not to be married to a killer. She's always worried too much what people think, which is probably why she jumped into a second marriage so quickly. Then she had to keep up appearances."

"How was he not nice?" Tempest studied Geoff's profile and noticed the tightening of his jaw.

"Oh, you know. Controlling. I think she was relieved when he got cancer and died."

Tempest made a face. "That's rough."

"Not as bad as it sounds. She and I have been relatively happy since. But she's still somewhat co-dependent, which is one of the reasons I haven't moved out yet. I just hate to leave her alone. She needs to be looking after someone, and I'm all she's got."

"You're a good son."

"It's not always easy."

Frank veered off the busier road onto a quiet residential street, and Geoff followed. It would be trickier now not to be noticed, so Geoff pulled over to give them a bit more distance. Up ahead they saw Frank pull into a parking lot near a square brick building.

"We'll need to get closer," Geoff said, "or we could lose them altogether."

They drove by the entrance to the parking lot, and Tempest saw Frank helping Edna out of the passenger side of the van. She thought she saw him look her way briefly as they passed, but she quickly turned her head. When she looked back, Frank and Edna were heading into the building.

Geoff leaned forward to read the name on the side of the building. "It's a long term care facility. Not so sinister."

"I wonder who they go to visit?" Tempest furrowed her brow. "I know Frank's parents have both passed, but maybe Edna still has a parent living."

"There's one way to find out," Geoff said. "Go in and ask."

"Frank will know."

"Chances are they'll be in someone's room, not near the reception desk," Geoff reasoned.

"I doubt they'll tell us anything though, for security."

"It's a shame to be this close and not at least give it a try."

"I suppose." Tempest sat for a moment considering the options. "We'll give it a shot, but if they won't tell us anything, I'll just have to figure out a different way to get the list of residents."

They got out of the car and walked up the wide cement sidewalk to the double glass doors. Inside it was cool and dark. Tempest took off her sunglasses and glanced around. The colors were muted and clinical, and there was the hollow echo of footfalls in a faraway hall. She noticed a sign pointing to the reception area.

She and Geoff approached the high counter, and Tempest placed her sunglasses on the ledge as she peered over its edge at the woman sitting behind it. "Excuse me. My uncle and aunt just came in, and I wondered if you could tell me who they came to see."

The woman narrowed her eyes. "If they're really your aunt and uncle you'd know."

"True, but -"

"What in blazes are you doing here?"

Tempest recognized the bellowing voice and slowly turned. There was no point in making a run for it. Frank Dunlop was no slouch.

"Frank," she said pleasantly. "I was just asking which room you went to so I could join you." She looked at the receptionist as if to verify her claim.

Frank arrived by her side. "I said, what in the blazes are you doing here?"

"What are *you* doing here?" Tempest countered with a tilt to her chin.

Frank looked from side to side. "There's a patio outside where we can talk." He turned to the receptionist. "I was just coming out to fetch a nurse. Can you send one?" Next he pointed at Geoff. "You stay here."

Frank grabbed Tempest by the elbow and maneuvered her toward a set of glass doors that led to a courtyard. "Edna will be expecting me back soon, so we've got to make it snappy."

Tempest twisted to look back at a bewildered Geoff. She lifted her hands in silent surrender and then continued with Frank.

Once outside, Frank directed her to a set of lawn chairs. She sat and waited for him to lower himself into the one opposite.

"I told you to stop digging," Frank began. When she opened her mouth, he held up a hand for her to keep silent. "But a good reporter never gives up, so in that way I'm proud of you. I taught you right."

"Thanks, I guess."

"I'm going to tell you something, and once I do, you have to promise me not to dig any deeper."

"Okay…"

"You already know I have a son."

"Yes, Johnny. You've mentioned him. He used to live above the garage, but when he moved out, you sublet it to me."

"Well, that's partly it."

"Partly? What do you mean?"

Frank paused then blurted, "Edna and I are here visiting him."

Tempest furrowed her brow. "Here? At a long term care home? But I thought you said he lived overseas?"

"I did. I lied."

Tempest took this in. "So, you're saying that Johnny is a resident here?"

Frank nodded.

"Why didn't you just tell me?"

"It's complicated."

Tempest shifted in her seat and waited for Frank to continue.

"Johnny joined the military. Edna begged him not to, but I thought it was a smart career choice. It would make a man out of him." Frank blinked. "Instead it ruined him."

"I'm so sorry."

"He had severe PTSD. Was never the same after coming back. Tried to take his own life more than once. " Frank's eyes began to well up. "The last time he almost succeeded."

All Tempest's bravado was knocked flat and she sank further into the chair. She had been suspicious of Frank, but had never dreamed of something like this. "What happened?" she whispered.

"Tried to poison himself with carbon monoxide right there in our garage. Used Edna's Monte Carlo. It's why she won't drive it anymore. It just sits there in the garage. The last thing Johnny touched before he turned his mind to mush."

"Oh Frank, I don't know what to say." A wave of compassion overtook her and she leaned forward, placing a sympathetic hand on Frank's knee. "But why keep it a secret?"

Frank shook his head. "In hindsight, maybe it would have been better if he'd succeeded. It would have saved… But he's my only boy, you understand?" He turned pleading eyes to her face.

"What are you trying to say?"

"He's been here for a long, long time, Tempest."

"Oh…"

"How much do you think a place like this costs?"

"A lot…" she supplied hesitantly.

"I couldn't afford it. Not on my salary, and Edna couldn't care for him at home. He's practically a vegetable. Like an infant. But he's still her son. Her only son. I had to do it for her."

"Do what?" She felt a coldness creeping into her spine, and she removed her hand.

"He promised me money in exchange for one little lie."

"Who promised you?"

"That I can't say. But I figured it didn't much matter. Your folks were good people, but they were dead already."

"My parents?" Tempest grasped the arm of the chair. The courtyard was suddenly spinning.

"There was no bringing them back and Johnny… He needed care."

Tempest clutched her head. "But, this makes no sense! What are you saying?"

"Your dad was a good reporter. He found out about some things. Things that he should never have let on he knew about."

Tempest looked slowly up at Frank's face. "It wasn't an accident, was it? You lied about what happened that night. Someone was seen running from the crime. A gun was found nearby!" A sob escaped and she placed a hand over her mouth.

"All circumstantial and hard to prove."

"How could you?" Tempest bolted to a standing position. "Especially once you knew I'd found out."

"The guy who hit them had been drinking, so he got what he deserved." Frank glanced around. They were still the only people in the courtyard.

"But, still! How could you look me in the face and lie to me all this time?"

"I thought I was doing you a favor. Believe me, I was. I am."

The warmth of the sun felt surreal against the coldness prickling her skin. "Did you know I was their daughter all along?" she asked between clenched teeth. "Is that why you hired me? Because you felt guilty?"

Frank stood slowly and tried to place a hand on her shoulder. She shrugged it away with vehemence. His mouth was a grim line, but he held up his hands. "Listen. Can you sit down again?"

Tempest blinked and then dropped back into the chair. Whatever he had to say, she needed to hear it, no matter how much she wanted to run screaming in the opposite direction.

"Thank you," Frank said. "Did I know you were Merlin Ross's daughter? Yes. Did I hire you because I felt guilty? Maybe, at first."

Tempest sucked some air in through her teeth.

"But you turned out to be a darn good reporter. And, if the truth be told, I'm fond of you."

Tempest ignored the sentiment. "Did Ryan have a hand in this, too?" she asked tightly.

Frank shook his head. "I swear, he didn't have a clue that I knew who you were or had any dealings with your parents or their story. I thought I'd just been given a chance by the Almighty to try to make amends. I was thanking my lucky stars."

"But you still didn't tell me," Tempest came back to that point.

Frank leaned forward. "For your own safety."

"So you say, but I'm still going to keep digging. You said yourself good reporters don't give up."

Frank grasped her hands in his. "Now, that's where I've got to insist. It's not just about a one-time pay off. They've been blackmailing me for years now, and there's no way out. They'll kill me, or Edna - or Johnny. And now you've stuck your foot in it, too. I tried to keep you out of it, but..."

"Does Edna know?"

"No!" he responded. "If Edna ever found out, it would kill her - if they don't get to her first. For your own safety, you need to stop poking the bear. You'll never prove anything, and you'll just end up getting hurt or worse. Now, that's all I'm gonna say." He stood up. "As it is, I'm gonna have to come up with some tale for Edna since I've been gone so long." He gave her one last stern look. "I mean it. Do not pursue this. And don't go blabbing to anyone. Not even the new boyfriend."

"He's not my boyfriend."

Frank didn't respond. Tempest watched him stride back to the glass doors and disappear inside.

She blinked, trying to settle her insides, not sure if her legs would carry her back to Geoff. Not sure if she could repeat what she'd just learned. Not sure if she should.

What in the world was she going to do now?

CHAPTER 26

*R*yan held the miniature flashlight in his mouth as he took a photo with his cellphone. Squeezed under a maze of pipes and tubing that transported the raw diamonds to the secure area for assessment, it was barely accessible. From what he could tell from the blueprints William Herschel had provided, it was the only part of the system with a joint that could potentially be tampered with. If someone was going to get their hands on a few diamonds without being caught, this might be the only way.

He shut off the flashlight and then touched the joint with his index finger. A bit more feeling around like a blind man, and he felt it. An inconsistency. What could be a trap door - albeit very small - that could be opened to let one raw diamond through at a time. He grunted as he tried to get a look at it, but there was just no way he could maneuver in the tight space to get his eyes on it. Instead, he held his phone in what he hoped was the right place and snapped another photo.

He heard a noise - the buzz of an access card unlocking the door and then the scraping of metal upon metal as the door opened. He stilled, pocketing the phone so as not to allow any extra light to alert anyone to his presence. This area was strictly off limits to all but a few with the highest security clearance.

He waited for several minutes while the security officer made his rounds and then let his breath out when he heard the door open and close again.

Suddenly his phone rang. He'd forgotten to turn off the ringer! He quickly hung up on the caller and fumbled to mute the phone. Before he'd managed, an incoming notification told him he had a text. Dirk Hillyer.

He looked down at the message and frowned.

Anne-Marie arrested for smuggling diamonds. Set up. Need help asap.

What in the world? How did that even make sense?

He shimmied on his back out from the cramped position and crawled a short distance until he could stand up. Hopefully, the security guard would be long gone.

He peeked out the small porthole window in the steel door and then slowly opened it. William had slipped him the access card, necessary on both sides of the door. The older man also told him in no uncertain terms that if he got caught, Ryan was on his own. William would have to play dumb. Well, he was almost there, so there shouldn't be a problem, and it looked like he had found the thief's access point. Once in the hallway, he would be home free.

Ryan unlocked the door and opened it just enough to slip into the hall. He'd only made it a few feet when a commanding voice boomed behind him.

"Stop right there!"

RYAN SAT ALONE on a chair in the inner security office, waiting. The mine didn't have a jail, per se, and he had not even been handcuffed, but a security guard stood just outside the door to the closet like room. Not that he hadn't been tackled by the strong young security officer who'd first caught him. The guy seemed to think he was on the football field or something. Ryan rotated his shoulder, still feeling the impact.

He'd already been questioned by the head of security, an older gentleman with a handlebar moustache. Naturally, he had denied everything. Explaining the security keycard had been a stretch. He'd said that he found it and thought he'd check to see what it opened. Sounded juvenile and the security chief hadn't bought it, anyway. Ryan wasn't sure what was next, but he knew it couldn't be good.

He drummed his fingers on the tabletop that separated the two chairs, the only furniture in the room. Another concern was the text from Dirk. He couldn't believe that Anne-Marie was guilty, so he had no other conclusion than to agree with Dirk that she had been set up. What he could do about it now was questionable. He had his own problems to deal with.

The doorknob rattled and Ryan straightened. He tried not to show his relief when William Herschel entered. He understood the necessity of the CEO remaining neutral.

"That's fine, Dean," William said to the security guard outside the door. "I don't need you to accompany me, and I won't be long."

As soon as the door was shut behind him, William strode to the other chair and sat down. He looked around the room. "I don't think this place is bugged, but I'll keep it brief. You don't need to worry about a thing. I'm accompanying you to Yellowknife, and we'll square everything away once we get there." He stopped for a moment and eyed Ryan intently. "That is, if you found what you were looking for?"

Ryan nodded. "I did. A small but effective trap door in one of the tubes. But you might want it double checked before you leave. If the thief is still here, he might try to cover it up or destroy it altogether."

"I'll have Dean shut that section off. Post a guard."

"Can he be trusted?" Ryan asked.

"I would hope so. Our security team is completely vetted and hand-picked. If security is in on it, then we really are in trouble."

"I still have my agent here. He might be of some help," Ryan said.

"Not sure how I'd do that without blowing his cover all together. I want to keep it in tact until we're sure we have caught everyone involved. I got word that they arrested someone in Yellowknife already, so it's a start."

"No, you've got that wrong," Ryan said. "I know the one they caught, and she's been set up."

"You know her?" William asked. "The nurse?"

Ryan nodded. "There is absolutely no way she is involved. She's been framed, and until we find out who did it, I'd say we better not trust anyone."

William rubbed his chin. "That does complicate things a bit."

"What do you mean?"

"Don't worry about it. Once we get to Yellowknife, I plan on telling local authorities that an international investigation is underway and that you're part of it. I just don't know who tipped off local police to make the initial arrest. If your nurse is innocent, then we still have no idea who's behind it, or why they would go to the trouble of implicating her."

"In other words, we have more questions than answers."

LOCAL AUTHORITIES WERE WAITING in Yellowknife as soon as the small private charter from Paragon landed. Two RCMP officers boarded the plane where it was parked on the tarmac, and Ryan was handcuffed. One of the officers recited his rights as he snapped the cuffs in place. Ryan glanced at William. He'd come on the flight along with two security officers.

"I'll be heading right to the station behind you, officers," William said. He looked at the security guards. "Accompanied by you two, of course."

Ryan recognized the one named Dean, a man in his forties, while the other one was the man who had caught him in the first place. He was younger and had an air of superiority about him, as if he had a chip on his shoulder or had something to prove. Sometimes 'rent a cops' had that attitude, he mused darkly. On impulse he twitched his shoulder, which still smarted from the tackle he'd taken, thanks to the younger man.

The ride in the police SUV from the airport to the police station afforded Ryan another view of the rugged scenery in the remote city with its jutting rocky outcrops, boulders erupting like dinosaurs from a prehistoric past. He wasn't accustomed to being on this side of the glass. Hopefully, William could get his position straightened out quickly with the authorities. One phone call to FBI headquarters in LA should do the trick.

One hour later, he was released from the interrogation room where he had been held when first arriving at the downtown police station. Officers had been civil, and for that he was grateful. He'd told them everything he knew, including his doubts about Anne-Marie's involvement. Now, he was meeting William in the main lobby.

"Not too worse for wear, I hope?" William asked as soon as Ryan came around the corner

Ryan's brows shot up when he saw who else was waiting for him. Dirk Hillyer. "I've been through worse," Ryan replied. His gaze went to Dirk. "You've met one another, I take it?"

"That we have. Your friend spins quite an interesting tale," William said.

His friend? Ryan grunted. Hardly, but then they'd been on the same side of things more than once. "I'll bet."

"He tells me you've worked together before."

Ryan's jaw twitched. "Can we talk here, or should we go elsewhere?"

"There's a restaurant just up the block," Dirk said. "If you think what I told you so far is interesting, just wait until you hear the rest."

Ryan zipped up his jacket and flipped up the attached hood. The temperatures felt milder than the last time he'd been in Yellowknife, but it was still definitely winter north of the 60th parallel.

They walked briskly without talking, making their way perpendicular from the station to a nearby cafe. The warmth of the interior enveloped them like a warm hug, and Ryan let his shoulders relax. He'd been hunkering down into his jacket subconsciously. Cold could do that. Make you tighten up without even realizing it.

The interior was rustic, with rough wood trim and plenty of northern artifacts on display. Once they were seated in a private booth, Ryan looked square at Dirk. "Start at the beginning."

Dirk clasped his hands on the table top. "We were at the ice festival, inside the castle listening to some music, when all of a sudden some police came up and started interrogating Anne-Marie. They searched her backpack and found a pouch that apparently contained stolen diamonds. We both got arrested. They haven't even let me see her, let alone talk to her. They finally let me go - which is another whole story - and that's when I called you."

"Any idea how the diamonds could have been planted?" Ryan asked.

"Who knows for sure, but I did see her hugging some guy just before we met up."

Ryan raised a brow. "Hugging some guy? Don't tell me you've lost your touch."

"Very funny. It's not like how you think. It seemed casual.

Maybe even awkward. She told me he was some executive from the mine."

"Richard Camry?" It was William's turn to look surprised. "They knew one another?"

"Apparently. I'm just telling you what I know," Dirk said.

Ryan turned to William. "What's your take on Camry? Could he pull something like this off?"

"He's a smart man, there's no doubt," William said. "But to admit that he has anything to do with it means I'm a very poor judge of character. I'd hate for that to be true."

"But you're not ruling it out?" Ryan asked.

"I suppose nothing can be ruled out at this juncture. I'm keeping an eye on both Dean and Wayne, my security men, although I'd almost guarantee it couldn't be them." He turned to Dirk. "What about your nurse? You're sure she's innocent?"

"I'd bet my life on it. There is absolutely no doubt in my mind," Dirk said.

"I'll vouch for her, as well," Ryan stated. "So, how did you get off so easily? I realize you didn't actually have the diamonds on you, but still, I'd assume they would at least keep you for questioning as an accomplice."

"I'm sure you'll find this part especially entertaining," Dirk replied, his tone sarcastic. "The interrogators wouldn't release me until I had…" He hesitated. "This is humiliating! They kept me until I went to the bathroom. You know. Number two? It got bagged and, not long afterward, I got released."

"That's disgusting." William shook his head.

"I'm thinking of filing a complaint. Maybe violation of my human rights."

"Interesting…" Ryan furrowed his brow.

"Oh, I knew you'd like that story," Dirk said with a self depre-cating laugh.

"It's interesting because Agent Leming said he heard talk amongst the workers about swallowing a condom filled with diamonds as a way to smuggle them off site. It could be how it's being done."

"This could be important. We need to find out who said it and alert the police right away," William said.

"Agreed." Ryan frowned. "It could explain how they're getting the diamonds off site, but it still doesn't tell us who our man is on the inside. Who's accessing the breech in the tubes I discovered earlier."

"You've lost me," Dirk said with a shrug.

"It's need to know," Ryan replied, giving Dirk a a pointed look.

"Of course," Dirk said. "What *I* need to know is, how are you going to get Anne-Marie off the hook? She absolutely did not have anything to do with stealing those gems, and I'm going crazy thinking about what she must be going through right now."

"I'll get my team of lawyers on it," William said. "I'm sure we'll be able to come up with something. Bail, if nothing else."

"We know she couldn't have had them in her possession when she left camp because of the screening, so it had to happen in Yellowknife, and Camry is our only lead. We still have no motive for Camry to plant the diamonds on Anne-Marie, though, if he is the one who did it. Why not just take then safely with him, since they were already off site?" Ryan rubbed his chin in thought. "We are definitely missing something important here."

CHAPTER 27

*A*nne-Marie raised her head as a key rattled in the lock. She swung her legs to the side of the narrow bed and fully sat up. The cell wasn't like the ones in the movies - or like the one she'd had to endure in Mexico, for that matter, with an entire wall of bars. It was a plain white room with a plain white door. She was still at the RCMP detachment because there was nowhere else for women awaiting trial to go in the territory. The door opened to reveal a female officer.

"Let's go."

Anne-Marie slowly stood. "Where are you taking me?"

"You're being released," the woman said curtly.

Anne-Marie's eyes widened. "Oh!" It wasn't what she 'd expected, but she would definitely take it. "Thank you, Jesus!" she breathed.

"If you think so," the officer said. "Now, let's get a move on." She waved her arm as if to shoo Anne-Marie along.

"My things? Will I get them back?" Anne-Marie asked as she passed through the doorway.

"All in due course."

They made their way down the cream colored cinderblock

corridor lined with similar doors. Anne-Marie wondered how many other women were waiting behind them. Women without hope, feeling desperate and alone like she had been just minutes before.

At a counter, she signed for her belongings and then was directed to a washroom where she could change. A nice hot shower and maybe a different outfit would have been nice, but she certainly wasn't going to complain.

Once changed, the officer escorted her all the way to the main foyer. Her eyes widened when she rounded the corner. There were several people waiting there, but she only had eyes for one.

With a cry of relief, she bolted for Dirk's waiting arms. The moment she saw him, the dam of courage she had constructed was breeched, and she sobbed into his coat like a baby.

"It's okay. You're safe now," he soothed, rubbing her hair.

When she finally pulled back, she registered who else was present. Ryan O'Toole and another older man she didn't recognize. "Ryan! Are you the one I have to thank for my release?"

"Actually, you can thank Mr. Herschel." Ryan gestured to the older man. "He's the one with the real clout."

Anne-Marie reached to shake Mr. Herschel's hand. "*The* Mr. Herschel, as in the CEO of Paragon?"

"You can call me William," he said.

"Thank you so much," she said. "I had no idea what was happening. Did you find the person who planted the diamonds on me?"

"You mean the fake diamonds," William clarified.

"What?" Anne-Marie looked from one man to another.

Dirk put his arm around her. "Come on. I think we should get out of here first before we go into the details."

"He's right," William agreed. "Your agent friend and I have a few more things to look into while the timing is right, but then we should all meet for dinner at the hotel. What do you say?"

Anne-Marie nodded. "Sure." A hot bath and change of clothes sounded like heaven right about now.

ANNE-MARIE WAS reluctant to get out of the tub, but she knew Dirk would be waiting to escort her downstairs to the hotel dining room. They'd shared a cab to the hotel, sneaking a few kisses on the short drive. Then he'd escorted her to her room, and several more lingering kisses later, she'd gone in to freshen up. All of her belongings were there, transferred from her previous, less expensive suite when she'd first landed for the festival. Trust Dirk to insist on the best. He was who he was, and she loved him - despite it or because of it. Sometimes a bit of both.

She took some time to look out the window once she was ready. The view was lovely, facing the downtown park than bordered Frame Lake, a smaller fresh water body in the heart of downtown. The other side of the hotel overlooked Great Slave Lake, which was the largest lake in North America next to the Great Lakes themselves, and where the ice castle stood. A knock sounded on her door, and with one final glance, she turned away.

It would be Dirk coming to pick her up. She grabbed a sweater, just in case it was cold in the dining room, and strode to the door. The moment she opened it, her heart did a little flip. He was so handsome! How did she deserve such a man?

She gave her head a shake. She would not allow herself to go down the route of insecurities again. That was a bridge she definitely wanted to burn.

"Hi beautiful," Dirk said and gave her a quick kiss.

"Hi yourself," she said and tucked her arm into the crook of his as they headed toward the elevator.

There was a huge polar bear standing on its hind legs in the lobby, obviously a photo-op for tourists. She hadn't noticed it earlier, she was so exhausted and intent on soaking in the tub.

"Want a picture?" Dirk asked.

"Maybe later. We shouldn't keep the others waiting."

The dining room was warm with a large stone fireplace in the center. Expansive windows along one entire wall brought the outdoors in with its view of towering evergreens, rocks, and of course, snow. William and Ryan were already waiting at a table along with another young man who looked familiar. Oh yes! She'd treated him on his first day on the job.

"Hello there," she greeted.

"Anne-Marie, Dirk, this is Jeremy Leming," Ryan introduced.

"We've met," Anne-Marie said. "And I know his grandmother." She smiled at the young man.

"Right." Ryan straightened his mouth into a line.

"Something I should know about?" Dirk asked as he held out Anne-Marie's chair.

"Only rookie agents who can't keep their cover intact," Ryan quipped.

"Let's order first and then we'll get down to business," William suggested.

There were many local and northern delicacies on the menu such as wood bison, moose, and white fish from Great Slave Lake. Once they had ordered, William began the story.

"The diamonds were actually fakes," he said, "which is why you were released so quickly once the analysis had been done."

"Fakes! Then why plant them on me in the first place?" Anne-Marie looked from one face to another. "And then call the cops to boot, I presume. Thanks a lot!"

"We think it was a decoy, allowing Camry to get a head start with the real diamonds," Ryan said.

"So, you *do* think it was Camry who planted the diamonds?" Anne-Marie asked.

"Fake diamonds," William clarified.

"He seems to be our best suspect, especially since he lied

about his whereabouts to Mr. Herschel this past week and now seems to have flown the coop," Ryan supplied.

"What do you mean by that?" Dirk asked.

"He took a flight directly from Edmonton to Cuba, where he apparently met his wife. From there they could be anywhere. On a boat, private plane... Who knows?" Ryan took a sip of his water.

"With my diamonds," William said.

"So, he got away." Anne-Marie couldn't believe how disappointed she felt about that. She sat back in her chair.

"Don't worry, my dear," William said. "He can't hide forever. He'll surface eventually."

"And when he does, we'll be ready," Ryan finished.

"Who was working with him? Any idea about that?" Anne-Marie asked.

Jeremy spoke this time. "So far we just have one of the haul truck drivers. He seemed happy to finally come clean, I think. He'd been the mule, so to speak, who carried the goods out of camp."

Dirk smiled at Anne-Marie. "Swallowed condoms full of diamonds. That must hurt on the way out."

"Seriously?" Anne-Marie looked from Dirk to Jeremy for confirmation.

"That's what he said," Jeremy affirmed with a shrug.

"If there are others on the inside, we'll find them," William said. "I've got a whole team flying in to comb over the security footage. Not to mention, the RCMP are putting every single employee under close scrutiny. Even security."

"Do an extra good job on Wayne, would ya?" Ryan asked.

"It looks like Camry was the brains, though, and by the look of it, he left the rest of them high and dry." William shook his head. "I hate to admit that I trusted him so implicitly."

"So, what does this mean for you two?" Anne-Marie looked from Ryan to Jeremy.

"Our job is done here," Ryan said. "So, it's home sweet home. Hey partner?" He gave Jeremy's shoulder a gentle punch.

Jeremy smiled, but his eyes weren't in it.

"You both did good work," William said. "If you get tired of working for the feds, I might have a job for you." His eyes swept the table. "All of you."

"Thanks, but no thanks," Ryan said.

Anne-Marie couldn't agree more.

~

"I CAN'T BELIEVE what just happened, actually happened," Anne-Marie said as she and Dirk walked from the elevator to her room. "I mean, I like adventure, but I think I've had enough of the kind involving smuggling and police for a lifetime."

"You and me, both," Dirk agreed.

They stopped at her door and stood for a moment, just looking at each other.

"And tomorrow?" Dirk asked.

"I need to go back to Edmonton to see my parents, I think. I left abruptly and not on the best terms, so I need to smooth things over with them."

"And then?" Dirk asked.

"Well… I know this really great guy who lives in Boston. I was thinking of taking a trip to see where he grew up. Maybe get to know him a bit better."

"Now that sounds like the best idea I've heard in a long time!"

With that he swept her off her feet and kissed her hard on the mouth. She was breathless when he let her down, but happy.

"I love you, do you know that?" he asked.

She nodded. "Yes, you do, don't you? And I love you, too."

CHAPTER 28

*T*empest waved to Geoff as he strode toward the park bench. She stood and led the dogs to meet Geoff halfway on the grassy open section. "Thanks for meeting me here. You didn't have to. I know there are plenty of places to take them near your - I mean 'our' - house, but they like it here. It just feels familiar."

"After what Frank said, I don't feel comfortable letting you walk alone," Geoff responded. "Especially in the evenings." Geoff took Paddy's leash and they started walking toward the street.

"I know." Tempest switched Jupiter's leash to the other hand so that there was more distance between him and Geoff. They still weren't comfortable with one another. "To be honest, I wanted to walk by Frank's house just to make sure everything is okay. I feel partly responsible for putting him and Edna in danger."

"You shouldn't. Frank made his own choices. Choices that had an impact on more than just him."

Tempest glanced at Geoff. She knew he meant his own father and potentially even himself.

They continued down the street and came to the area where

the trees and shrubbery impeded the sidewalk. Tempest let Jupiter take the lead on the sidewalk, while Geoff and Paddy hung back. The house behind the tall hedge was almost not visible due to the overgrowth. "I often wonder why the city hasn't done something about this yard," she said. Geoff didn't respond, but Paddy let out a sharp series of barks. She turned to see what was happening.

Suddenly, a hand clamped over her mouth, and she was jerked into the hedge. She tried to cry out, but the glove over her face was covering both her mouth and nose, and she could hardly breathe, let alone respond to the pricks and scratches jabbing into her flesh from the bush. She heard Jupiter let loose with a volley of menacing growls followed by a man swearing, some scuffling, and a yelp. She jerked side to side to try to get away, but her arm was only forced further behind her back, and she cried out silently into the glove.

"That's enough out of you," a man said into her ear and gave one last jerk for good measure.

She was dragged up several wooden steps and shoved into the semi-darkness of the abandoned house. The smell was musty, and dust particles floated past the shards of light that were trying desperately to infiltrate the boarded up windows.

"One noise and I'll blow your boyfriend's brains out," the man said. He slowly removed his glove from her face, and Tempest gulped in the stale air.

"Who are you? What do you want?"

"No talking!" the man hissed. She still hadn't seen his face, but she did make out Geoff and another figure in the dimness. The other man was wearing non-descript clothing and a ski-mask over his face. He held Geoff in an arm lock.

"Okay, okay!" Tempest said quickly. So far, she hadn't actually seen a gun, but she wasn't about to test the theory.

"Now, move toward the basement stairs."

She did as she was told. With hands in the air, she walked

forward and then bent to navigate the narrow steps into the even danker basement. She coughed, her throat suddenly constricting with mildew. The basement had obviously gotten damp over the years, and the smell was almost overpowering.

"On the floor." Tempest toppled to the floor as she was shoved from behind. Geoff landed in a similar heap beside her. "Up against the wall." She scooted on hands and knees to the outer perimeter and turned to lean her back against the cement bricks of the basement wall. She could see her abductor now. He looked very similar to the other man, since both had their faces covered, and he was definitely holding a gun. The cold from the wall filtered through her thin jacket, and she shivered.

Geoff's abductor bound their hands and feet and then he secured gags around their faces while the other kept his gun trained on them. "That should do it," he said and stood upright. "I'll take the first watch down here."

"No way," the one wielding the gun said. "That big dog got away, and you know what the boss said. We either capture the dogs and muzzle 'em, or kill 'em."

Tempest gasped.

The man who'd manhandled her looked at her. "That's right. The little mutt is upstairs. He bit me, too, and if he causes anymore trouble, I'll gladly put him down." He was clearly the one in charge. He turned to the other. "You need to get out there and look for the big dog. He could lead someone straight here."

Tempest smiled inwardly. Way to go Paddy and Jupiter!

Tempest's abductor tromped up the steps without further discussion.

"You might as well get comfortable," the one left behind said. He dragged a rickety chair a few feet away and sat down.

Tempest glanced over at Geoff. He looked about as comfortable - and as frightened - as she felt. She stared at him until he acknowledged her, trying to communicate somehow that it was going to be alright. How, she wasn't sure, but it was important for them both to believe it.

~

TEMPEST WASN'T sure how much time passed. Maybe an hour. It had become fully dark now. She heard a door scrape open upstairs. Probably the other culprit. She felt her heart beat quicken. What if he'd found Jupiter? What if he hadn't…

"Stay put," their guard said as he stood up. "And don't go anywhere." He laughed, then took the steps two at a time.

Geoff made a muffled sound, and Tempest looked over. He motioned with his head to a pipe sticking out from the wall, the leftovers from some plumbing. He bumped on his behind over to the pipes and maneuvered his face until he was able to slip the pipe up under the cloth gag, grunting with pain as he scraped his face. Somehow, he managed to get the gag loose. He took a couple of deep breaths.

"You want to try it?" he whispered.

Tempest shrugged.

"Unless…" Geoff bumped his way closer to Tempest. "Just hold still." He leaned in, his face hovering close to hers. Tempest jerked back, alarmed. "Don't worry," he whispered. "I'm not trying to kiss you. Just trust me."

Tempest steeled herself and waited as Geoff got close again. He grasped her gag with his teeth and then pulled. Tempest held her breath. It was too intimate - almost like a kiss, but without any of the pleasure.

Suddenly the gag slipped, and she sucked in a breath. "Thank you," she managed.

"Welcome."

"What if he comes back?"

"Just lower your chin, like this." Geoff demonstrated by ducking into his gag. "It's dark, and hopefully they won't notice."

"I wonder if he found Jupiter. I wonder…" Tempest choked on the words. She couldn't voice the possibility.

"Jupiter is a smart dog. He'll be fine," Geoff said.

"I hope so." She'd lost her cat Zoe in terrible circumstances. She couldn't think about losing Paddy and Jupiter, too.

"What do you suppose they want? Do you think this is related to Frank's involvement?"

Tempest nodded her head. "I imagine so."

"What should we do? Try to escape?"

"I don't want to be negative, but how would we do that? There aren't any windows, and we'd have to get past those guys upstairs. They have a gun." Tempest looked at Geoff. "There's not much we can do but pray."

CHAPTER 29

"Thank you." Ryan retrieved his credit card from the woman at the hotel's front desk. He stuffed it into his wallet and turned to Jeremy. "You did good work. I had my doubts at first, but you turned out to be a good partner."

"Thanks." Jeremy hefted his duffel bag a bit more securely onto his shoulder. "I've been thinking. There's something I need to tell you." He gestured with his head for Ryan to follow him a few yards away to some couches.

Ryan rolled his own bags behind him and parked them beside the couch. "What's up?"

Jeremy put his hands in his pockets. "I'm not coming with you back to LA."

Ryan's eyebrows rose. "Your uncle isn't going to like that. What's going on?"

"I'm staying on for a bit. Since I'm so close to my grand-mother, I thought it was a good opportunity to connect with my roots, you know?"

"I thought you looked a bit glum about going home when I mentioned it last night. Have you cleared it with your uncle Reynolds?"

Jeremy just shrugged. "I will, soon enough. I just thought I'd tell you before we got to the airport. I'm heading a different direction once we get there."

"Well, I hope it goes well for you. I'll deal with Reynolds for you, I guess."

"Um… there's actually something else. Something I want to come clean about before you go," Jeremy said.

Ryan furrowed his brow. "Okay…"

"Let me start off by saying, I love my uncle and would do anything for him, so you have to understand that from the outset."

"My, my. This is getting more dramatic by the second."

Jeremy opened his mouth to speak, sighed, and shut it again.

"I take it what you have to say isn't very pleasant," Ryan offered.

Jeremy squared his shoulders and tried again. "He put me on this case because I've been to the area and I'd blend in, not just because I'm his nephew. You have to believe that."

"I know, and I believe it now that I've seen you in action. So?"

"But there was another reason." Jeremy held Ryan's gaze for a moment.

"Another reason," Ryan repeated.

Jeremy sighed again. "I don't know how to put this delicately. My uncle thinks you might be dirty. He says the inconsistencies in recent cases have your finger prints on them."

Ryan felt his insides beginning to boil. "I know there are inconsistencies. I've been trying to root out the cause myself. And he sent you along to keep tabs?"

Jeremy nodded. "He thought this case might be a temptation to someone like you. A carrot. A way to set you up; to show your true colors since so much money was at stake. I must say that when you first got arrested, I thought he was right."

"But now?"

"I just can't believe it's true. My uncle would call that weakness, but I don't care. I believe you're as honest as they come, and I'm sorry. I wanted to come clean before you head back to LA."

"And I suppose you've been in communication with him behind my back this entire time?" Ryan asked.

Jeremy nodded again. "He knows my true feelings now, though. I just didn't tell him I was going to tell you."

Ryan stared out the large hotel windows to the swirling snow beyond. "He and I have never quite clicked. I don't know what it is about him, but…" He looked away. "Oh well. I guess you can't get along with everybody all of the time."

Jeremy cleared his throat. "I think he may have an issue with your friend, Andy Coates, too." He held up his hands. "I really shouldn't be saying all this, but there's just something not right, and I feel as if I need to warn you in advance. Not saying that my uncle is dirty or anything. Just that he didn't get to the top by being friends with everyone."

So, Reynolds wasn't above using his own nephew to get what he wanted. Maybe Ryan's sights needed to be trained in another direction once he got home.

"Thanks. I appreciate the heads up. And thanks for being honest." Ryan held out his hand.

Jeremy looked down at the proffered hand and then up again. "You're not angry? I know I would be."

"There's no point. I wish you all the best. In some ways I envy you that you aren't going back to LA. You sure you're not just trying to get out of meeting your uncle?"

"Maybe just a bit." Jeremy grinned and shook on it.

Ryan's telephone beeped, and he glanced at the caller. Andy. "Hey, can you hold our cab?" he said to Jeremy.

"Sure."

Ryan watched the young agent stride out the doors to the cab that had just pulled up. Jeremy walked with a confident stride, and Ryan really did wish him all the best. One couldn't help one's relatives.

He swiped the cell to answer the call from Andy and held it to his ear. "Hey, man. I'm just leaving Yellowknife. Should be back in LA sometime in the wee hours. What's up?"

"You're not going to like this," Andy said.

"I already don't."

"I went by Frank's house earlier this evening. I came across Jupiter, wandering alone. He was still wearing his leash."

Instant alarm bells rang in Ryan's brain. "Where was Tempest?"

"I don't know. That's the point. I'm going to go to Frank's directly. See if I can get some answers."

"Be careful. I don't like the sounds of this."

"You and me both."

Ryan hung up and strode through the doors to the waiting cab. One crisis averted, another on the horizon.

CHAPTER 30

Tempest's head lolled to the side and she jerked it up again. Pain shot clear from her neck down her spine into her buttocks and legs. She had dozed off more than once, but her body had been stuck in the sitting position on the cold cement floor for too long. One or the other of their captors had come down to check periodically, but they hadn't looked too closely.

"You awake?" Geoff asked quietly.

"Mmhm."

"I was thinking. If I die, I want you to know something. The truth, I mean."

Tempest glanced over to where Geoff's voice was. She couldn't see him very well, just his outline in the darkness. "Don't be silly. We're not going to die."

"Well, just in case."

"Okay..." Tempest shifted again. There was no way to get comfortable, but the restlessness she felt couldn't be contained.

"My mom. She has reasons for wanting me to find a girlfriend."

"Most mom's do."

"No, I mean reasons beyond the…norm." He hesitated. "It's been hard for her having a son like me."

"We all have baggage."

"Not my kind of baggage." Geoff sighed. "You don't know what it's like."

"Then tell me."

"You might not want to be friends anymore once I do."

"I doubt that."

"I think I'm gay." Geoff sighed. "There, I said it."

Tempest stilled. Whatever she was expecting, it wasn't this.

"I know what you're thinking. How can I be a Christian and still be gay?"

"I wasn't thinking that."

"I mean, I've never acted on it, but I have these… these feelings, sometimes. And don't think I haven't tried to suppress it. To control it. I've prayed and prayed and prayed. There's no hope for me. I guess I'm doomed to burn."

"Don't say that!" Tempest hissed, cognizant of the fact that they still needed to be quiet. "Don't you remember what Randall said? Having certain feelings and acting on them are two different things."

"I know, but for how long? It would make my mother very happy if I was suddenly 'cured'. Had a sudden and miraculous change of feelings. But so far that hasn't happened. And what's the alternative? Celibacy?"

"Maybe God wants you to focus on other parts of your life right now. Maybe this is a test of how much you love Him. Life doesn't have to revolve around sex, you know."

"Says the straight girl," Geoff said with a cryptic laugh.

"I'm sorry. That was insensitive. You're right, I don't know what it's like, and I cannot pretend to. But I do know there are plenty of single Christians out there. People who are remaining celibate, as you say."

"I suppose. It seems like a bleak future, though."

"All I know is, God doesn't make mistakes. I'm not saying He made you the way you are, but I believe He has a plan and a future for you. With time and prayer, He'll show you the way."

"If we make it through this," Geoff said.

"Should we pray?" Tempest asked. She'd been praying silently most of the night, but perhaps verbalizing it would help.

"If you want. I don't think I have any words right now," Geoff said.

Tempest took a steadying breath. "Lord, you made us, and you have a plan for our lives. You know the trouble we're in, and we pray for a miracle, God. Help us. Send someone to rescue us!" She didn't know what else to say, so she ended with, "In Jesus name, Amen."

"Thanks. You know, sometimes I find it hard to see God as a loving father. My own father abandoned me and then, well…"

"Yes?"

"Never mind."

"What is it? You can tell me, Geoff. Whatever it is."

"It's too hard."

"Is it about your stepfather?" She wasn't sure why she knew to ask that, but for some reason, she did.

"He said he was a Christian," Geoff said, his voice still and quiet. "At times I believed him. Then at other times, I can't believe that the spirit of Christ could live in that… that kind of person."

"What did he do?"

"No, I don't think I can."

"Oh." A coldness swept over Tempest's body and it wasn't just from the cement. "Did he… abuse you?" she asked quietly.

"Yes." The one word came out small and scared, like a little child.

"Oh, Geoff, I am so sorry."

"It didn't happen that often, and he mostly just had me touch him."

"That's sexual abuse, Geoff! There is no 'just' about it."

"He said he was teaching me how to be a man." He let out a strangled laugh. "I guess that didn't work out so well."

"Did you tell someone? Your mom?"

"I couldn't. I was so ashamed. And I certainly couldn't tell my real father." He sighed. "I think she knows, though. I think in her mind, if I just got a girlfriend it would reverse whatever effects it had on me. Maybe she's right."

"I'm glad you told me," Tempest said. "And for the record, if I wasn't already in love with someone else, maybe I'd be interested."

"You're just saying that."

Maybe, but the fact that she'd just admitted she was still in love with Ryan was a breakthrough, even if it brought little comfort.

A crashing sound upstairs jolted her back to reality. It sounded like some kind of scuffle and then it settled down again.

"We'd better stop talking now," Tempest whispered.

Geoff nodded, and they both ducked their chins into their gags as best they could. A minute or two later, one of the men thumped down the steps. Tempest tensed her body when she could feel his presence.

A flashlight glared into her eyes, and she squinted, keeping her chin low. There was a moment of scrutiny, then the beam swung back to the stairs. "They're fine," he called as he headed back up.

Tempest relaxed against Geoff. She felt a sob growing in her throat, and she tried to tamp it down. *Oh, Lord. If ever I needed you, it's now!*

Tempest heard a noise and roused herself groggily from sleep. At some point in the night, she had leaned her head against Geoff's shoulder. His revelations clicked with so many signs she had noticed, but could never put her finger on. She was not repulsed or judgmental, either. She did not know all the answers, but for now, it was enough that she felt compassion and a deeper connection with him than she had felt before. He would always be her friend.

Her neck had a terrible kink, and she tried rotating it to alleviate some of the discomfort. Dawn was breaking, and she blinked to adjust her vision in the dimness.

"Well, isn't this touching."

Tempest's gaze darted to the stairs and she grimaced at the pain it caused. Then she sat upright when she saw who it was. "Assistant Director Reynolds! Thank goodness! I knew someone would rescue us."

Reynolds was lounging against a post at the bottom of the stairs, arms folded across his chest. He pushed off from the post with his shoulder and came to stand directly in front of her. "I see they didn't do a very good job of gagging you." He shook his head.

Tempest blinked, her mind trying to make sense of what he'd just said. "Um... can you untie us now, please? I really have to pee."

"They didn't even afford you the decency of a washroom break?" He clucked his tongue. "It's so hard to find good help these days."

Cold fear crept into her stomach and the need to relieve herself vanished along with her relief at being rescued. "You're not here to rescue us, are you?" she stated quietly.

"Smart. Frank Dunlop knew what he was doing when he took you under his wing. Unfortunately for you, a little too smart for your own good."

"You're the one paying for Frank's son's medical expenses," Tempest said slowly as the truth dawned. "So, that means you had something to do with covering up the circumstances around my parents' deaths, too. But why?"

"Too many questions." Reynolds looked at his watch. "I want to know what's taking O'Toole so long. He should be back in LA by now."

Ryan! Her heart leapt into her throat. "What makes you think he'll come looking for us?"

Reynolds shook his head. "I know everything. Don't think I didn't know his buddy Andy Coates was snooping around and then telling him everything. He's upstairs, by the way. I haven't quite figured how I'm going to eliminate him, but… accidents do happen." Reynolds began to saunter back and forth in the small space in front of them.

Tempest's eyes widened. "You're going to kill him?"

Reynolds laughed unpleasantly. "The hazards of getting too cocky."

"What about us?" Geoff shifted his position.

Reynolds glanced their way as he walked. "I hear you're both religious, so there shouldn't be a problem. I'm just helping you meet your Lord and Savior a bit early."

Geoff let out a small gasp.

"Poor Geoff has nothing to do with any of this. You wouldn't kill an innocent man?"

"He should have steered clear from the beginning. The moment he started playing detective with you, he lost his innocence."

"But what is the purpose of all this? I don't understand! Surely, if you're going to kill us anyway, we deserve an explanation. You owe us that much."

"I don't owe you anything," Reynolds replied. He stopped and perused them with an icy stare. "But what the heck? You'll be taking it to your graves, anyway. When O'Toole shows up playing the knight in shining armor, he'll end up taking a bullet. Of course, I'll make it look like he was the jealous boyfriend, and I showed up to stop him from doing something stupid - too late, of course."

"But why? What has he ever done to you? He's a good agent! Honest and hardworking!"

"Too honest and too hardworking for his own good. Your Ryan O'Toole has been acting the hero for too long in this agency. Sticking his nose where it doesn't belong. I hoped to get rid of him up north, implicate him in a diamond smuggling ring and put him away, but that didn't pan out quite the way I'd hoped. So, this is my next best option. He knows too much and needs to be eliminated."

"Knows too much about what? You've been dirty for years, haven't you? Even as far back as when my parents were killed."

Reynolds shook his head. "You're just like your old man, you know?"

"You knew him?"

"Of course I knew him. He was a fine reporter, but like you, he didn't know when to quit. He figured out I was syphoning evidence and was going to go public. What was I supposed to do?"

"You mean you were behind...?" Tempest felt the room spin. She thought she might be sick. "But how?"

"It seems ridiculous to see all that cash and product go to waste, just sitting there for years or even decades, when it's perfectly useful."

"You were taking drugs and money that was supposed to be kept in evidence and making a profit on the side." Tempest shook her head. "Of course."

"You make it sound worse than it is," Reynolds said.

"But my parents? How did you manage to arrange a car accident?"

"That was real. I had someone in the car waiting for them when they came out of the concert, or wherever they went that night. I can't quite recall. Anyway, your dad tried to get the gun, and that's when he swerved into oncoming traffic."

"My father," Geoff supplied.

"Poor stooge. I couldn't have arranged for anything so perfect!" Reynolds gave a snide chuckle.

"So, the person witnesses saw running away was your gunman."

"Now, that took some doing, to get Frank onboard. His son had just tried to commit suicide, and they had doctor bills coming out the yin-yang. Poor bugger would have done anything at the time to try to save his boy. Too bad it hasn't worked out…"

"And you've been using him ever since."

"It's a good arrangement. Don't think Frank hasn't benefited. He's in so deep now, he couldn't get out if he wanted to."

"Dirty bastard."

Reynolds looked at Geoff. "Tut, tut. Such words coming out of the mouth of a fine young Christian man as yourself."

"You ruined my life. If it wasn't for you, my father might not have gone to jail. My parents might not have gotten a divorce. My stepfather…" His voice cracked and he stopped.

Reynolds held up a hand. "Enough of this chit-chat. Your man better show up soon, or I'll be forced to go to Plan C."

"What would that be?" Tempest asked.

"I can't reveal all my secrets." Reynolds stood for a moment surveying his captives. "I suppose I better fix those gags. As much as I'd like for O'Toole to hear you scream, I don't want the whole neighborhood hearing it, too."

"Wait -" Tempest's words were cut short as Reynolds retied her gag, this time with no chance of letting it slip. He did the same to Geoff, took one final look as he stepped back, and then headed up the rickety stairs.

Tempest closed her eyes. She'd been praying for rescue and imagining that Ryan would be the one to swoop in like a super-hero. Now she prayed that he would stay away.

CHAPTER 31

*T*he moment the airplane touched down, Ryan switched his cellphone off flight mode and checked for any messages from Andy. There were two texts, the most recent almost three hours old. Andy said he was going to check on something suspicious at a vacant house near Frank's place. Then nothing. Ryan had expected that Andy would be there to pick him up at the airport, too, but there was no sign of him, and he wasn't answering his phone.

Something was definitely not right. As soon as Ryan got his luggage, he hailed a cab. Going to his place and getting his own wheels was the sensible thing to do, but something inside told him he needed to hurry. At least he had the firearm that had been in his checked luggage.

The taxi pulled up across the street from the vacant house in question. Trees and bushes had overgrown the property for some time, creating a visual barrier that shielded the house. "Wait here," Ryan instructed as he got out of the vehicle. He shoved a large amount of money toward the driver, but took note of the cab number in case things went south and the driver bolted with the luggage still inside the trunk of the vehicle.

With calculated steps, he approached the yard and then ducked past the hedge. Most of the windows were boarded up, and the weeds all but masked the sidewalk that led to the front door. Hunching low, he scurried to the side of the house and then plastered his back against the rough siding. One foot over another, he sidestepped into position until he got to the slanted wooden steps at the foot of the entrance and then proceeded to advance upwards. One of the boards creaked. He halted, waiting and listening.

He reached out to grasp the doorknob. It was unlocked, and he gave a slight push. The door swung open with a groan. Stepping gingerly inside, he gave his eyes a moment to adjust to the dim light, sweeping the room for signs of life. A sudden muffled yell had him swiveling left toward the sound.

"Andy!"

His friend and partner was gagged, his clothes disheveled. He sported a blackened eye, and blood trailed from his nose into the gag across his mouth. A goon wearing a ski mask was holding him upright. Before Ryan could respond further, he heard another sound. A gun being cocked to his right.

"Took you long enough."

Ryan recognized the voice instantly. Assistant Director Reynolds. Without moving his body, he shifted his gaze right and saw the older agent with a gun pointed directly at him. "Reynolds. You're not here as part of the rescue party, I take it?"

"I hoped your friend would lead you here, but unfortunately, he was stupid enough to try and be the hero before you arrived. Another casualty in your jealous rampage."

"What are you talking about?" Ryan's gaze darted about, but he didn't see anyone else.

"Drop your gun, and I'll tell you all about it," Reynolds said.

Andy made another frantic protest, but got another blow for his efforts.

"On the floor with it, and then kick it to me," Reynolds

instructed. "That's nice," he said when Ryan complied. Reynolds picked up the gun with his gloved hand. "Now walk straight ahead and down those stairs. Nice and slow, or I shoot your friend."

Ryan led the way down the narrow steps into the semi-darkness of the old basement. All the windows had been boarded up, and very little light filtered through the cracks in the sheeting. Still, the moment his line of vision came into contact with the lower level, he recognized Tempest, her legs curled under her as she sat on the cold floor against the far wall. "Tempest!"

"Not so fast," Reynolds warned.

Ryan stopped his advancement. He heard Andy's grunt of pain behind him as he was pushed down the last few steps. Another goon sat on a nearby chair with a gun resting in his lap.

Ryan watched as Andy was pushed toward the two prisoners huddled on the floor. Tempest and her new boyfriend, Geoff. Jealousy jumped forward, but he quickly tamped it down. This was life and death, and his training needed to take over. He couldn't let his personal feelings get in the way of their safety. "Are you hurt?" Ryan asked, looking directly at Tempest. She could only shake her head, since she and Geoff were gagged.

"I ask the questions around here," Reynolds said. He gestured to the goon holding onto Andy. "On the floor. Against the wall with the others," he instructed.

The man shoved Andy forward against the wall, and he stumbled, hitting himself on the cement as he tumbled into a heap.

"Now, which one do you want to shoot first?" Reynolds asked.

"You talking to me?"

"Who else?"

Ryan let out an unpleasant laugh. "I'm not shooting anyone. You can't force me to do such a thing."

"Of course not, but *I* have your gun." Reynolds held up Ryan's handgun. "With your finger prints all over it."

"You'll never get away with this," Ryan said between clenched teeth.

"Of course I will. You got a tip from your friend about your ex's little after hours rendezvous with another man in this abandoned house. I also got the tip from Andy, because he was worried about your mental stability. Once I shoot them with your gun, I'll use my own weapon to shoot you. It'll be self-defense - the only way to stop you after your jealous rampage. Unfortunately, Andy got caught in the crossfire." He turned to the other two men. "And I'll have witnesses to back up my story."

Ryan stared at the men in ski-masks. "You're agents?"

"Regular police. You didn't think I was working solo, did you?" Reynolds laughed. "You'd be surprised at the number of dirty cops in this city."

"But you're the mastermind." Ryan snorted and shook his head. "I should have seen it."

"You should have been more careful, but you let your personal interest in Frank Dunlop's protege get the better of you. Now, let's see... the boyfriend first? It probably fits the timeline best, although the girl would also be a good option. I'll leave Coates till last. Use another gun to make it seem more plausible, as if he just got caught in the crossfire."

Ryan glanced at Reynolds. The Assistant Director had Ryan's own revolver trained on Geoff. The two goons behind were wielding their own guns at Ryan. The chance of someone getting hit with a stray bullet was high, but he couldn't just let Reynolds kill three innocent people without some kind of fight. He couldn't let him kill Tempest. All of this flashed through his mind in a milli-second.

He took a sudden gulp of air and simultaneously threw his body against Reynolds. The crack of a gunshot split the air, but Ryan didn't stop to analyze it as they toppled to the floor, and he wrestled with Reynolds on the cold cement.

Another gunshot echoed in the tiny space. More scuffling and the oomph of bodies crashing and thrashing registered in the far recesses of Ryan's mind, but his own faculties were needed as he and Reynolds vied for dominance. Reynolds was still fit and tough as nails, despite the fact that he was a decade or so older. Suddenly, Reynolds flipped and grabbed Ryan around the throat in a choke hold. The room began to spin as the dim shades of grey faded to black.

Another shot rang out followed by a voice yelling over the reverberation. "Reynolds! It's over!"

Ryan felt the pressure on his neck relax, and he coughed, gasping for air as he flung himself away from his captor.

He shook his head as he sat up to survey the damage, clutching his throat with one hand. One of the masked thugs had removed his mask and had his weapon trained on Reynolds, who was still prone on his back. His dark completion was difficult to see in the dim interior. The other thug was writhing on the floor. Blood seeped from a wound in his lower body, probably his leg. Andy crouched nearby with Ryan's own weapon pointed at the immobilized hoodlum.

"What just happened?" Ryan asked.

"First things first," the captor turned savior said. "Let's cuff these two and then free the others." He reached inside his jacket with his free hand and pulled out some handcuffs. Then he gestured with his head at Reynolds. "Him first. I don't trust him as far as I can throw him."

"Agreed." Ryan caught the cuffs and none too gently hand-cuffed Reynold's hands behind his back. "I take it you're undercover?"

"Eugene Gear, LAPD," the big black man said. He looked at the other thug. "Homer should have his own pair on him somewhere."

Andy patted Homer, the other assailant, until he found the cuffs, and then proceeded to handcuff him as well.

"Go easy!" Homer cried out.

"You should have thought of that earlier," Andy quipped.

Ryan moved to where Tempest and Geoff sat wide eyed. "You're safe now," he said gently to Tempest. He took in the tears that glistened as he removed the gag and wanted nothing more than to take her in his arms right then and there, despite the fact that her new boyfriend sat inches away.

"You came," was all she said when her voice was released.

He searched her eyes, his own wanting to mist over with relief until he straightened his spine. "Of course I came," he said gruffly. He turned his attention to Geoff and removed his gag as well, although perhaps with less care than he had done for Tempest. Next, he freed their hands and unbound their ankles.

"Back-up is on its way," Officer Gear said. "Is everyone okay?"

"I really have to pee," Tempest said with a nervous laugh.

Ryan helped her to her feet. She seemed unsteady, undoubtedly from being in such a cramped position for so long. "Do you need help up the stairs?" he asked.

"I'll go," Geoff piped up.

Ryan's jaw tightened as he watched the two of them shuffle toward the steps.

"Don't go far," Gear called.

"If you were undercover all this time, you could have gone easy on me, Gear." Andy laughed then winced. He was still sitting on the floor near the other abductor.

"Sorry. Had to make it look real," Gear replied. "You, on the other hand are one crazy son-of-a… The way you threw yourself at Homer, we all could have been killed. It's a good thing you didn't disable me, or the whole thing would have gone sideways."

"That's what you get for not telling me you were undercover in the first place," Andy replied. "You could have given me some kind of sign somewhere along the line."

"Too risky."

Ryan looked from one to the other, his mind still in a fog. "Exactly what happened here?"

"When you jumped Reynolds, his gun went off, and then your friend, here, decided if you could play the hero, he could too, and he lunged at Homer, hands tied behind his back or not! It's just a good thing that stray bullet didn't land somewhere nasty."

"Not so sure it didn't."

Ryan turned his attention to Andy. "Are you hit?" He strode to Andy's side and held out a hand to help him to his feet. As soon as he saw the blood on Andy's shirt and the way he favored his side when he stood, he knew. "You *were* hit! You crazy -! What were you thinking?"

"Trying to save the day, I guess." Andy laughed and then winced again, taking in a sharp breath as he did so.

"How bad is it?" Ryan asked.

"Just a flesh wound, I think. Nothing to worry about."

"Crazy…" Ryan repeated.

"Help will be here soon," Gear repeated. He looked over at Reynolds. "You're being awfully quiet."

Reynolds narrowed his eyes. "This isn't over. You may think you've won today, but things run so deep you'll never root everyone out."

Gear shrugged. "Maybe not, but it's been a good day's work as far as I can tell."

Ryan heard sirens approaching in the distance. "Let's get these thugs upstairs," he said.

What Reynolds said was true. Organized crime and police corruption went far deeper than one simple arrest. But Reynolds was a key player, as far as he could tell, and he'd take whatever victory came his way. The biggest victory was that he'd found Tempest, and she was still alive.

TEMPEST HUDDLED into the blanket that had been placed around her shoulders and stroked Paddy's fur where he sat in her lap.

He'd been muzzled and locked in a room upstairs in the house, but was no worse for wear once he'd been found. "You were a brave boy," she said into his ear, and he yapped a happy response. Jupiter was apparently safe and sound at Frank's house with Edna. Poor Frank, on the other hand, had been taken down to the station for questioning.

She searched the street for Ryan. The normally quiet neighborhood had been transformed into a circus of flashing lights from police cruisers and ambulances, cordoned off by crime scene tape. A crowd of law enforcement and medical staff milled within its borders. It was a scene not unlike a TV drama, but one she would have gladly watched from the outside, not from within.

She spotted Ryan a few yards away by Andy's side. Andy was sitting in the back of an ambulance, his midriff wrapped in gauze, talking to Ryan and another agent while the medical attendant finished up.

She'd already had her turn talking to police, but Ryan had given her strict orders not to leave the scene. What she really wanted was a hot shower, some food, and a few hours of decent sleep - if her nerves would actually settle enough to afford such a thing.

Geoff tapped her on the shoulder, and she glanced up from her vantage point on the curb to where he stood. "I've been cleared to leave. How about you?" He lowered himself to her level and stretched his legs out in front of him.

"Yes and no. Technically, I'm free to go, but Ryan asked me to stick around until we can talk."

"Of course. I can wait with you, if you like," Geoff offered. He scratched Paddy under the ear.

She smiled at him. "Thanks. I appreciate the offer, but I think you should get home before your mother really starts to worry."

He scrutinized her face for a moment. "You sure? I'm here for moral support if you need me."

She nodded. "I know."

"But you need time with Ryan alone," he said. "I get it. See you later, then?"

Geoff went to stand up and Tempest grabbed his hand. "Geoff… what you told me last night is strictly between you and me. When you're ready to tell others, I'll be there for you."

Moisture sprang to Geoff's eyes and he blinked it back. "Thank you. Just knowing that is going to give me strength for the future, no matter how it unfolds."

"I believe in you, Geoff. You're a good man. What your stepfather did was wrong. Don't let it define who you are."

"Thank you. I've been too scared to tell anyone, even a counsellor or our pastor. But now I realize I need people to pray and support me. I can't face this on my own."

"I'm here for you. And thank you for being such a good friend."

Geoff gave her hand a squeeze and then backed away, letting her hand drop as he distanced himself. She watched him turn and walk away. She didn't know what Geoff's future held, but that was the same for everyone. Counselling to deal with his abuse was a given, but beyond that, she had to leave it in God's hands.

Someone cleared his throat nearby, and she glanced up. Ryan. Paddy barked hello.

"Sorry to interrupt." He tousled Paddy's furry head.

"There is nothing to interrupt," she replied. "How's Andy?"

Ryan lowered himself to sit beside her. "He was lucky. Just a graze. Officer Homer's injury is a bit more substantial. Gear shot him in the leg."

"And Reynolds?"

"Hopefully, he'll be put away for a long time. I'm not sure if he'll talk, but we're hoping Homer will be more cooperative."

Tempest brushed a strand of hair from Ryan's forehead where a gash had been taped over. He also had a black eye, and there was bruising on his neck. "I meant, how are his injuries. I was wondering which of you got the worst of it."

Ryan looked over at her and grinned. "I'd say we're equally battle scarred. Why? Do I look that bad?"

"No. You're a sight for sore eyes. I've never been happier to see you." She let her hand drop to her lap. Just touching him brought back all the feelings she'd been bottling up inside, but he had made it clear before he left on assignment that he wasn't interested anymore. Just because he had rescued her didn't mean he wanted to take up where they'd left off. He was a man of honor and was just doing his duty.

Ryan shifted his gaze to the street in front of him. "I don't imagine Geoff would like to hear you talk like that."

"Geoff and I are just friends."

He looked back at her and searched her face as if to see if she were telling the truth.

"I mean it. We've never been more than that and never will be."

"O'Toole!" Someone called Ryan's name.

He sighed and stood up, offering her his hand so that she could stand also. She set Paddy down and then let herself be hoisted to her feet.

"Listen, I have to go," he said. "But I really think we need to talk some more. Somewhere private, once you've had some time and rest."

"Okay. I'll call you?"

He nodded. It looked for a moment like he might say more, but then he clamped his mouth into a line and strode away.

She watched him go before turning to Paddy. "Well, boy? What do you say we find your brother and then head home?"

Paddy barked his agreement.

The only trouble was, where was home?

CHAPTER 32

$\mathcal{R}$yan hung up the telephone and rubbed his chin. It was good to be back in his own office at the agency, but in some ways it left him feeling melancholy, too. To think that Reynolds had been orchestrating so many falsehoods right here, under his nose. Like a dark channel running deep under a fresh current. It was disturbing, and it made him wonder about what Reynolds had said back at the house. How many more dishonest players lurked in the agency? In the police force in general? In the entire network of law enforcement? A knock sounded on the glass door of his office, and he snapped back to reality.

"Still at it?" Andy asked, entering the space. He had some discoloration on his face from bruising - as did Ryan - but he was walking straighter without favoring his side, as he had been the first day after the incident.

"How come you keep coming into work? If you didn't earn at least a couple days off, I don't know who did."

"Said the pot to the kettle," Andy quipped. He eased himself into a chair. "So? What's the latest?"

"Reynolds confessed to working with Richard Camry, the

Director of Operations from Paragon. Not only was he into drug money, but diamond money, too."

"I guess dirty money is dirty money." Andy shrugged. "It seems strange that he'd send you to investigate if he was part of what was going on."

"You know what they say about honor among thieves," Ryan replied. "I think Reynolds had something else on Camry, so when he knew the next diamond heist was about to go down, he convinced Camry to try and fix it so I'd be implicated. Maybe even be killed accidentally in jail. Fortunately, it didn't stick. Meanwhile, Camry was supposed to get away safely with the diamonds, and they'd divvy up the score. But Camry got the best of Reynolds there, too. He managed to get away with the real deal while planting the fakes on Anne-Marie Fletcher."

"Quite the twisted mess," Andy said. "What about young Jeremy Leming? Was he part of the plot?"

"They're still investigating, but my gut says no. This whole thing has been hard on Leming. He was going to take some time up north with his grandmother, but he had to come home. A guilty man would have just stayed put. Plus, he confessed to me that his uncle sent him north to keep an eye on me. I think he was sincere in not knowing what his uncle was actually involved in."

"Let's hope so, for his sake," Andy said. "I like the kid."

"Me, too."

"And what about our intrepid reporter, Frank Dunlop? How is he fairing in all of this?"

"So far he is cooperating fully with the police investigation. Frank is a fountain of information, and because of it, I think they'll go easy on him. He might even swing some kind of plea bargain. Yes, he took money, but it was all for his son's medical bills and long term care."

"Hope so. I like him, too," Andy said and laughed.

"Next you're going to say you like Reynolds and hope they go easy on *him*," Ryan said with a smile.

Andy shook his head. "No, I won't go that far. I hope he gets everything the law can throw at him and then some." He hesitated for a moment before continuing. "Speaking of Frank, Tempest has moved back into her suite above his garage."

"I know."

Andy's eyebrows rose. "You do? Oh. I wasn't sure how much communication you've had since the incident. I thought you'd be happy she moved out of Geoff Vanguard's place, but moving back to Frank's seems like a strange choice."

"She has a soft spot for Frank, and now that he's in custody, she wants to make sure Edna is alright. This has been extra hard on her. She had no idea that their son's care was being paid for with illegally obtained funds."

"Sounds like you've been communicating well enough," Andy observed with a nod.

"Only over the phone. Hopefully, that will change after tonight."

"Plans?" Andy asked.

"You could say that," Ryan replied.

"But you're not going to tell me about them."

"You got that exactly right." Ryan smiled.

TEMPEST RELEASED the filmy curtain and let it swing back across the window. Ryan's car had just pulled into the driveway. She straightened her blouse and touched her hair, then waited with clasped hands by the door for his knock. Her stomach was fluttering, her heart was pounding and her hands felt shaky. She hadn't been this nervous in weeks. Maybe even months.

She'd left the downstairs door to the garage open, and she heard his footfalls on the steps as he climbed them two at a time.

She took a deep breath, waited for the knock and then grasped the doorknob and swung the door wide.

Naturally, the boys started barking the moment they heard the knock, but once Ryan entered, they stopped and just waited on the futon with thumping tails.

"They're happy to see you again," Tempest said with a laugh as she twisted her hands.

"I see that." Ryan strode right to the dogs and spoke to each one in turn along with giving each a pat on the head. That seemed to satisfy them, and they settled down again. He turned back to Tempest, but just stood there by the futon, hovering.

"Can I get you something? Some herbal tea?" She walked forward and stopped. The awkwardness in the room was palpable.

"No thanks," Ryan replied. He ran a hand through his hair.

"At least sit." She gestured to the futon.

He looked down at the somewhat lumpy surface, as if he was considering it, but straightened. "Look. I have something I need to get off my chest. I've been thinking about if for… well, weeks, but… You know how things have been. I had no choice."

"You're not making any sense."

"When we broke up I said some things that were hurtful. About you not letting go of the past. I only did it to make sure you thought I was serious about breaking up with you. It was for your own safety."

"It's okay. I *have* held onto a lot of pain from the past. It's made me skittish. Unable to trust."

"I shouldn't have said those things to you. We all have baggage, and I had no right. I should have found another way to keep you safe. I obviously did a poor job of that, anyway."

"Don't blame yourself. Who could have known? In fact, I think it did me some good. I realize now I haven't truly forgiven them. Any of them. Even my parents. Sometimes I feel angry at them for leaving me the way they did, as if they had a choice in the matter."

"That's understandable."

"Maybe, but not logical. Anyway, it's good riddance to all those twisted feelings along with all my past relationships gone wrong."

Ryan's eyes twinkled. "Just how many are we talking about? Should I be jealous?"

Tempest laughed. "No. They were, shall we say, unhappy subtexts, but of no real consequence. I'll tell you, sometime."

"You can if you like, but honestly, I don't care about your past relationships. I'm only interested in the here and now. With you."

"What do you mean?"

"I never stopped loving you. And when I proposed to you that time, well… I meant every word."

Tempest felt her heart flutter again. She watched in slow motion as Ryan got down on one knee in front of the futon. "I meant it then, and I mean it now. I want to marry you, Tempest Ross. Will you marry me?"

One simple nod was all it took for Ryan to catapult into a standing position and envelope her in his arms. She had wondered where home was, but now she'd found it. Right where it had been all along, in the arms of the man God had ordained for her.

*T*empest stood looking up at the cross at the front of the church. Light angled in through the stained glass windows, creating a prism of color that seemed to envelop the holy symbol.

A burst of laughter rose up from the chatter at the back of the church, and she smiled. Cherise and Stella were here, of course, along with their husbands, Zane and Blue Shepherd. Who else would she have chosen as bridesmaids? Other members of the wedding party were also gathered since they had just finished the rehearsal.

"Thank you, Jesus," Tempest whispered, still staring at the cross. They had been through so much together - she, Stella and Cherise. God had brought them together at boarding school, and now each one had accepted Christ and found the love of their lives. "You have been so good to me."

"Tomorrow is the big day."

Tempest spun around and smiled at Anne-Marie. The other woman stood about six feet away with her hands clasped in front. "Yes. Yes it is."

"Thank you for inviting me," Anne-Marie said.

"Of course. Why wouldn't I?"

Anne-Marie shrugged. "You have a complicated history with Dirk."

"True. I have a complicated history with all of them," Tempest said and laughed. "I'm just glad God has seen fit to get me out of my own way."

"I could say the same thing. I was jealous of you for a long time."

"You needn't have been. There was never anything between me and Dirk. Not in that way."

"I know that now. I was just surprised when Ryan asked him to be a groomsman."

"You and me both. But besides Andy, Ryan doesn't have a lot of close friends, and he's an only child. I suppose he felt like Dirk was instrumental in bringing us together. He *is* the one who introduced us the first time."

"He told me that story," Anne-Marie said with a smile.

"And I'm sure he put his own spin on it!" Tempest shook her head. "The things we've been through. And now, here you are in Boston, too. Planning to stay?"

"The jury is still out on that," Anne-Marie said. "But wherever we end up, it'll be together. I finally relented and we're engaged."

"I'm so glad." Tempest reached out and took Anne-Marie's hands in hers, squeezing them before letting go.

"I'm surprised you're having your wedding in Boston, actually." Anne-Marie looked around at the the opulent stained glass. "I thought you were from LA."

"When my parents were killed, I moved to Boston to live with my Great Aunt Rose. I went to boarding school here, too. It's where I met Cherise and Stella."

Anne-Marie nodded. "The famous threesome."

"Yes. She died last month. My Aunt Rose, I mean."

"Oh. I'm so sorry to hear it."

"It's okay. We didn't really get on that well, but she was good to take me in when she did. She left her estate to charity, so I won't have anywhere to come to after this. But it just seemed right to honor her - and my time in Boston - this way. And as I said, it's where I met Ryan."

Ryan approached. "Not getting cold feet, I hope."

Tempest shook her head. "No. You're stuck with me, I'm afraid."

"Anyway, thanks for everything," Anne-Marie said. "Both of you. I should probably go and join the others now." She gave a small wave and retreated back down the aisle to where the rest of the wedding party and their spouses waited, Dirk among them.

"Come on!" Andy yelled from the back of the room. "As the best man I feel it's my duty to move this party to a new location."

"Coming!" Ryan yelled back. He turned to Tempest and put his hands at her waist, holding her at arm's length. "I'm looking forward to saying my vows for real tomorrow."

"Me, too."

They leaned toward one another for a kiss and were met soon after by catcalls and whistling.

Tempest laughed and took Ryan's hand in hers. "We better not keep them waiting."

"I'd make them wait all evening if I had my way," Ryan said.

It had been a tumultuous few months, tossed by the waves of doubt, insecurity, and an insidious evil. But now the clouds had parted. The future looked bright.

MORE IN THE SERIES

There's more to this series!

In Book One, Tempest and her best friends Cherise and Stella get embroiled in a dangerous international drug ring and almost lose their lives while also juggling complicated romantic relationships and much more.

Three Strand Cord is the book that starts it all!
https://www.tracykrauss.com/books/three-strand-cord/

The saga continues in Book Two with some unexpected romantic entanglements and a Mexican drug smuggling ring. **Blood Ties** continues where **Three Strand Cord** leaves off.
https://www.tracykrauss.com/books/blood-ties/

OFFER

Join Tracy's mailing list and get up to date info on all new releases, promos and giveaways when they happen. You'll also get a free book!

https://tracykrauss.com
- fiction on the edge without crossing the line -

If you enjoyed this novel, or any of Tracy's books, please consider writing a review online. Reviews help readers find books they'll love and are tremendously helpful for today's authors. Thank you in advance!

ABOUT THE AUTHOR

Tracy Krauss writes contemporary Christian romance with a twist of suspense and a touch of humour. Her books strike a chord with those looking for a hard hitting yet thought provoking read. Her work has won multiple awards and has been on Amazon's bestsellers' lists. She also writes stage plays tailored to a high school audience, and has contributed to several anthologies, devotional books, and one illustrated children's book. Tracy has a Bachelor's degree from the University of Saskatchewan and taught secondary school Art, Drama and English—all things she is passionate about. She is a member of ACFW, The Word Guild, and Inscribe Christian Writers' Fellowship, a Canada wide organization for writers of Christian faith. She and her husband have lived in five provinces and territories including many remote and unique places in Canada's far north. They have four grown children and now reside in beautiful Tumbler Ridge, BC where she continues to pursue all of her creative interests. Visit her website for more: https://tracykrauss.com

ALSO BY TRACY KRAUSS

<u>Novels</u>

Wind Over Marshdale

Lone Wolf

Play It Again

Conspiracy of Bones (And the Beat Goes On)

My Mother the Man-Eater

Neighbours Series I

Keeping Up with the Neighbours Series II

Three Strand Cord

Blood Ties

Tempest Tossed

Aliens Among Us

Out of This World

<u>Stage Plays</u>

Dorothy's Road Trip

Ebenezer's Christmas Carol

Hook's Nemesis

Ali and the Magic Lamp

Mutiny On Mount Olympus

A Midterm Eve's Phantasm

The Western Tale

Little Red In the Hood

King William Travels The World

Non-Fiction

Life is a Highway: Advice and Reflections On Navigating the Road of Life

Thirty Days of Targeted Prayer

Divine Appointments: Daily Devotionals Based On God's Calendar

Children's book

The Sleepytown Express

www.ingramcontent.com/pod-product-compliance
Lightning Source LLC
Chambersburg PA
CBHW020946260626
47169CB00006B/1844